DOCTOR ALIEN

DOCTOR ALIEN

THREE TALES

RAJNAR VAJRA

WFP

WordFire Press

EBook ISBN: 978-1-68057-268-1
Trade Paperback ISBN: 978-1-68057-267-4
Dust Jacket Hardcover ISBN: 978-1-68057-269-8
Case Bind Hardcover ISBN: 978-1-68057-270-4
Library of Congress Control Number: 021951070

Cover design by Rajnar Vajra
Cover artwork images by Adobe Stock
Kevin J. Anderson, Art Director
Published by
WordFire Press, LLC
PO Box 1840
Monument CO 80132

Kevin J. Anderson & Rebecca Moesta, Publishers
WordFire Press eBook Edition 2022
WordFire Press Trade Paperback Edition 2022
WordFire Press Hardcover Edition 2022
Printed in the USA
Join our WordFire Press Readers Group for
sneak previews, updates, new projects, and giveaways.
Sign up at wordfirepress.com

CONTENTS

DEDICATION

My heartfelt thanks to Doctor Stanley Schmidt, my lifelong friend Gerald S. Beyer, to my agent Christine Cohen, and above all to my wonderful wife for infinite reasons, D.L. Ainsworth.

INTRODUCTION TO
A DOCTOR ALIEN TRILOGY
STANLEY SCHMIDT

W e're often told that truth is stranger than fiction, and I usually think there's a good deal of truth in that. Sometimes, when I'm reading Rajnar Vajra, I'm not so sure—and I mean that in the nicest possible way.

Science fiction is about imagination, but rooted in science; and sometimes writers underestimate just how wide a range of possible realities science allows. Rajnar likes to seek out the boundaries and poke at them to see what happens. He obviously has fun doing it, and so do the readers who go along for the ride. I know I did when I was editing *Analog*. Whenever I saw a new submission from him, I knew I was in for a treat, but I seldom knew what *kind* of a treat. His imagination, and the ideas he explored, and the tones of his stories, were all over the map—often surprising, but never dull.

Who else, for example, would imagine a human psychiatrist building a practice on treating a motley assortment of extraterrestrials of species he'd never encountered before? A human psychiatrist treating human patients at least has some idea of what constitutes "normal," and can view that as a goal of his treatment. But what if he has no idea what is normal for a new kind of patient? (And why would aliens seek out a *human* to help them, anyway? I won't answer that, but the answer can be found in these pages.)

I've long thought that the "completely incomprehensible alien" is one of the most overworked and least plausible notions in science fiction. There are certain very basic things that any living being must deal with, and most of his/her/its actions are ways of dealing with those needs. If you don't understand its actions, that's unlikely to mean there's no logic to them, or even no logic that human minds can grasp. It's far more likely that you simply don't understand the underlying premises—or, in one of our vernaculars, "where the alien is coming from." If you take the trouble to do so, things will probably make sense.

Dr. Alien's patients may seem as baffling a lot as any you'll ever meet, but they make sense on their own terms. I think you'll enjoy meeting them. And who knows? Maybe truth is more like Rajnar's fiction than most of us think!

A DOCTOR ALIEN TRIO

THREE TALES BY RAJNAR VAJRA

The initial premise of the Doctor Alien stories is that a human psychiatrist winds up acting as a psychotherapist for three extraordinary extraterrestrial aliens.

So, let's get to the fun!

But perhaps best not quite yet.

Due to what I call the "Fourth Law of Existential Physics," which states that "To do anything, it is necessary to do something else first," we should at least glance at what might make this premise ... well, not utterly impossible.

Then we can have fun.

Astronomers believe that something on the order of one septillion star-orbiting planets inhabit the currently observable universe. A septillion can be written as one with twenty-four zeros following it like baby ducks. Some astronomers predict ten times more planets!

The idea that intelligent life only exists on Earth strikes me as so gigantically absurd that it's only surpassed by the idea of life of any kind only existing on our world. The fact that terrestrial creatures thrive near oceanic hydrothermal vents in 113-degree temperature—Celsius!—shows how flexible and resilient life can be.

But considering the astonishing number of light-years separating extrasolar planets, direct contact between us and extraterrestrial beings, barring some astonishing coincidence, would require a mode of transportation bypassing Einstein's speed of light traffic restriction, and also some way that intelligent species could find each other in a universe so large that averaging out the total amount of matter in it would result in a sum so minuscule that it could reasonably be rounded down to zero.

So, how do we push Einstein aside even speculatively?

Science fiction writers have offered various possibilities such as traveling in some extra dimension, usually named "hyperspace" or "subspace," or altering the physics of the spaceship to remove annoying details such as inertia, or my idea of creating an alternative reality around a spaceship allowing it to pass through normal spacetime without interacting with it as certain forms of neutrino are suspected to do.

Perhaps the most likely candidate for offending Einstein is some flavor of teleportation, creating or finding cosmic wormholes that act as dimensional loopholes, permitting a spaceship to directly jump between distant points in our universe.

We don't *know* that any of these ideas are impossible, so let's brush the speed of light restriction aside, adding an appropriate apology.

As to how one intelligent species could find another, say, ten thousand light-years distant? I've got an idea although it would require an absurdly advanced technology, a currently undiscovered property of spacetime, and our trusty light speed bypass.

We know that the physical universe shapes our minds. Our experiences of distance, time, weight, direction, color, texture, and almost everything else depend on external input mediated by our senses, which work with only a tiny percentage of the information available. Human vision, for example, registers such a pitiful portion of the electromagnetic spectrum that on

4

a world with truly gifted beings in the visual department, we'd likely be classified as legally blind.

In the end, all we can be aware of is consciousness itself. All else, including data from our most clever instruments, remains at best secondhand information, perceived by the senses evaluating that information, interpreted by our conditioned education, and experienced by ... that which experiences all experience.

But is it possible that our relationship with the universe works both ways, that our minds directly influence, even in a most trivial way, whatever external reality exists?

If so, it might be possible for some ultra-advanced device to detect, in real time—again sneaking past poor old Einstein—the influence of consciousness on spacetime.

Now that we've wriggled past those obstacles, that still leaves another improbability standing between us and the required suspension of disbelief we may need to enjoy our three Doctor Alien tales:

How could any human, however well trained in human psychology, act as a therapist for any extraterrestrial intelligent being? Wouldn't any such be far too different from us to even begin to comprehend?

Now there, I can offer an answer that might be entirely probable.

Given that these ETs live in the same universe we do, affected by the same basic properties, they might well evolve with enough mental similarities for our therapist to make some educated guesswork. Admittedly, it might require an improbable degree of luck for this guesswork to be useful to troubled extraterrestrials.

So, I may have cheated a bit to provide Doctor Alanso J. Morganson, our protagonist psychiatrist, a bit of extra serendipity. I hope you'll forgive me for any probability overreach.

Ready?

Let the fun begin!

DOCTOR ALIEN

Funny thing about emotions. While they can be blended ten thousand ways, the basic ingredients are so very limited. Example? Fear. In my case, I'm terrified of performing a fairly ordinary human activity: public speaking. And here I was, about to step into a situation outside all human experience, yet I felt *exactly* the kind of sick fluttering in my stomach I get every time I'm pressured into addressing my fellow psychiatrists at an APA convention.

Of course the door in front of me, the inner portal, opened in the direction I least expected, sliding straight downward into a previously hidden slot in the floor. *How much more intimidating*, I asked myself, *can this get?* Then I realized that in this setting, the top wasn't necessarily the top.

I'd been warned the thermostat here would be set lower than I'd find comfortable—at least my hosts-to-be had conveyed that much—so I wasn't surprised to find the airlock chilly after it had pressurized and I'd stripped down to my hooded smartsuit; but as that inner door descended, whoa! A shock of coldness slapped my face, numbed my cheeks, made my eyes water, and stuffed my nostrils with tiny icicles. No problem. My smartsuit reacted and buried wires radiated

7

warmth. I patted my chest pocket to make sure the photo of my wife and son hadn't overpowered the valence zipper and fallen out, gave my vacuum gear tucked into the airlock's safety netting a longing glance, picked up my case, then cautiously stepped into the alien space station.

Still light as fluff, I tiptoed over the blue "neutral" band acting as a kind of foyer and pushed through a filmy decontamination membrane. I took one step out onto dark, rubbery matting and *thud*. The large case I'd been toting by its carrying strap was snatched from my hand and hit the floor, hard. I nearly joined it. Normal gravity would've been a shock after eight hours of mostly the micro kind and suddenly I weighed half again my weight on Earth, a nice trick since the station wasn't spinning. The Tsf had been specific for once about the weight increase to expect, but honestly, I hadn't believed synthetic gravity would feel so genuine. And despite a crash course in Tsf Trader culture, I hadn't imagined Trader headquarters in our solar system would smell like burnt vanilla beans or be as noisy as a plague of cicadas.

My ignorance wasn't NASA's fault. These aliens hadn't revealed much about this station. And until now, no woman, man, bug, animal, or plant from Earth had ever been invited here into the Parent Ship, although it had been right in our backyard, orbiting the moon for the last three years.

But I sighed with relief because no one greeted me. Among Traders, any welcome visitor was supposed to stroll into a Tsf dwelling as if they owned it. Should one of them have been waiting by the entrance, even holding out a Hawaiian lei, it would've meant I wasn't wanted, conceivably a fatal condition for a human dealing with this species. Unless said human had, say, a loaded bazooka. Some enterprising thieves had learned that the hardest way in a Tsf outlet on Earth.

My case, unscathed, automatically unfolded into a multipurpose acceleration couch, slower than when I'd seen it demoed at the Kennedy Space Center. It began following me like a faithful basset when I ignored the implied invitation and staggered forward.

The room before me was an extremely long and rectangular box, rather tunnel-like and mostly ivory colored, with blue and russet equipment or perhaps furniture laid along the floor in tidy linear patterns, everything fastened in place with bolts that could've supported the Golden Gate Bridge. I glanced up. The high ceiling held more equipment in similar patterns and with identical bolts. Interesting, I'd never thought of gravity control as a means to squeeze more use out of a room. Wall panels glowed, casting a bright, faintly pinkish illumination. I hoped my upgraded DM, its icon curled around my right ring finger, was functioning properly and recording every detail; I'd studied pictures of several Earth-side Trading Posts, and they'd looked nothing like this. But then, they'd been set up for human esthetics.

I counted a dozen Tsf fifty yards ahead and was grateful to have a moment to adjust to their appearance before having to interact. They were more grotesque in the flesh than in photographs, which is saying something.

None were taller than me, most several inches shorter, but each took up more floor space due to having ten outer legs plus three central, somewhat hidden ones directly supporting the "gondola" containing their circulatory pump, cranium, and digestive mechanisms. They resembled neither spiders nor octopi. The jointless outer limbs were thin but muscular and descended in a smooth arc. Halfway down each one, a thick bundle of cilia wriggled, reminding me of those fiberoptic threads used for hokey Christmas trees. According to our science gurus, sensory organs tipped the medium-sized hairs while the longest ones were used as hands and fingers. The shortest and most numerous ones, only an inch or so long, made clicking sounds as they changed position, the Tsf way of speaking. I was the only person in the room wearing clothes.

So far everything was going by the book, line by paragraph.

Sure enough, I could breathe the air, handle the gravity, and keep my lunch down. My only real problem, aside from anxiety enough for two cowards and the dissociative numbing to be expected in such a surreal situation, was that my mission still made no sense to me. I told myself that more experienced human heads than mine knew what they were doing.

It wasn't until I'd lumbered halfway to my alien hosts that my confidence in the experts nosedived. They'd told me, with a certainty only possible for people who planned to remain safe at home, that the Tsf would ignore my presence until I initiated conversation, but now most of the medium-length hairs in the room pointed straight at me. And the clicking chatter sped up, evidently, every Tsf talking at once—foolish me, I'd thought they were loud before. Sounded like a thousand car mechanics ratcheting away. Next time, I promised myself, earplugs. Better yet, no next time.

My case-couch nudged the back of my knees, but I still didn't take the hint. I certainly felt the extra eighty-six pounds I carried right now, but I keep myself very fit, I *have* to, so I didn't need the support ... yet. I stopped anyway. My hosts were turning back and forth in place, a dozen slow-motion ballerinas, while their sensory cilia kept themselves aimed at me with the steadiness of telescope clock-drives. My anxiety blasted off without so much as a countdown while my buck-fifty weight made me feel horribly weak. For the first time in my life, I had a visceral sense of what it might be like to be morbidly obese. Which was humbling since I'd *treated* obese people and had pretended to understand them. But there's nothing like terror to deflect mere humiliation, and what scared the shame out of me was two Tsf suddenly barreling my way in high-gravity-defying leaps.

They slowed to a halt, standing distant enough so that I didn't quite panic and make a futile break for the airlock, but close enough to me to learn that they smelled like curry, which implied the burnt-vanilla odor wasn't coming off them. Each was distinct enough in shape and coloration for me to easily tell them apart, but all their fingers, their longest cilia, were lavender, so if my information was correct, they were both males at the moment. The smaller alien held a Tsf interpreter: a device shaped like a doughnut with bicycle spokes. The larger Tsf clicked away, and the machine provided a running translation in a version of English that meandered from obsolete to bizarre, with frequent side trips to stuffy and obscure. Plenty of slang; most of it antique. Traders, I guessed, had done the cliché thing and had been monitoring our radio and TV transmissions. For at least a century.

"Regrets and apologies," the largest one chattered. "Our bad. We never intended such staring rudeness. Here's lies the skinny: each of us, unknown to each other, was so hot to see it happen. As true as I am called Deal-of-ten-lifetimes, which you know I am, and my comrade is known as Best-offer, which you'll bet he is, we all hang our gondolas in shame."

Hot to see *what* happen? And while Deal's words were disarming, the tenor voice the translator used for him sounded cold, almost sullen; I tried not to read anything into it. Still, as far as my fundamental expectations went, I was back on semi-solid ground. Deal's oblique introductions fit what I'd been told was the Tsf sense of propriety. The idea was that we were already familiars, making a straightforward exchange of names inappropriate.

Of course, NASA had already told them my name, but I was supposed to not-introduce myself anyway. I usually go by "Al" or "Doc" but had been told to use the official moniker for this first greeting. "As certain as my name is Doctor Alanso J. Morganson, I noticed no rudeness whatsoever." I hoped their culture had no taboos against the paler sort of lie. "Um, if I may ask, what were you hoping to see?"

"You may indeed ask. Anything and always. Curiosity, as Traders say, brushes wisdom." Again, the words were friendly, if eccentric, but the tone came across otherwise. Deal, in a gesture lost on me, lifted a leg and lightly swept its tip across my forehead. Considering Tsf abilities, he could've poked a hole through my skull just as easily. "We believed you'd be altering your size to make yourself more comfy in this gravity field."

"My size?"

"Isn't a human of your profession referred to as a 'shrink'?"

"Ah. We seem to have a slight misunderstanding. What's supposed to shrink, if I do my job right, is my patient's emotional problems." Didn't seem wise to tell these walking craniums that the term was short for "headshrinker."

"Go figure. Our bad, again."

I lowered my voice. "Is my patient somewhere in this room?"

That got a reaction; Deal shuddered all over. "*Awk*ward," he said. "We Traders maintain stable emotional orbits and suffer no mental flaws."

"Sorry, I thought—wait! You mean my patient isn't a Trader?"

"Most assuredly correct. In fact, if you will forgive me for expressing it so harshly in your terms: no way, Jose."

That "Jose" threw me. Why would they use my middle name?

"Doctor, I wonder if our interpreting machine is functioning with full propriety." I was wondering that myself. "It seemed you referred to your patients in the singular."

Uh-oh. "I've got more than one?"

"It is a unique happenstance, but we have recently collected a triad of beings, no two alike, and all unfamiliar to Traders. We cannot comprehend their behaviors nor have yet ascertained their planets of origin."

Three aliens utterly alien to these aliens. Oh. My. God. I'd never remembered to ask what NASA had asked in trade for my services but hadn't much cared since I wouldn't be earning it. But now it dawned on me with that classic sinking feeling that if I screwed up here by doing some actual harm, my failure could jeopardize Tsf-human relations. And with three total unknowns, how could I even guess what might cause harm?

I tried to sound calm. "Please tell me more."

"We have little to relate. We rescued two of your patients from damaged starcraft, the third was a chucknoland found on a world similar to your Mars."

"I'm sorry. What's a ... chucknoland?"

Deal hesitated. "Our translator has failed? Let me elaborate. I refer to a being forced to abandon their vessel who attempts to thrive beyond civilization."

I snapped my fingers and every Trader in the room clicked loudly. Had I made a faux pas? Or were they were all just saying, "Bless you"?

"Sorry about the snap, didn't mean anything by it. And I don't know how the translator came up with chucknoland, but I think you mean a castaway."

"Then we have attained a bitchin' mutual understanding. Now, I must sound a klaxon. Shortly, within six of your minutes if we comprehend your temporal and counting systems, and we do, we must make all Trader occupants of this station four and three-fifths times heavier for five and two-thirteenths minutes."

That news upset me and not because of the picky fractions. The Tsf had informed Earth about the periodic gravity boosts but wouldn't say how much or for how long. My handlers had guessed light and short. They'd had no idea why the aliens weren't more forthcoming.

"Dig this," Deal continued, "our muscles would soon atrophy and our skeletal fibers de-mineralize in this wimpy gravity without frequent relief."

"Why not stay heavy all the time?"

"If only. That would be prohibitively energy expensive since each added dollop of gravity requires exponentially more power." His translator coated the statement with condescension. "May I show you to your stateroom where we can send you real-time images of your patients while you remain immune from increased weight? Or would you prefer to see them directly? Or ... you might care to leave our Parent Ship and forget everything the Master Traders have employed you to do."

"I'm getting the impression you don't think I'm up for it." If so, Deal and I were in perfect agreement.

"I *think* you are wasting your time and mine. The finest Tsf minds are focused on these problems; what could a human possibly add? But my thoughts are weightless since I'm not in charge. So, of the three options I offered, and I do recommend the final choice, what's your cup of tea?"

So much for the famous Trader politeness, but the question was good. And so was another: could I handle the upcoming change? I'd trained on a scaled-up centrifuge, a carnival ride designed by sadists as I'd described it to my wife, working up to three minutes at 7G, which jacked my 172 pounds to about 1,200, double what my NASA coaches claimed would be "worst case" conditions. I was the only mental-care professional on their short list who could handle anything approaching that—ironic considering my condition—so I got hired. By hired I mean drafted.

But since the gravity here was already too strong for my comfort, the coming increase would leave me nearly as heavy as during my training and for almost twice as long. Even with a smartsuit-cum-G-suit, inflating as needed to keep blood from pooling away from my brain, the experience sounded ghastly. Also, I'd "grayed-out" more than once during my carnival rides, temporarily becoming colorblind. What if color provided important clues concerning my patients?

What was I thinking? *My* patients? Was I really moronic enough to continue with this farce? I'd had no idea how I was supposed to provide therapy to Traders, and we knew a *little* about Traders. This would be a shot in the dark, blindfolded.

Anyone with the intelligence of a squirrel or less would've chosen Deal's third option, pled incompetence, and bowed out fast.

I just couldn't bring myself to do it, not yet. Deal's contempt had invoked what my wife calls my "stubborn edges." Foolish, I know, but sometimes I'm a fool. Still, I didn't have to be stupid and squished. I opened my mouth to accept the stateroom invitation and then had two nasty thoughts. What if one or more of the mystery aliens was in some sort of crisis and lack of proximity hid important cues? Also, it might be useful to learn how well I could operate under the extreme condition.

"I'll visit your guests in person. Could you let me know a minute or so before you turn on the heavy?"

"You bet your bippy. If you desire to experience failure, please follow me."

Strange. Deal's hostility went against everything I'd heard about Traders. Also, what was a "bippy" and why would I want to bet it?

––––––––

A large sheet of transparent material separated the large room and its two occupants from the rest of the station. That seemed a good thing, not only because one of said occupants appeared dangerous as hell, but because the yellow-brown smog tinting the room's atmosphere didn't look like anything I'd care to inhale.

"I suppose," I said, "the big one's my patient?"

Deal waved a few legs around. "Yes, the other is a mechanical entity whose only function, to our knowledge, is disposing of the organic entity's wastes, a useful task since the organic refuses to utilize our lavatory facilities."

"A sanitation robot."

"An apt but unnecessary description. From its increasing

torpidity, we believe its power is failing. Soon we will remove it and attempt to restore its mojo."

The machine resembled R2-D2 from the antique *Star Wars* movies so much, I would've laughed if the thing next to it wasn't so frightening.

My patient stood eight or nine feet tall, face like a tiger, but with steely spikes jutting from its scalp. A punk predator. The larger spikes on its back implied defense against something I didn't care to imagine. It had six limbs not counting its long flat tail, four of which served as arms with six-fingered hands, and an upright body that seemed equally feline and reptilian. No clothes, but short brown fur with variegated green stripes; no visible sexual organs. Claws eased out of the fingers, gleaming metallically. The tiger-lizard stared at me with yellow, yellow eyes then became anything but still, jumping every which way while providing a soothing accompaniment of God-awful howls and screeches."

"What's the gravity in there?" I asked.

"Presently, no different than out here."

Yikes. Jumping that high under these circumstances was impressive. And alarming. The phrase "bouncing off the walls" popped into my head, which annoyed me; thinking in clichés in here could lead to a clichéd and utterly inaccurate diagnosis. Even with the glassy barrier in the way, the noise rattled my teeth and drowned out the distant clacking from the main room. My latest responsibility drooled.

I turned toward Deal, to my right. Best-offer flanked me on my other side. "You sure," I shouted to be heard over the racket, "this, um, individual is intelligent?"

The tiger abruptly quieted down; otherwise, I would've missed the translation. "Our guest," Deal said, "is seldom so exuberant and may have been excited by seeing you." Right, the way a lion gets excited by a gazelle. "We found him or her or it alone except for the robot in a damaged spacecraft with appointments and controls obviously designed for this specific species under microgravity conditions."

"Why only under microgravity?"

"If the craft were logically oriented on a solid planetary surface, the controls would remain out of his, her, or its reach unless he, she, or it, constantly performed acrobatics big time. As you see, our guest has the requisite chops, but we feel such bouncing would be impractical for operating that ship's form of complex manually-controlled navigation system."

"I suppose. Speaking of impractical, can we agree to use, um, 'her' as the pronoun?"

Deal and Best-offer exchanged a series of clacks that weren't translated. "A consistent gender-defining term would be groovy with us in the interests of efficiency, always bearing in mind that we dare not conclude childbearing abilities due to an absence of well-hung attributes. Consider my own presently subtle genitalia."

That little speech seemed to rattle around in my head for a minute before it dropped into the comprehension chute. "Have you been able to communicate with her at all?"

"You are uptight that you may be in a first-contact situation rather than a therapeutic one, where we have no basis of communication?"

"Well, yes." Deal understood me better than I'd expected.

He waved a leg expressively, or at least gracefully since I had no idea what the gesture expressed. "Chill out, Doctor, although in another of your cases your fears may just possibly have merit. We have deciphered this patient's language—logically, it must be hers—by the usual means, and have had similar success with the third patient you will see, but neither has been willing or able to speak with us. This is one reason we suspected emotional impairment in both cases, likely due to trauma, which impelled my superiors to request human assistance." He didn't *quite* add "bad idea."

Deal's clacking quieted as though turning confidential. I

had to concentrate to catch the translation, which also grew quieter. "Your species reputedly suffers an astonishing array of such impairments, so our Council of Masters foolishly believes you must be the galaxy's foremost experts in the field. No offense projected."

I fought back a grin. "None taken. But what *is* the usual means for figuring out an alien language?"

"You don't know?"

The superior tone galled me. "It's not the sort of problem we've had to deal with yet."

"So primitive, and yet I am here to answer your childish questions. The technique involves activating and studying an instructional protocol embedded in the alien vessel's data management system. Of course we rely on our own data processor for initial deciphering."

"Huh. Why would anyone put language lessons on their own ship's computer?"

Deal tapped one leg against the floor, I'd bet impatiently. "Most starfaring species capable of even rudimentary foresight will anticipate spacecraft failures and possible rescue by helpful but unknown aliens. Therefore they make it practical to open communications."

I shook my head. "How's that even possible?"

Deal's tapping sped up. "If I must educate you, such instruction, typically visual, is activated when the potential rescuer demonstrates ignorance of the damaged vessel's operating systems."

"You mean when someone starts pushing buttons at random?"

"If you mean 'buttons' in a figurative sense, Doctor. Instruction most often commences with simple counting of objects to reveal the numeration symbols and number base involved. Then the mathematical operators are defined through their operations, again demonstrated visually, which leads to an array of prepositions and predicates. From there, context supplies an expanding field of comprehension with ever more complex axioms. Often live actors or animations of living beings act out various—"

My patient emitted a particularly loud screech and began chewing on her own tail. I lost track of Deal's spiel although I'd already gotten the gist, but I noticed when he wound down.

"So to get back to my question, you haven't been able—"

"To communicate with her, no. Our exchanges have been limited to one success: by offering a variety of nutritional substances, solid and liquid, we have learned to feed her." I got the impression Deal was embarrassed by their failure to do more. "Likewise, we have not yet found sufficient navigational cues in her starship's data array to identify her home world."

"Hmm. Maybe they don't necessarily want strangers knowing where they live."

"Spot on, although obvious. I have also been ordered to mention that this one has recently begun displaying an attribute we've never encountered before. My superiors think it best for you to see this for yourself and draw your own conclusions before we offer our more sophisticated ones."

"Okay. What I need to take a stab at this job is some idea of what constitutes normal behavior for this species. If you found language lessons in movie format on her spacecraft, did you find any other visual recordings?"

Deal rubbed three legs together. "Gnarly logic, I must admit, and the answer is yes. A series of such recordings await you in your stateroom, frequency-shifted for the limited human optical range. Would you care to go there now, or would you prefer misunderstanding another of your patients?"

Mainly, I wanted to stop seeing patient one. She scared me. "Let's move on to the next. I'd like an overview."

"Righteous. But I must warn you, as you demanded, that a therapeutic gravity bump is due in one minute."

I nodded and lay down on my self-propelled furniture. "Thanks." Now I'd find out just how therapeutic my acceleration couch was. I gazed at my Data Manager icon and muttered an activation phrase. The luminous ring uncurled and floated upward, expanding into a virtual touchscreen displaying a fish-eye view of the area. My two flanking Traders neglected to gasp or at least click in wonder at this demonstration of human technology. But then, they couldn't see it. I reached up and pushed the target cursor onto the distorted image of Deal then poked a finger through the impalpable enter button. It was a relief to let my hand drop since my arm was getting very heavy.

"Lead on, please," I said as my weight relentlessly increased. I ignored the prompt for continuance and after a moment the touchscreen shrunk, curled, and resumed its post around my ring finger. "This contraption will follow you now." So I hoped. The new CPU element of my Data Manager was far more advanced than any upgrade you'd find at Electronics-R-Us, and its increased features gave it more scope for errors.

Deal backed away and, glory be, my craft rolled along behind him. Without turning, the Trader moved in a dead straight line down the middle of the hallway, a trickier feat for someone without a ring of eyes. My back support, which had felt delightfully comfortable when I lay down, morphing to match my contours, felt harder every second.

The smartsuit tightened around my legs, and I helped by tensing my leg muscles; the brain, like Dracula, needs its blood. But everything was starting to ache. And I had nearly five minutes of weighing over 1,000 pounds to go.

"Do you remain in vibrant health?" Deal asked, the translation sounding bored.

"Yes," I lied in a choked voice. It's hard to breathe in high-G let alone talk; the diaphragm tends to clench as part of an overall Support-the-Spine-At-All-Costs instinct, a kind of hyper-Valsalva effort. I imagine one could experience something similar by lying supine with a hundred-kilo Olympic weight or three on one's tummy. How, I wondered, did those rare unfortunates on the far end of the obese bell curve manage? I've heard of cases where people weighed more than I did right now.

"Sadly for you, our science isn't yet capable of isolating individuals from the surrounding gravity without limiting their spatial movements."

"I just. Wish. We could. Control. Gravity. At all."

"Do you? Then why didn't your government require that information as payment for your ... expertise?" The translator did a fine job of expressing sarcasm.

I would've let my jaw drop except I wasn't sure I could close it again. "You'd. Trade—"

"Trading is what we do. Goods, services, information, anything. *If* you can deliver, and even you must know how probable that is. But bide! Look behind you. Your first patient is performing the unique maneuver I mentioned."

"Walk back, please. Can't turn my head."

"You are tragically weak." Deal stepped around me and returned to the transparent shield. My go-cart spun around and followed. When it stopped, I ordered my DM to put the couch into voice-controlled mode. Although by then, I didn't have much voice to work with.

"Turn. Clockwise. Don't mean you, Deal. Stop. Still not you, Deal. Raise head."

After all this hassle, I saw no change in my punk tiger at first. Then, slowly, its coloration intensified and kept getting increasingly vivid. The claws and spikes turned luminous, and the golden eyes blazed enough to resemble searchlights.

"What?" I croaked.

"Keep your peepers peeled, Doctor. Truly, I've never seen her perform this feat nearly so powerfully. She keeps improving at this and doubtless even a primitive will find the results totally rad."

Rad? Short for radish? Or radium? And nothing happened except I began losing my battle to stay calm, and on two fronts.

One was my growing irritation with Deal. The other and more immediate concern was air. I kept assuring myself that I was getting enough but didn't find me convincing. And sure enough, just then my peripheral vision flickered and went out and the blindness gradually crept its way inwards. Which is why I thought my eyes were playing tricks when my patient became a ghostly shape, losing all color and most of her solidity. I could see right through her.

"There!" the Trader announced, clicking with extra force. "Isn't that special?"

"What—ah! That feels *good*." 1.5G was easy now. My chest hurt, but it was lovely to breathe again. The tiger reappeared but cloaked in no more than her initial glory. "What happened?"

"We resumed normal operating gravity."

"I mean, what happened to my patient."

"Consider that for yourself while we mosey to your next appointment."

I hadn't a clue, and that statement applied to this entire fiasco. What the hell was I doing? I hated to admit that Deal was right, but I really was useless here. And still, my pride wouldn't let me call it quits. When I got home, I'd be sure to buy *The Complete Idiot's Guide to Idiocy*, if such a book existed. It's not that I wasn't doing splendidly on my own, but it's always good to sharpen one's game.

———

We didn't have to "mosey" far, which was nice since my leg muscles trembled when I got off my couch and stood up. Patient two appeared comfortingly simian if you overlooked trivial details such as six arms, two thick legs in front and a scrawny one in back, mottled turquoise hair, and two pairs of surplus eyes. I guessed this one might be male, judging by the way its tunic-like wrapping bulged in the front crotch area, and Deal agreed to use the masculine gender but grumbled that appearances among aliens not only could be deceptive but usually were. At least I was no longer the only clothed person in this nudist colony.

I couldn't begin to interpret the ape's behavior. He stood calmly as he stared at us with the top two eyes, the brown and green one, while all six of his hands moved incessantly, flicking sideways as if pushing aside some little nuisance or flipping up and down at random. If this was some form of sign language, why didn't he stop and wait for some return gestures? And if the only signs were those of desperation, why was he obviously more focused on his hands than on us. The constant motion reminded me of water flowing down a steep streambed, cascading over the larger rocks. It also reminded me of something else I'd seen. I couldn't pinpoint what....

"This being is the one we found on an otherwise uninhabited planet and whose language we have been unable to unfurl through no fault of our own," Deal said. His clicking had a stiffer and more precise cadence than usual, reminiscent of marching band snare rhythms. "The only spacecraft we could find was a miniature spiraling lander such as many alien voyagers use in emergencies." *Voyagers*, I thought, *who didn't get dizzy.*

"No Berlitz lessons available, I take it?"

"Minimal electronics, but a sizable cache of consumables."

"Does he stop gesturing when he eats?"

"No, but if you insist on hassling me with irrelevant questions, his paw motions diminish by one-third because he requires two paws to handle his nourishment. And he constantly rotates the pair he uses."

I observed the castaway for a few more minutes but learned nothing except that his gesturing became hypnotic after a while. I was surprised the Traders, with their super technology, hadn't been able to spot the starship he'd evidently had to abandon, assuming it was orbiting the world where he'd been rescued. Then again, without knowing the starship's shape, albedo, composition, or orbital distance, perhaps it wouldn't be easy to find.

Where *had* I seen hand movements like that before?

"Will I have time to see my next patient before the next gravity change?" I asked.

"Surely. Follow me."

Deal's body posture altered the instant I mentioned visiting patient three, and when I glanced over at Best-offer, he'd changed similarly. Both Tsf had pulled their legs in closer to their gondolas and stood taller. Their new positions struck me as defensive, but I didn't have enough arrogance to trust my ability to decipher an extraterrestrial body language.

––––––

Still, something about my final patient clearly had a big impact on my tour guides. It—and we agreed that "it" was the bon mot in this case—sure had an impact on me. The two previous rescued souls had seemed highly exotic, but alike enough to terrestrial life so that I could compare them to Earth animals. I could relate. This new one was something else. Alien in the spookiest sense.

For one thing, it was flat enough to ooze out from under a door or a rock, practically two-dimensional. Talk about your flat affect. For another, it was unbelievably slow, creeping across the room with all the haste of a tired slug. It wasn't nearly as pretty as a slug, not with all those translucent, twisted protrusions placed seemingly at random on that nearly shadow-thin gray body; not with so many rotten-cucumber-green claws or hooks, most scattered over the protrusions, some projecting directly from its torso, the universe's ugliest picture hangers. Small discolorations that could've been sensory organs or ulcers completed the ensemble, and I'm embarrassed to admit that the sight of my patient left me nauseated.

On impulse, I decided to take a chance and turned toward Deal. "What makes this specimen more important to you than the others?"

The Trader went rigid. If I'd guessed right, this might help my reputation here, which just might prevent my stock from plummeting to zero point nothing when—not if—I failed at my main job. But Deal wasn't clicking, and I started worrying. Then Best-offer spoke up, which startled me since he hadn't thrown a click in my direction until now.

"As my esteemed associate remains muted from his shock and disappointment, I will assume his diplomatic duties on the basis of a brief stewardship." The translator device used a deep, raspy tone for Best-offer's voice. "Is that hunky-dory with you?"

"Um. Sure. Why's he shocked and disappointed?"

"I am honor bound not to spill the beans. Unless you have something worthwhile to trade for the legumes in question?"

At least I was consistent: I didn't understand anyone or anything on this station. But I had the feeling I'd just missed something significant. "I—just tell me about this alien."

"Super. We found the dude adrift on the galactic attenuation adjacent to your planetary system. His ship, an organic-electronic, had been trashed by a collision and most of its atmosphere had flown the co-op."

"The coop?"

"Whatever. The surviving data organisms, after some sweet-talkin', provided language instruction and some general information, but were too whacked to do their thing with navigation, life-support, propulsion, and repair. We checked out the traces of atmosphere. Unique."

"How so?"

"No trace of water vapor. Every intelligent life form we had previously encountered in our travels requires some amount of dihydrogen monoxide. There may be clever crystals or sentient flames hangin' out somewhere, but we have never consciously crossed their paths."

"So I imagine you're keeping my patient dry in there?"

"Duh. Water is almost certainly toxic for an entity adapted to such an arid atmosphere."

Interesting, but were my hosts evading my original question? "And the importance of this species?"

Best-offer didn't go mute, but he spoke slowly as though weighing each click. "The ship's data organisms were royally screwed, Doctor. Aside from the abstract visual patterns automatically generated when we triggered the language lesson sequence, we could glom on to only one distinct image: a star map with a heap of color-coded connecting lines."

"I don't—wait. You figure you've stumbled onto some galactic empire?"

"Not close and no cigar. We doubt it's coincidental that we use very similar maps."

"Oh. Another species of traders?"

On my other side, Deal returned to life. "From the map and the starship's cargo," he said, "we are confident they operate much as we do."

"A rival."

"Conceivably. But frankly, dear Doctor, we don't give a damn because that's not the big deal. Will you bite?"

"Will I what?"

"Are you hearing, language, or attention impaired? To rephrase, are you *interested*?"

Couldn't help it, I laughed. "Okay, I'll bite."

"Their star map, however rotated, didn't match the configurations of our galaxy. Our guest, we believe, is a visitor from another." Now his clicks came fast and loud. "I doubt you have the capacity to understand, but the trading possibilities are awesome. And a ship from even a relatively near island universe, perforce, likely utilizes propulsion techniques far in advance of ours and perhaps communication techniques equally advanced, although these issues are uncertain considering the time scale commensurate with your patient's movements."

Strange to think of the Tsf faster-than-light drive being second rate to anyone's. My NASA advisors would've chewed off their own legs for a practical *near* light speed drive.

I gazed at my patient with new eyes. How could a creature that moved like cold syrup, however technologically advanced, do business with faster folks? At least it wouldn't make any hasty bargains. "Do you know which galaxy the map shows?"

"We are working on that, but the project is complex since the image is limited and the map supplies no directional cues such as the position of what you humans call the Great Attractor."

I had a thought. "It must've taken forever for the language instruction sequence to finish."

"Hardly. The program was interactive. The student set the pace, and our student, this station's data controller, is a quick study."

Damn. If it weren't for that interactivity, I might have some notion of how fast this fellow *should* be operating. Still, I saw another possible angle. "Did the instruction include audio?"

Deal lifted several legs in sequence, another gesture that was lost on me. "You wish to know if we can produce the creature's actual speech."

"Right."

"An obvious question and the answer is yes, with the assistance of our translator doohickey."

"Have you tried setting your translator to speak *very* slowly?"

"Of course. And we have essayed communication in written form. Assuming our guest digs this particular language —and why provide language instruction otherwise?—it hasn't responded to us. Nor has it eaten although we've offered it a variety of dehydrated substances. Thus we suspect some mental or emotional defect, perhaps stress-induced, which may also account for its remarkably torpid movements."

Following an old and bad habit, I tried to gnaw on a knuckle but tasted smartsuit instead. "I'm going to have to, um, chew on all this for a while. Could you take me to my cabin now? I'd like to see those movies you found on my first patient's ship."

"Groovy. Follow me."

———

The décor in my room was too loud. Literally. The Traders had arranged an elaborate virtual Earth environment with all the comforts of home—if your home is set on the edge of a precipice with a view of a giant waterfall on one side and a redwood forest on the other. *All it needs for perfect corniness*, I thought, *is, well, a unicorn. And a rainbow.* Then I looked more closely and by gum, found a rainbow lurking in the mist ahead. It was the waterfall making all the racket.

But it felt like heaven when I stepped inside. The weight of a world seemed to drop off my shoulders. At first, Earth gravity felt trivial, as though I might float to the cloud-spattered ceiling. The room had been adjusted for human occupancy, or at least Inuit occupancy since it was no warmer than the rest of the station. Deal showed me how to summon a bed, which I wouldn't need thanks to my faithful couch. Likewise a chair, likewise unnecessary. And he explained how to access the "pantry" and a bathroom, which I definitely needed. This last required stepping off the precipice onto apparently empty air and I was grateful that Best-offer demonstrated because otherwise I might've stalled until my bladder ruptured.

From inside, the doorless entrance to my stateroom was a rectangular phantom, visible through the virtuality, but I couldn't see an inkling of the actual walls. I was even more impressed by the bathroom when I excused myself to honor my kidneys. This room, too, had no door, but since I couldn't see the Traders waiting ten feet away, I told myself the environmental illusion gave me privacy. Everything from toilet to shower had been cloned from some four-star hotel. I opened a wrapped minibar of soap to wash my hands, stared into the mirror above the sink, and wasn't pleased with the face looking back, the tight lips and tighter jaw, the sunken eyes, that little bulge between the eyebrows.

Snap diagnosis: this subject feels an overwhelming sense of futility but too much pride to admit it.

I didn't need a mirror to gather that. Even before I'd learned that NASA had so badly misunderstood what the Tsf expected me to do, I'd known this mission was absurd. How could I even begin to evaluate extraterrestrial problems? Despite all my training and experience, I barely understand my fellow humans.

To be honest with myself, I'd accepted this assignment out of curiosity and, yes, pride. I'd wanted to be the first human to see the Parent Ship and to visit with aliens on their space station. I'd been attracted to the adventure despite my fears, and the publicity would boost my reputation. But now that I was here, and both the challenge and possible rewards were vastly more extensive than I'd thought, that face looking back at me projected nothing but bad news. Yesterday, I'd hoped I might have at least a microscopic chance for success. Now I'd convinced myself that I had no chance at all. Accurate diagnosis requires open-minded, clear-eyed observation on the part of the diagnostician, and constantly telling myself the job was impossible narrowed my perception and created a self-fulfilling assessment. If I wasn't going to pack up and go home, I needed to change my attitude.

I took a breath in and slowly exhaled, visualizing my certainty of failure dissipating in the frigid air. I repeated the procedure ten times. Mining just *one* useful insight about any of my patients would make me a winner. *Suspend judgment and look*, I told myself. For once, I listened. Returning to the party, it felt as though my personal magnetic poles had flipped.

An unfamiliar Tsf, obliquely introduced to me as Great-bargain, was waiting with my former playmates in the main room, but she left after passing me a little coppery disk. Best-offer silently demonstrated how to use the thing, which proved to be a self-contained multimedia player and data-storage unit with a projected virtual user interface. When activated, the menu presented a long list written in a Tsf script composed of Braille-like dots. Each item, Deal assured me, represented a video retrieved from my first patient's starship. I selected one haphazardly and the menu screen displayed five tiger-lizards engaged in assembling something mechanical and intricate while a snarly voice apparently provided commentary. None of these engineers jumped around, howled, or performed a semi-vanishing act. Something really did seem wrong with my patient.

I had a question, but Deal beat me to the punch: "Have you assembled a theory as to how your initial patient renders herself insubstantial?"

"Not really. But I got the impression she has to make herself *more* substantial before she can ... thin out."

"An obvious observation, but at least you are following our line of thought on the subject. I doubt you will arrive at the correct destination. Now we will abandon you to your futile research. The pantry is stocked with human foods, both solid and liquid."

"I appreciate your hospitality." No sense in returning the rudeness.

"Courtesy is the parent to trade. Call out if you require anything."

"Thanks. I'll do that."

My guides departed, and I tried to think.

Two things we'd learned about Traders: they took verbal

contracts very seriously, and they believed in the principle of mutual benefit. While they'd haggle and leave their customers responsible for understanding the details of any transaction, they weren't deceitful and never tried to cheat or gain unfair advantage. So it seemed at least theoretically possible for me to earn something incredible for the human race. All I needed was a miracle. I'd no idea what the Earth authorities had actually requested for my services, but surely, artificial gravity was worth far more. Did anyone back home know that the Tsf would trade in knowledge? Was it possible the reason we'd learned so little about them and this station was simply that we hadn't offered to trade anything for detailed information?

I shook my head and considered the little disk in my hand. Impressive technology. Yes, my implanted DM can appear to produce similar effects, but that's an illusion. The glow around my finger, the touchscreen if initiated, and the responding voice, all are subjective. It's not my field, but I know how it's done:

After a customer provides blood samples, the "router-rooter," a tiny piezoelectric capsule wrapped in a gene-modified stem-cell matrix, is surgically implanted near the customer's spine and attached to several multifidus muscles and the crura, which allows the capsule to be powered by simply breathing. Stem-cell filaments grow, seek out the spinal cord, and merge with it. That part is permanent barring risky surgery. Then, the system operates by wirelessly networking the person's nervous system with an external CPU; in my case, the fist-sized CPU buried in my couch. The result: an interactive computer that's essentially a controlled-hallucination generator. And if several people have such DMs and desire it, they can share hallucinations.

This disk was powered by God knows what, worked God knows how, and any seeing being could make popcorn and watch the movies it projected. I shook my head. No sense in getting bogged down in minor mysteries when bigger ones were more important. I didn't have any popcorn, but I sat down and loaded a video anyway.

———

Four documentaries later—or soap operas for all I knew—I stood and paced around the room, or rather around the couch since I still wasn't comfortable stepping onto apparently empty air. I'd seen enough punk tigers to make up for a lifetime of having seen none. Thin ones, chubby ones, exceptionally muscular ones who probably spent hours in gyms pumping something heavier than iron. Maybe lead. Or thorium.

Perhaps from too extensive a stay in microgravity, my patient appeared scrawny compared to most of the brutes I'd seen, but not uniquely so. And yet, and yet ... something was different about her, and I couldn't figure out what.

Sure, her peers didn't jet around like punctured balloons, but that wasn't it. No surprise that she behaved differently from them. While the Tsf had placed her in environmental isolation for her own good, she might not see it that way; simply being imprisoned could affect any being's psychology. And speaking of stress-induced quirks, I'd been traumatized by the big squeeze earlier and hated the idea of leaving this haven, but damn it, I needed to observe my patient again and compare ...

I grinned because having confirmed I was an idiot, it seemed better to be the grinning kind. Why leave my cozy cliff-side retreat when I could study her right here? I called my Data Manager into virtual screen format and played back that first encounter with patient one. Perfect recording: clear and seamlessly tiled despite the subject moving around so much, and that it had been shot from the fixed low angle of the lenses set into my couch. But when she jumped high enough, her head popped out of frame. The videos I'd watched earlier hadn't showed any tiger-lizards from so close-up.

And the answer was right in front of me, I *knew* it but couldn't see it.

"Doctor alien?" The voice seemed to come from nowhere, but it sounded deep and raspy.

"Best-offer?"

"Got it in one. What's happenin'? Your life signs are wigging out a bit."

Odd not to hear any clicks beforehand. And I felt uneasy about being so closely monitored. "I'm fine, just getting slightly frustrated."

"Stay cool. But there's been a change in your second patient. I could flip video your way, but would you care to check it out live?"

"Um, when's the next gravity surge?"

"We'll wait until you complete your examination before applying therapeutic force. We observed how bummed out you got last time."

"Thanks, but won't that hurt your health?"

"Our health will keep. If you can dig it, Deal-of-ten-life-times will meet you in the Arcade of Healing. Even-steven and Trader-joe shall join you ASAP. They're non-shrinking doctors."

Even-steven? Trader-joe? Had the Tsf selected such names simply to make me comfortable? If so, it wasn't working. "Okay. I'm leaving right now."

———

Best-offer was right about patient two, the simian had certainly changed. He'd lost perhaps a third of his hair, and where his mottled skin was exposed, it resembled freshly plucked poultry. Diseased poultry. He'd stopped the incessant hand twitching, his lowest two eyes, the only ones open, looked as if they'd been whitewashed, and the way he sat slumped on his tripod legs practically screamed of despair through the body-language barrier.

"How long has he been like this?" I asked Deal.

"I am unsure of the precise time interval, but ahoy! Here come the medicos."

The "medicos" were both currently female—green-tinged cilia—and they streaked down the hallway, arriving in seconds. Even without prompting I might've guessed these were doctors. No white coats or tongue depressors, but they had that harried, behind-schedule vibe. Each toted an arsenal of small but complex-looking devices. Diagnostic, I assumed.

"Trader-joe," Deal asked the newcomer slightly in front, "when did this patient suffer a state-change?"

Trader-joe also carried a translator, so I got her answer in stereo. "In human time, nine minutes and eight-thirteenth seconds from when you finished asking me the question."

Huh. The Tsf all seemed to have built-in chronographs and a savant's ability to instantly convert their time units into ours. For some reason, that notion struck me as highly relevant and for an instant, I wobbled on the threshold of remembering exactly where I'd seen hand movements similar to the ones my patient had stopped making. The second medic, Even-steven, addressed me before I could clarify the memory.

"We waited to learn if the aberration would resolve itself before subjecting this subject to the potential trauma of direct evaluation."

"So you'll examine him now?"

"Only with your permission, Doctor. He is your patient. If you wish us to proceed and to accompany us, you must don your vacuum suit. His atmosphere contains enough chlorine to discomfort a human to death."

"I think we should act immediately, so please go ahead without me."

Both doctors moved to lean against the subtle barrier separating the patient's space from ours, and they seemed to slowly melt through and into the room. The three-legged simian didn't react, even when Trader-joe and Even-steven unfolded their machines and began attaching clamps and probes to and in him. *Unipolar depression or possibly bipolar disorder*, I thought, then reminded myself to distrust my instincts. But damn it, it looked like some form of depression.

"Cheese it," Best-offer said, barely clicking. "The cops."

I didn't get the cheese reference, but the "cops" became obvious when two more Tsf joined us in the corridor. These two were the largest Traders I'd seen. They moved nearly in unison, and neither was introduced to me, not even off-handedly. They halted behind Deal and lurked there, watching everything with presumably steely sensory organs.

"Why the company?" I whispered to Best-offer, but Deal answered.

"My whimsical associate misstated the role of the individuals who have joined us. These are Masters of Propriety here strictly to make sure our doctors follow established protocol in what is clearly a medical emergency. Should this subject kick the bucket, we would find it desirable to have evidence of our good faith attempts to preserve him."

Right. If Traders ever located his species, they wouldn't want to alienate, so to speak, a potential trading partner. So no experimental neck tourniquets. But the "cops" reminded me of just how deadly the Tsf could be.

Two years ago, a year after the Traders had put this station into circumlunar orbit and opened up Trading Posts near Beijing, Delhi, and Manhattan, there'd been an incident unreported in any human news media. I'd only found out about it myself two weeks ago. Some crime syndicate had tried to rob the Manhattan Trading Post, which was understandable considering all those exotic treasures just sitting there on all those shelves. This Post, like the others, was only open an hour at a time, three times a day. During those hours, its environment was adjusted for human comfort. At all other times, the environment was set to duplicate conditions on the Tsf's high-gravity home world. Which, from what I now knew, implied that it was more practical to increase gravity on a planet than on a space station.

The heist was perfectly organized, executed, and timed, and the eight masked men who rushed into the open-for-business Post carried the most reliable and powerful automatic weaponry any mob could afford.

Until that moment, the Traders had seemed harmless, self-effacing, friendly, and unarmed. It hadn't occurred to many humans that ambulatory beings who'd evolved in high gravity would not only be strong and tough, they'd also have reaction times like oiled lightning. Maintaining balance under multiple Gs, even with multiple legs, requires super-quick reactions because everything falls *fast*. And if you want to avoid a predator, or catch prey, or even catch a ball....

To make a long and gory story just gory, the three Tsf present in the Post moved like rockets and tore the eight men to bloody paste, bones and all. I watched the Trader recording of the event, which they released to the US Justice Department who hot-potatoed it to the FBI, evidently with instructions to bury it deep and only decant it for intimidating psychiatrists. I'm fairly sure one of the Tsf got hit with a bullet or two, but it didn't even slow her down.

Yes, the Traders could've simply disarmed the bad guys, captured them, and turned them over to our police, and it says something about Tsf psychology that when presented with a clear threat, they obliterated it. Another point of interest was the method the Tsf used to clean up the mess: they released a cloud of blue gas; when it dissipated, the Post was spotless and only the carnage was gone.

I needed a distraction. "Why do you think," I asked Deal, "your medical tests will be meaningful on a life form so unfamiliar to you?"

"The data now being collected can be compared to the data

we gathered immediately after we rescued this individual. We expect to find significance, but aren't counting on it."

"I—good Lord! *Counting on it.* That's the key!"

For a few seconds, Deal kept as still as the security personnel behind us. Then he clicked, "I fear our translator has failed. I failed to grasp the import of your last few statements."

"My fault. I'm just—I think I know what my patient was doing with his hands before." I had to fight off a childhood tendency to stutter. "Do you know what an abacus is?"

"Only if you refer to the counting frame referred to as a *suanpan* in China, a *soroban* in Japan, a—"

His condescension no longer bothered me. "That's the thing."

"What about it?"

"Years ago, I visited a school in Tokyo where students were trained to perform all sorts of arithmetic calculations on, um, sorobans and do them in seconds."

"I still await enlightenment."

"Not for long. When the students got really proficient, their teachers took their sorobans away. After all those years of intensive practice, the students could visualize the beads perfectly, and I watched a roomful of kids multiplying four-digit numbers, fast and accurately, on imaginary abacuses."

"That what you talkin' 'bout." The voice sounded worried. "You believe your patient was employing a similar technique. A curious notion, but what problem would require three separate counting frames?"

I nodded, relieved that Deal hadn't stomped on the idea. "You told me you'd only found his landing craft, so I'm guessing he was somehow keeping track of his main spaceship and trying to give you the coordinates. It would take three, right? Finally he gave up."

Deal stiffened, and I thought he was going to clam up on me again. "An improbable theory although it conforms to all known facts. But even given the numbers, how could we determine the zero point to which the coordinates relate?"

"I don't know. Or maybe I do. You found him on a planet? If I were him, I'd have used the spot where you found me as the reference point. Either that or the planet's center."

"You foolishly assume he has unprecedented powers of spatial and temporal orientation. Please bide while I discuss this matter with my superiors."

I expected Deal to go off to find these superiors, but he stood right there, clicking like a Geiger counter in plutonium. The Tsf way of speaking carried quite a distance because I couldn't see the Traders who began clicking back in return. The interpreting device ignored all this byplay, but Deal gave me a summary in his own sweet way.

"Here is our plan: We will play back earlier recordings of this being, analyze the image of his moving hands, and deduce the bead arrangements of the counting frames he was visualizing, and the three continual sets of results." He made it sound as though the idea was his. "Then we need only vary dimensional axes and numeration systems until his results become meaningful and consistent in relationship to a moving object. If one of the logical zero points such as galactic center proves correct, a few sets of solutions will allow us to plot his ship's course or orbit. If this is successful, we will then retrieve his spacecraft. Personally, I very much doubt this approach will accomplish anything but waste time and energy."

I had to admit that the Traders had evidently caught my insight and run with it farther than I could, all the way to the goal posts if everything worked out. "I have another idea. Do you have or could you build anything resembling an abacus?"

"Why?"

"I'll have to show you."

Deal hesitated. "The project seems unnecessary. But I have been ordered to obey your whims. Certainly we have wires and beads. Hang loose, this won't take long."

Deal leaped away, leaving me alone with Best-offer and two grim shadows until the medicos finished their research and squeezed back into the passageway. Without waiting for me to ask, Trader-joe began rattling off—it sounded like rattling—test results, all expressed in human measurements but too fast for me to follow. I interrupted to ask some questions but just then Deal returned, passed me an improvised abacus, and everyone who wasn't already silent became so and watched to see what would happen.

I glanced at the toy in my hand. It had once been a Tsf translator, but the spokes had been ripped out, the frame bent rectangular and restrung with fifteen parallel wires. Each wire held fifteen hollow rings, all emerald green except for the black top two. Fast work, putting this together.

I hoped my patient would see it and realize that we'd caught on, but first I had to catch his attention; he seemed to have withdrawn a light-year into himself. So I stood in front of him and waved the impromptu abacus like a madman. Slowly, his eyes focused on it. I flipped a few beads and all his eyes popped open, colors instantly replacing what had resembled cataracts. I'd never seen such a rapid, spectacular transformation. In that instant, he jumped to his feet, all three of them, practically radiating joy and health. I could've sworn his hair was already growing back on his bare spots. He pointed to the abacus with three arms and Deal took it and pushed it through the isolation membrane into his hands. The simian held it so that we could see the emerald beads and hid three of them under a hand.

Deal made an especially forceful click. "Base twelve, it seems," he said, no pleasure in the tone. "Other possibilities exist, but this may save us time. Would you care to return to your stateroom now, Doctor?"

"Oh. Sure. Guess I've been holding up your gravity therapy."

"You think? But apparently the Masters have found a

champion in you. Come, I will accompany you to lightness." Deal's legs practically dragged as we moved along, but his partner seemed to skip.

"Doctor, you da man," Best-offer click-whispered to me.

———

My room hadn't changed, but I had. "Deal-of-ten-lifetimes," I said, standing between Deal and the doorway, a joke if he wanted to leave. "You clearly have a problem with me, and I want to know what it is."

"I will tell you, if you insist."

Best-offer, who'd entered behind me, hopped onto my couch without asking my permission and rode it to its usual spot. I had the feeling he found this confrontation vastly entertaining.

"Here's me," I said, "insisting."

"Very well. I chose to wager against your success, which required a large amount of exchange credit to show any significant profit."

I stared at him for a second. "Let's see if I understand you. You made a bet that I'd fail and had to bet a pile because the local bookies were betting the same way."

"In essence, yes."

"I, on the other hands," Best-offer volunteered, "wagered against the odds, risking little and earning much exchange. Deal-of-ten-lifetimes should've hedged his bet with a side wager."

Deal shook a leg at his partner. "Thanks for nothing, friend of friends. Your advice is as tardy as it is obvious."

I held up my hands. "Okay. We've cleared the air. So how about we stop bickering and make the best of things?"

"I see no reason why we can't all just get along," Deal said, his artificial voice expressing resignation. "I was only trying to insure a positive outcome. For me, that is."

"You weren't exactly encouraging."

"I provided my best shot. Now, my smug associate and I have duties and must leave you alone to enjoy your victory. I will not underestimate you again."

The pair hurried off, and I found myself ravenous. So I opened my couch's fridge, which didn't need to cool anything here, and pulled out two half-frozen pea-protein sandwiches on true whole-grain bread. To wash them down, a chocolate oatmilk drink. True, my stateroom pantry had plenty of human snacks, but they were all high-glycemic-load items crammed with sugar and saturated fats. As biologists learned nearly a century ago, every meal counts. Since I was living on borrowed time and wanted to make it a long-term loan, I couldn't afford treats that would stimulate a cascade of inflammatory agents. But those damn chocolate-chip macadamia cookies in the pantry threatened to burn a hole in my will power.

Frankly, I felt damn good. Not only had I taken a large step toward solving patient two's problem, I'd earned my first gold star from my hosts. Plus, I had a new hope. Perhaps I didn't stand a chance of resolving alien neuroses, but what if one or both of my other patients had a more ... mechanical sort of difficulty, the sort of simple thing only a technological primitive such as yours truly might spot?

Then I had to laugh at myself. From Doctor I-think-I-can't, I'd turned into a wild-eyed optimist when my success had really been the dumbest sort of luck. If I hadn't visited that school in Tokyo, I wouldn't have had a clue, and my chances for similar victories, realistically, were none to nil. But Deal's mention of analyzing the image of hands had given me a notion....

I hadn't wanted anyone monitoring this room to think I was talking to myself, but I'd reached the point of needing someone to bounce ideas off of, someone without hidden agendas. That left me one choice.

A year ago, putting my standard DM into vocal-interaction

mode had been fun because of a popular fantasy liveapp I'd downloaded and customized, ostensibly to entertain my son whose DM was, naturally, on my family-and-friends list. I'd say the codeword "Aladdin," see and feel a lamp in my hands, rub the thing, and watch smoke rise up and congeal into Carl Jung. The system I now used had been designed originally for military use, and I doubted it would accept any fun control mods such as Aladdin Live or my wife's favorite, One Ring.

But my NASA handlers had waxed enthusiastic about this DMs having new "bells and whistles" and then, perhaps suspecting that psychiatrists don't recognize metaphors, they explained that they referred to improved cognition and pattern-comprehension rather than to any annoying musical accompaniment. Also, my unit came with a choice of four designer personalities: Diana, David, Dane, and Doris. I'd had two weeks to get to know them all and to learn the control procedures.

"Diana, Diana, Diana," I said quickly, the redundancy preventing accidental activation should some breathing Diana drop by. Right now, I didn't want David's philosophical ramblings, or Dane's jokes, or Doris's constant concern for my well-being.

"How can I help you, Al?" The alto voice, adjusted to my preference, sounded friendly but businesslike.

"Last time I was in this room, I watched some videos that the Tsf had retrieved from an alien spaceship. As I understand it, you're recording everything happening around me, so I assume you recorded the recordings?"

"If your rising inflection indicates a query, my answer is yes."

"Great. When I say "go," please display random images of the aliens from those videos one at a time—just one image per second and on only half your screen, um, the left side. On the other half, show me the first patient I saw today, the one similar in appearance to the recorded aliens."

"Do you wish to see your patient in real time or from my memory?"

I blinked twice. "How could you display my patient in real time?"

"I am receiving a feed from the Parent Ship."

"Huh. Real time, then. Go."

The virtual screen appeared, as did the images I'd requested. "Stay with this grouping," I ordered after a minute. "Zoom in on the leftmost alien until it's the same size as the one on the right and put its actions on a ten-second loop."

I'd chosen that particular tiger because its body posture matched my client's. I watched it reach out to adjust a complicated mechanism on a black stand, and then watched the whole thing again three times. Damn. The two aliens had individual variations, plenty of them, but I saw no fundamental physical difference between my patient and, presumably, a healthy tiger-lizard. Yet I knew I was missing *something*.

Suddenly, a big difference. My patient started her intensifying routine. Only this time, she kept it up so long and became so vivid that I half-expected her to burst into flame. *Tyger, tyger, burning bright* ...

"Deal," I shouted, "if you can hear me, I'm heading out to patient one. I think something's gone wrong with this one, too."

I sprinted out my doorway, not thinking, and then the extra eighty-odd pounds hit me. I yelped from a horrible twinge in my right knee. That leg gave out, and I slammed into the floor as if some steroid-bulked-up pro wrestler had thrown me down. I'd felt at least one rib crack and for far too long, I couldn't breathe. But I finally managed to gasp in a little air and struggled to my hands and knees, intending to crawl toward the hospital corridor if I couldn't stand. I was no longer proud of myself.

The DM screen re-formed before me; I'd forgotten to close it, but Diana had minimized it while I'd been moving. An instant later, my couch tapped me on the ass. Dr. Dignity here. I glanced at the screen and forgot everything else. The left-side tiger kept adjusting that same machine every ten seconds; but on the right, my patient's room contained one robot and no patient.

To my far left, past the screen, Deal skidded into view, reached me in two giant bounds, and used four legs to set me on my feet. He'd only needed one, I'm sure, but the extras made the hoisting gentler on me. "Are you injured?" he asked, a bit late to earn his EMT merit badge, but it was strange to hear him express any concern for me. "We saw you fall."

"I'm all right." At least I could stand on my own. And breathe, sort of. "But look!" I pointed to the screen.

Yes, the kind of fool that would dash from one gravity field into a much heavier one is just the sort to point at a virtual object only visible in his head.

"Sorry," I said. "You can't see what I'm seeing because—"

"Au contraire. Your data management system and ours have linked. Mine is showing me what yours is showing you."

"Oh."

"Plus, the original feed is ours, so I already knew of your patient's absence." Now his words were smugger than his tone.

"Maybe she just ... thinned out to the point of invisibility?"

I could've sworn the translator prefaced his response with a raspberry. "We scanned her room for life signs. We doubt she has ceased processing gasses, ceased making even the slightest sounds of organic involuntary activities, ceased radiating and absorbing anything on the practical electromagnetic spectrum, stopped—"

Now *that's* the Deal I'd grown so fond of. "I get it. She's gone."

"Also, we found traces of her elsewhere. You stand askew, are you certain your fall did not damage you?"

I shrugged and the tiny motion hurt my ribs. "Maybe a little."

"Then return to your stateroom and recuperate; there's naught you can do at the moment to aid in searching for the ding-a-ling."

"Did you say 'ding-a-ling'?" If that was obsolete slang for a mental case, it made no sense to me.

"Yes. Perhaps this translator provided an inapt metonymy."

"Let's just move on."

"Done. If you need assistance in healing, our medical team trembles from readiness."

I envisioned overeager "medicos" inserting their probes into me. "Thanks, but I'll be fine. Wait! Why should you have to *search*? Don't you have ... sensors or something that can locate her?"

Deal brushed his gondola with a leg in a thoughtful, jaw-rubbing kind of way. "They have, many times. But when we arrive, she has already relocated."

"Good God. Teleportation?"

"We believe she becomes tenuous enough to pass through walls, explaining her escape."

I just stared at him and after a moment he continued. "Frankly, we are surprised she can absorb our atmosphere. Yet she travels with great vigor."

"Have you tried pinning her down with gravity?"

"You betcha. With no success. Don't assess her capacities by measuring yours. Before I rejoin the search for our rolling stone ..."

He paused until I caught on and said, "That one works."

"... may I assist you to your room?"

We all need someone we can lean on.

———

45

My body hurt less the instant I entered my cabin. Deal galloped away, and I lay down on my couch, which as usual had tailed me in. The screen automatically re-formed, directly over my head because of my supine position, but I barely glanced at it.

How, I wondered, did the Tsf recognize an alien distress signal? Was some kind of super-science aetheric siren the usual ploy? And on reflection, it seemed implausible that the Tsf had located three unknown, stranded aliens within a short period of time—Deal had claimed they'd all been recovered recently. He'd also referred to this triple play as a "unique happenstance," but wasn't it far more likely that all the victims had been involved in a single accident? Perhaps they weren't unknown to each other and had been meeting to arrange a trade deal, and something had gone wrong. Or gone sour.

Three travelers. One, judging by the strange star maps, from a distance even the Tsf couldn't reach; one capable of complex three-part running calculations; one who could drift through walls. All three appearing to surpass the usual three-dimensional limitations. A possible connection?

A spasm of honesty made me admit that all this speculation was largely my attempt to forget there was a crazed tiger-lizard wandering the ship. *Get a grip, Al*, I warned myself. *You may be on to something, but it has nothing to do with why you were hired.*

But if a trade deal *had* melted down like the standard TV drug deal, maybe patient one was seeking the others, and not to cheer them up. I sat up too fast and my ribs let me know. After a second, the screen reappeared but it showed nothing new.

"Diane, Diane, Diane. Can you communicate with Deal-of-ten-lifetimes through the ship's DM?"

"Yes. What do you desire to communicate?"

"Tell him patients two and three may be in danger from the first one."

Deal's audio response came almost instantly. "Doctor, we already guard them. Rest yourself! Over and out."

Human cliché, and wrong. "Over": it's your turn to talk.

My patients were safe, but was I? Needing another distraction, I came up with a potentially useful one: studying Diana's video of patient three, the squeaky wheel who moved too slowly to squeak. "Diane, close all current images and show me what you've got on that flat alien with all those hook things."

And there it was in all its repulsive glory. Its body design didn't seem functional. How could it possibly use those twisted, almost two-dimensional protrusions as limbs? For the first time, I noticed how it … ambulated: by slowly rocking forward on its lowest protrusions rather like someone in a potato-sack race determined to lose.

"My problem," I said, complaining out loud, "is that this thing is *too* alien. I've got nothing to relate it to, let alone compare it to. So how am I supposed—"

The question was rhetorical, but Diana interrupted. "Physically, it relates somewhat to tardigrades."

That stopped me in mid-rant. "How? Tell me about tardigrades.

"They are tiny, segmented, invertebrate animals. Phylum Tardigrada."

"Are you claiming patient three looks like one of those little monsters?

Something in her programming made Diana sound a tad disapproving. "They were discovered on Earth in 1773. All people educated in biological sciences should be aware of them." Make that disapproving plus snooty. I refrained from mentioning that I only knew they existed from "Ant-Man" movies I'd seen many years ago where they appeared after various characters violated good sense and physics by radically shrinking.

"Under conditions," Diana continued, "lethal for virtually

all other species including hard vacuum, drought, and temperatures near absolute zero, tardigrades can survive by entering an extreme state of suspended animation called a *tun*. In this condition, they are nearly indestructible."

"Huh. You re-learn something new every decade. Detailed pictures, please, with more info below in a fast crawl."

I watched a parade of these weird little guys, most resembling a cross between a caterpillar and the contents of a tackle box, and the crawl mentioned that they were nicknamed "water bears," and "moss piglets," which didn't quite convince me the things were adorable and cuddly. Plus bears and piglets weren't known for thinness. But when I read details about the *tun* state, I felt my eyes widen. Then I burst out laughing but stopped immediately thanks to rib pain. If patient three's resemblance to tardigrades was more than skin-deep, and I had the strongest hunch it was, the Traders had made an incredible blunder. Admittedly, I was basing a lot on appearances. But what struck my funny bone so hard was how easily I could perform a second miracle "cure" if I was right. Hell, I could do it with both hands tied behind my back.

Then the lights went out along with the gravity. My virtual hideaway became as black as a subterranean cave, and I instinctively anchored myself by grabbing the first two couch-straps my scrabbling hands could find. I was scared, and it didn't help that in utter darkness, it felt like I was falling. Something was wrong—unless the Tsf enforced a weird sort of curfew.

"Activate your DTB," I ordered Diana, faking bravado because I knew someone might be listening to me. "Let there be light!" And there was light, but it wasn't good.

Even in my own home, having my civilian genie light my path, say, to the bathroom at night to avoid waking my wife, direct-to-brain illumination makes me edgy. When a Data Manager applies a DTB interface to provide the illusion of seeing, it's actually replaying visual patterns that have previously entered the eyes rather than present reality. So on my way to the toilet, the floor can appear perfectly clear of obstructions, and then I can trip over my wife's shoes, or the wife herself if she happens to feel her own call of the bladder. It's a character flaw, I'm sure, but invisible objects and people tend to creep me out.

In this case, my fancy-schmancy DM was only partly relying on visual memories for information. Electromagnetic eyes and ears along with more ordinary lenses studded this couch like a dog collar. Calling up this unit's DTB vision without specifying limits gave me the *entire* optical recording. So when my stateroom became visible, it looked bizarre and out of focus, its virtual forest and waterfall superimposed upon a moiré pattern of fine white lines projected onto gray walls, which shimmered with hints of colors beyond human vision. Dizzying.

Then I felt myself sink into the couch again, much deeper than usual, and the ceiling brightened with a bit of genuine light, which provided yet another layer of optic stimulation. Everything seemed to vibrate. Between the sudden weight and the visual weirdness, all I could do was lie flat and yell.

"Diana! Shut off your DTB *now*. Thanks. Much better." The cabin had become simple but was still unfamiliar. Minus the faux landscape, it was roomier than I'd thought, a cube about fourteen feet per side, which gave it a surprisingly high ceiling. "Okay, now tell me what the *hell* is going on?"

"My link with the Parent Ship's data controller has been severed, therefore I can only report on events prior to the disconnection."

Enhanced conversational abilities, my sore ass. "So what happened?"

"Your feline client, in attenuated form, passed through the area housing the station's master CPU, generating an electromagnetic interaction. At that point, the controller went offline."

That didn't sound good. The Parent Ship was so huge that it seemed unlikely my tiger-lizard would've accidentally stumbled across the controller. Which suggested deliberate sabotage....

A Tsf appeared in my doorway, and it took me a moment to recognize Deal in the dimness. He wasn't carrying a translator, so I gathered that system, too, was dependent on the master CPU. Deal made his usual noises anyway, and I told him that I couldn't understand what he was saying, which I doubted he understood.

"Do you wish for me to act as an interpreter?" Diana asked.

"What? Do you suddenly ... read clicks?"

"I have gathered sufficient information through your previous communications with the Tsf to provide adequate two-way translation."

I mentally withdrew my nasty thought about Diana's conversational skills. "Great! But how will he hear you?"

"Like you, he has an internal DM; but unlike yours, which is me, his retains some autonomy even when disconnected from its primary CPU. While I cannot establish a conventional wireless connection because our frequencies are too disparate, our present proximity allows transmission via induction."

"I get it. No long-distance calls. What did Deal say?"

"His remark was addressed to me rather than you. He asked if I'd gathered sufficient information to provide adequate two-way translation, and if I could use induction to transmit—"

"Stop!" I partly withdrew my withdrawal. "Please just tell him—"

"Your exchange will proceed more rapidly if you simply speak, disregarding my role in the process."

The Diana personality reminded me of my first secretary. She, too, had been brusque, organized, and subtly scornful. "Fine. Deal-of-ten-lifetimes, I'm glad to see you."

"Most understandable," he relayed via Diana. "I truly apologize for how long it took us to activate emergency energies. And I apologize more deeply that we can no longer isolate this room and have been forced to apply a degree of gravity to the entire station that you surely find onerous. This is the minimum we need to maintain our physical integrity on a long-term basis."

I'd meant that I was glad to see *him* but decided to let it go. "What do you mean, 'long-term'?"

"Several of your hours, but it should not come to that. We seek your escaped patient with full diligence now and refined technique. Once we secure her and render her harmless, we will take our master controller out of self-protective mode. It will then re-coagulate, and all systems will return to functionality. I suggest you find patience and remain here where you will be safe from potential violence."

Diana's interpretations weren't nearly as colorful as those of the Tsf translator, but they'd given me a sickening premonition about what Deal intended. Evidently, I wasn't the only one to suspect sabotage, and I'd seen how Traders reacted to an actual threat. They hadn't even needed weapons to kill the thugs who'd tried to rob them in New York. Government analysts, who'd studied the massacre video in slow motion, lucky them, had concluded that Tsf skin and certain fascial membranes could harden tremendously, turning limbs into triangular clubs or, with maximum tension, something very like knives.

My patient had become *persona non grata*, and soon would lose her persona status. I opened my mouth to ask Deal if his people might consider an alternative to lethal force, but the doorway was empty.

———

I felt horribly heavy. From the pressure on my back, I estimated my present weight at over three hundred pounds. Thanks to this and my rib woes, breathing wasn't fun. I tried shifting position to give my diaphragm a bit more freedom, but nothing helped. Then I remembered just how well stocked this couch was.

"Diana. Get me a pain pill, really strong, and some liquid to wash it down. Um, I'd better do my swallowing sitting up, so lift my back up, please."

As I was hoisted into position, mechanical arms handed me a pill and a small, straw-pierced container. The quick-dissolving pill felt like lead going down, and the liquid nearly choked me. But after only a minute or two, the agony in my chest began to drain away.

That's when I noticed the smell: part floral, part grassy. Not at all a scent I'd associate with a large predator. So when my striped client coalesced into visibility, I wasn't exactly prepared. The "tyger" eyed me for a moment, then screeched so loudly, I'd thought my eardrums had had it. What was it about me that got her so agitated? She jumped upward, banging her head on the ceiling as hard as a pile driver, and then hung there, suspended by her skull-spikes, until her weight in the new gravity pulled her free. Quite comical, maybe, but I wasn't chortling. She landed lightly on her feet and jumped again, but only high enough to brush the holes she'd left earlier.

Her huge body seemed to take up all the space in my cabin, and for the first time in my life, I was so damn terrified that I couldn't move or even yell. Something in the back of my heart begged me to spend my last moments remembering and appreciating my wife and son while I had the chance, but the only cogent thought in my head was a terrible regret that I'd failed to share my guess about patient three with Deal.

My visitor leaped sideways. I saw that this time, she'd be landing directly on me, surely crushing me despite my cushion. But as she fell, my couch, or rather my DM controlling the couch, acted. Four flexible mechanical arms, two above my shoulders and two below my feet, erupted from the mattress, catching my patient in midair at her chest and thighs.

She screeched, quietly for once, and it sounded oddly like a squeal of delight. For a moment neither of us even blinked as she gazed straight down into my eyes, her body suspended above mine but extending almost to the doorway. Then her claws slowly emerged. My body remained petrified with mortal fear, but my mind seemed to sputter then catch like one of those old gasoline engines. Suddenly I blazed with insights, my thoughts rocketing along fast enough to escape the gravity grip of ignorance.

At close range, I saw that her claws, especially the tips, were quite shiny. They seemed plated with actual metal. If this was natural, wouldn't a being with internal electroplating abilities have to be able to generate an electrical charge? If she'd been holding any charge while drifting through the ship's master controller in some incorporeal form ... well, even the best shielding would be useless against direct penetration. And just maybe, this alien's ability to go intangible was also related to ...

Lightly swinging one paw, my patient raked her claws down my torso, slicing through my smartsuit and the skin below, from my left nipple almost to my public bone. I didn't feel the claws sink in very deeply, but the cuts were long and the pain excruciating.

I yelled, and my attacker added insult to injury by drooling onto my face; some of it fell into my open mouth.

An avalanche of nastiness. As I choked on hot coppery saliva and blood gushed from my wounds, sparks shot up from my torn smartsuit and its heating units failed. Some detached, observing part of my mind speculated on exactly what would win the race to kill me: bleeding out, getting my head bitten off, poison if "tyger" spit was toxic, or freezing to death.

Maybe the sparks scared her, or she hated the scent of human blood. Whatever the reason, my patient stared at me

⸀ a second longer while doing her intensifying trick, burning bright despite the surrounding dimness. Then she jumped away, yowling, and leaped out of the room.

Feeling both tremendous relief and a lot of pain, I swiped a hand across my chin before the alien saliva could freeze on. I glanced at my soggy hand and, just like that, I knew. None of the many tiger-lizards I'd seen in the videos had drooled. *That's* what I'd seen without seeing. And I knew precisely what it meant. I should've figured it out hours ago.

———

Bleeding, chilled to the marrow, and crushed by my own nearly doubled weight, I desperately wanted to stay put and try to patch myself up. But I couldn't wait this out. The Traders were about to make a second grotesque mistake, one that could never be undone. I pulled the torn ends of my clothing together, doing some weightlifting just moving my arms, and pressed the material down over as much of my wound as possible.

"Deal!" Squished by my own bodyweight, I couldn't manage much of shout. "Best-offer? Anyone? I need to talk to someone!" I listened and didn't hear the tap-tapping sounds of approaching Traders. No good.

"Diana, reshape this mattress so it covers me, neck to toes. Tightly." That should hold in my body heat and maybe stop the bleeding. "Meanwhile, get this crate rolling down the hall toward the hospital corridor. Now!"

The smart mattress neglected to shape-shift and my carriage didn't budge an inch. "Diana? Diana, Diana, Diana. Damn it, what's up? Get this bastard moving."

"I cannot at this time. My CPU regulates your protective garment; the two form a unitary system."

"So?"

"The damage to your smartsuit has evoked a safety

protocol requiring a full diagnostic assessment, which will be complete in ten minutes and twelve seconds. Meanwhile, as a further safety measure, some of my functions have been disabled including control of your couch. I am currently seeking a work-around."

"Oh, shit. *Ten* minutes?"

"And four seconds now. I may find a work-around earlier."

"I can't wait that long. Don't suppose someone packed crutches or a walker in this stupid loveseat?"

"That would have been redundant since the couch itself possesses mobility."

I kept my response to myself and levered myself upright as carefully as possible, but my wounds reopened, giving my belly and legs a fresh coat of blood. Just standing was a massive effort and as for getting enough oxygen, forget about it. I tried to use techniques I'd learned at NASA's training center, taking in only a modest amount of air at a time, and expanding my lower ribs in all directions at once, "three-dimensional" breathing. Thanks to my former injury, happy day, knives seemed to stab into my chest every time I inhaled.

I fought down panic and a growing urge to hyperventilate, which would only make matters worse.

Taking tiny, shuffling steps and leaving a little river of blood to mark my trail, I made it to the hallway. By then, my legs shook with exhaustion, and I had to support myself against the walls to keep moving. I kept telling myself, just one more step, just one more ...

The dim lighting to either side appeared to pulse in sync with my heartbeat. I glanced back and was horrified by how short a distance I'd come. And fuming because all this effort shouldn't have been necessary. Why in God's name didn't the Traders post a guard for *me*?

Maybe they had. In my mind's eye, I saw my patient arrive as something less than a mist and drift through my wall while two oblivious soldiers played the Tsf equivalent of gin rummy outside my room. I saw the "tyger" dashing past them, her claws dripping and red, and the guards chasing her until she faded from visibility.

It all seemed so real until I felt an extra coldness on my spine and realized that my eyes were closed, and I was sitting, feet splayed out in front of me, back supported by the wall behind me. Scared alert, I forced my eyes open. I'd slipped into a dream without knowing it. How strong had that pill been? Or was the effect due to blood loss?

There was no way I could get back on my feet, but I kept trying and kept slipping back down. I had no breath left for even a groan let alone a yell and kept hoping someone would show up. No one appeared. I suppose they were all searching for my patient, minds fixed entirely on killing her.

Then I had as much inspiration as a dying man could hope for. I snapped my fingers.

Back in my intern days, I'd flirted with becoming a neuro-surgeon. My resident advisor had me practicing surgical tech-niques on cadavers daily for a year, even after my most grueling shifts. The experience turned me off to anything involving sutures, but all that gripping gave me strong hands. So while I felt weak as a newborn possum, my snap was loud and clear. And it must've carried just fine because from a great distance, I heard what sounded like a million snaps in return.

I closed my eyes, and when I opened them, Deal was bounding toward me with the medico, Trader-joe, coming in a close second. Both carried translators, so repairs had happened. In my fuzzy state, they seemed more like cartoons than living creatures, and I giggled, imagining brakes screeching when they came to a stop. My analgesic had found a fourth gear.

Deal splayed out his legs to lower himself to my level. "Doctor, you are impaired." Impaired. Right. "You must allow Trader-joe to evaluate the damage." He shifted aside and my new personal physician took over.

Should be Trader-*Josephina*, I told myself, and the thought struck me as infinitely witty.

I have to admit she was competent, precise, and gentle, but her sensory cilia tickled when she pressed them against various parts of my anatomy. I got the impression she had built-in stethoscopes.

"You have the following injuries," she reported. "Three shallow, parallel cuts traversing from your thorax to your abdomen." I raised a mental eyebrow, in a humorous way, at Diana's fussy syntax. "Also two cracked thoracic bones, many exhausted muscles, and an increasing degree of hypothermia." Shouldn't that be a *decreasing* degree? I snickered again at my cleverness.

She continued. "The hypothermia must be addressed, but none of your injuries are intrinsically life-threatening. Still, you have lost and continue to lose your vital nutrient-carrying liquid at a fatal rate."

Deal started clicking, but he wasn't talking to me; maybe he'd noticed just how impaired I'd become. "How could the doctor have sustained such damage?"

"From the size and spacing of his cuts, I am certain our furred guest was responsible."

Deal shook three limbs at the medic. "You are mistaken. When I left the human previously, the furred one had already been discovered in section three. Since then, our entire security staff formed a wide perimeter and has been gradually closing in, posting sentries with sensitive detectors in every room should she attempt evasion through walls."

"I state the facts and have no responsibility to explain them. But you must have suspected my services could be needed when we heard the doctor's distress signal, or you would not have brought me here."

"The cuts are facts, your conclusions otherwise."

Trader-joe rose up. "If you feel better qualified than—"

"Stop," I said as forcefully as I could, barely a whisper,

which was as good as a shout with Diana doing the translating. The argument seized up nicely. "Maybe my patient can ... throw her magnetism or something. The doctor's right, she sliced me." I smiled to show that I bore no one in the universe any ill will.

Deal had gone very still. "I fail to understand how that is possible, but she will do no more slicing. We do not permit one guest to harm another. And her life was already forfeited by the previous damage she caused."

"You really don't understand. She isn't—oh, shit, she's *right behind you*!"

My pill-induced euphoria popped like a bubble. The creature stood, growling quietly, shifting her weight from side to side, turning her golden gaze on each of us in turn. Deal leaped at her so fast, it should've made a sonic boom.

She reacted almost instantly but still too late. Deal latched onto one of her arms by wrapping the end of a single leg around her wrist. I hadn't realized his limbs were so flexible.

The scene turned surreal. The tiger-lizard towered over the Tsf and looked to be twice as massive and ten times as powerful. But though she desperately tugged on her trapped arm and flailed at her captor with her three others and one leg, she couldn't budge him, lift him, hurt him, or get away. What I saw appeared physically impossible, even with Tsf muscles, until I looked down and saw three of Deal's legs splayed out and sunk far into the rubbery flooring material. He'd evidently turned his feet into stakes and anchored himself solidly. But damn, he only needed *one* limb to hold her.

When I looked up again, the Trader had become a living nightmare.

Four of his legs were raised high and angled toward the tyger's chest, their leading halves narrowed and hardened into organic swords. His entire body radiated tension and deadliness. For the first time, I saw a Tsf gondola clearly. It wasn't the blubbery, octopus-like head I'd imagined, but more like a purple wrecking ball with crocodile skin, and had at least five ugly mouths, some vertical and others horizontal, one with three-inch fangs. My patient began making a noise like the keening of a housecat in terrible distress. Her body kept brightening and dimming a little but didn't fade to mist. Something about the contact blocked her abilities.

God knows how I did it. I wasn't aware of making any particular effort although I heard myself grunt, but I was on my feet, grabbing one of Deal's improvised sword-arms, not too near the tip. Might as well have been trying to pull down a bolted-in steel beam. Could've done chin-ups on the damn thing had I the strength.

"Wait!" I panted. "She doesn't mean ... harm." My voice was probably too weak to be audible even without the keening, but Diana would get my point across.

Using a spare leg, the Trader gently pushed me away. "You are unwell and thus confused."

"No. You promised. Not to underestimate me. Look. Even now. She's keeping her claws in."

In the background, Trader-joe sounded like a frantic chicken except clicking not clucking.

Deal lowered his blades very slightly. "This much is true. And unexplained. If she means no ill, why did she cut you?"

"Didn't mean to. See her fur? About an inch thick. I think she was only trying to ... groom me. Bet she got interested in me—" I had to pause to catch my breath—"because I'm the closest thing ... she's seen to one of her own people. Ever since. Damn. I'm not being clear. She's only a ... toddler, Deal, barely more than a baby. Still drools. Can't use a potty."

"An astonishing theory, but experience contradicts it. Disabling our primary controller cannot have been accidental. Our safeguards are such that no fledgling could have disabled them. And you cannot believe that her finding our control center was coincidental."

"Why not? On my planet, unlikely accidents ... happen all

the time. But maybe something about your DM ... or the place where you keep it ... attracted her. Besides, *you* offered proof she's immature."

"When? I did no such thing."

"You said the controls in the spaceship ... where you found her ... were set too high for her to reach. Without jumping. Word to the wise. Her parents may be ... on the large side."

Deal's swords stayed just as sharp, but some of the tension went out of him. "You raise reasonable doubts. So now I am sorry, but she is too dangerous to release yet cannot be constrained by any means known to us."

Without warning, my vision blurred and the hallway seemed to dim. Bad news. It was clear what Deal had meant: he might feel regretful, but he was still planning to kill my patient. It was up to me to save her, and I had a good idea how. But now I was running out of time....

I took as deep a breath as I could and willed the darkness away. "We *can* confine her. Can't you see? She'd fade out now if she could. All you have to do is hold her until ..."

To my horror, everything went black, and I felt myself falling. "Diana. Her robot. Give it power. Tell him." I wasn't sure I'd gotten the words out. I prayed I had, and that Diana had enough bells or whistles to understand. Then I was gone.

———

Clouds drifted high above me when I opened my eyes, and a waterfall roar tickled my ears. Yes. I was in my stateroom, lying on my back, warm, comfortable, and feeling blissfully light. Sleepily, I glanced down at my body. The smartsuit was whole and obviously working. My skin beneath felt a little tight where I'd been cut, but pain free. I tugged on the valence zipper, opening the fabric just far enough to see the uppermost part of my wounds. The separated skin had been glued together. Nice.

Then memory flooded in, and my heart seemed to lurch.

Deal's question seemed to come from nowhere. "How the heck did you know?"

"Deal-of-ten-lifetimes? I recognize your—the voice your translator uses for you." Which was obviously working perfectly since "heck" has gone the way of the stegosaur. "And I hear your clicks so you must be in here, but I don't see you."

The Trader seemed to step right out of the landscape. "My bad. I've been here so long and kept so still, the controller blended me into the virtuality."

"Oh. How's my patient?" I asked nervously. "The striped one?"

"Most excellent. Back in her room and we are providing her appropriate care. But how did you know the robot would restrain her temporal mass-shifting abilities?"

Relief is such an underappreciated emotion. My "tyger" was alive! Grinning from eyebrow to eyebrow, I opened my mouth to ask what the hell "temporal mass-shifting" meant but then thought better of it. It was time to start working for my own species. Seemed reasonable to expect the Traders to pay me more if they respected me more. Remuneration commensurate with reputation, as Diana might've phrased it. So I needed some pondering time.

"If you don't mind," I said, levering myself off the couch. "I'll tell you after a short visit to the bathroom."

"Be my guest, which you are."

I felt a bit light-headed but otherwise fine as I walked past Deal. Moving must've oiled my brain cells because I had a possible answer before I'd reached the bathroom. My guess: Deal's people figured that the tiger-creatures possessed some extra-dimensional aspect that would allow them to withdraw their own substance from their future selves and concentrate it in the present moment. Then, when they'd caught up to that future, their bodies attenuated enough to move through solids. In a weird way, if this was true, I suppose they could be considered time travelers. Or time borrowers. Handy talent if you make your living by stalking and pouncing. And ... yes! Maybe it even explained why my cub got left behind.

Liking the fantastic idea better and better, I used the Earth-style toilet and flushed it, washed my hands, and returned.

"How?" Deal prompted in case I'd forgotten the question.

"Nothing to it. Once I realized that my patient was a toddler, the robot's role became obvious." Time to make hindsight and guesswork look like brilliance. "Here's what I think happened: My client was traveling with only one adult. When the spaceship became disabled, the grown-up had to use its time-phasing ability to seek help." *How*, I wondered, *does a disembodied body move itself?* "Are you with me so far?"

"I have not departed. How could this person seek help?"

Improvise, Al, improvise. "I'm thinking an time-shifting adult, but not a child, could move their body back through their own timeline to wherever help would be available."

"Interesting. Perhaps this adult might find another computer-controlled starship since these beings do appear cyber-tropic, as our master controller learned to our regret. But please explain your understanding about the robot."

Good thing he didn't ask me to explain "cyber-tropic." "Easy. If you had to abandon a child, even temporarily, wouldn't you make sure she was fed and kept clean? And if that child could walk through walls into vacuum and get lost, or killed after the mass-exchange thing wore off, wouldn't you make sure she'd stay put? I'd say you underestimated that robot even more than you underestimated me. And I'll bet momma or poppa is going to show up here when they find baby gone—uh, presuming you posted a star map in their spaceship showing where you took her?"

"Of course we did. And it may enhance trade when they learn we have not slaughtered their progeny. Most excellently reasoned!"

"There's more," I said. "You told me my patient didn't start her vanishing act until recently. Isn't that when the robot began losing power? All you needed to do was charge it up."

"So simple! Yet we failed to dig it. Doctor alien, you are a wonder."

I studied him for a moment. "You're not angry any more about losing that bet?"

"I might be bummed out if I hadn't placed a whopping new wager on your continued success before the odds changed. Thanks to you, I am now glutted with exchange credit."

"Look, maybe it's just the translator, but you don't *sound* all that happy."

"That is because I must give you some sad news."

Uh-oh. "Tell me."

"When we found you, you were near exsanguination and required far more blood than your body could hustle up. Our medics took samples and gave you a transfixion."

"You mean transfusion."

"How are hyper-nuclear processes involved in this?"

"Never mind, go on."

"I regret to report that your blood has been severely contaminated. We believe your patient was the disease vector although her claws are currently free of the contaminant." Deal's body practically drooped. "We dared not attempt to rid you of the infection because the organisms involved, which appear to be synthetic, are unknown to us. Also, samples were unaffected by our finest antibiotics and antivirals. We fear disastrous consequences for your health in the near future and suggest you hasten back to your own medics, who may be of more assistance. Again, my most sincere regrets. It has been an unexpected pleasure knowing you and quite profitable. Please have a good death, and I must congratulate you again. Your successes have been phenomenal. As you people say, 'Two out of three ain't bad.'"

This relief thing, I could get addicted. Keeping a straight face I said, "Actually, three out of three is better."

"You understand your *third* patient's needs? You blow me away! In fact, you qualify for whatever is the grandest compliment among humans. I am asking my DM to search out the appropriate phrase."

"Can't wait to hear it."

"So what is your solution to the final problem?"

Okay Al, I told myself, *grab every inch of credit you can steal, and pretend your victories weren't part luck, part Trader insight, and the rest Diana's doing.* "Solution indeed. As it happens, we've got tiny creatures back home with a strong resemblance to your flat guy. If the similarity means anything, here's how you fix it: just add water."

"I don't understand. We found it in an atmosphere devoid of moisture."

"That's the point. You described its starship as 'trashed,' right? On Earth, the miniature look-alikes go into a special dormant mode when the environment turns hostile. They dry up, and in that state they can endure almost anything. I bet the DM on Mr. Flat's inter-galaxy cruiser dehydrated the vessel after the accident to save its life. So hydrate the poor fellow, but slowly in case I'm wrong."

I laughed. "And don't worry about my blood. I've got a condition called leukopenia, which means my bone marrow can't make enough white blood cells to fight off infection, and the disease, as my doctors put it, hasn't responded to conventional treatments. So those little biomechanical bugs you found in my blood are all that's keeping me alive—them and an unpleasant amount of clean living."

"Cool. I'm pleased as punch. As to patient three, I have relayed your instructions and technicians are already following them. I am delighted to report that patient three already appears to be inflating. And I have garnered that ultimate human statement of admiration: Doctor, you are the bomb."

I stood near the airlock and fidgeted. Every Tsf I'd met, and many I hadn't, waited to see me off, and no one had brought up the delicate subject of remuneration. I wasn't even sure what to ask for or how. A crazy idea had gotten into my head and, like a bad houseguest, wouldn't leave.

Perhaps Deal read my mind. "Before you depart in glory, Doctor, have you decided on your fee, or will you cling to Earth's initial bargain of simple trade goods?"

Oh hell, everyone said the Tsf were dead honest. "I'm not sure because I don't know how much I've earned or how much the things I want are worth."

"The solution is simple. Tell us what you want, and we will assess their value against your performed services. I suggest you not be penny wise and Euro foolish as your saying goes."

"Okay. Gravity control as you suggested?"

"Done. That technique plus the original trade goods still leaves us mucho in your debt due to the unprecedented opportunities you've opened up."

"Really?" I took a breath. *Shoot for the stars, Al.* "Then I've got a big one: faster-than-light propulsion."

He waved a leg. "Too big. FTL entails not only technology but astrophysical information still unknown to human science. And it involves a small risk to us. Eventually your kind may become trading competition."

"I understand." It had been so much to ask for that I was surprised at feeling a pang of disappointment. How greedy could I be? Wasn't the secret of generated gravity enough for a day's work? And the thought of someone in my soft field bringing home the hard-science bacon tickled me immensely.

"But your surplus," Deal continued, "will make a handsome down payment."

"What?"

"Should you choose to earn the balance, we have a proposition. We will set up a clinic with various controllable environments, provide you a staff of useful beings, and bring you only the most challenging patients. Certainly, you can treat your human patients there. If you do a fraction as well as you did here, your species will soon be flying high and fast."

"You plan to add my services to your ... trading portfolio?"

"Right on."

A fantastic offer, a thrilling offer. But I saw a personal pitfall ahead that could make me one miserable shrink, namely helping the human race at the cost of losing my family. "Where," I asked slowly, "would this clinic be located? Could I bring my wife and son along, or at least have them visit frequently?"

"They could visit with ease. We shall set it up on Earth near your residence to maximize your convenience. Does the proposition appeal?"

Psychiatrist to the stars.

"Appeal? My God, *yes*." I was flying so high and fast myself that I forgot the one cautionary note about dealing with Traders: make *sure* you understand every detail of a transaction. I didn't ask what Deal meant by "staff of useful beings" and the thought of my neighbors' reactions to such an institution on their turf never crossed my mind. But I wouldn't discover my mistakes this day.

I smiled. "I can't promise anything close to this success rate, but I'd love to try." I doubted I'd ever again get this lucky.

"Then this could well be the start of a symbiotic friendship."

DOCTOR ALIEN'S FIVE EMPTY BOXES

You're not the first person in town to ask me what kind of crazy contraption I'm driving these days. But in your case, Pastor, if you wouldn't mind, and have the time, I'd feel better telling someone the *whole* story. I've never been completely open about some of it, not even with Sunny. My wife's been through more than enough. Does that nod mean you're willing to listen? In that case, I suppose it never hurts to start off with a bang.

—————

If you'd asked me that Wednesday afternoon, I wouldn't have said that everyone in my neighborhood hated my clinic. You didn't, far as I know. Sunny merely felt "jittery" about it, or so she claimed; Mrs. Murphy, living directly across the street from the main building, never uttered a complaint; and our son, Alex, even labeled it "groovy," a word he'd hijacked from one of the more usual unusual visitors to the institution. Of course, Ember Murphy suffers from multi-infarct dementia, and Alex recently turned eight. And while I'm being candid, an unprofessional condition for someone in my profession, I'd grown a bit sour about the place myself.

Still, I was surprised that anyone felt so strongly about it that they would try to kill me.

I picked myself up off the parking lot pavement, stared at the smoldering remains of my one-month-old car, and then turned toward Tad, the extraterrestrial gripping my right arm with a hand longer than my torso. My shoulder hurt and I was breathing hard, but at least I was breathing.

My ET companion, a female1 Vapabond from what I'd come to think of as the wrong side of our galaxy, gazed down at me with her big brown eyes and a grimace that may or may not have been sympathetic. What? You've never seen a Vapabond? Think seven-foot-tall gorilla with two appropriately hairy arms and legs but then add a torso covered in armadillo shell that expands and contracts hugely with every breath, *plus* a walrus head with three shrunk-down tusks. Throw in size 22 footwear with an improbable resemblance to huaraches as the only articles of clothing, and a pungent odor only an elephant might find sexy. That puts you in the ballpark if not quite in the infield.

"How did you know, Tad?" I asked her. At that moment, I was only mildly perturbed. What had happened was too surreal to take seriously. Besides, maybe my first guess had been wrong and some fluke, rather than someone with a grudge, had ignited the car's fuel cells.

"Scent. Explosive," she said, finally releasing my arm.

Tadehtraulagong was a being of few words, or rather few words at a time. She was supposedly fluent in English and Spanish, but you'd never have guessed; perhaps her jaw structure and tusks made human languages uncomfortable to chew on. When in the mood, Tad acted as a clinic nurse and was my official security officer. Now she'd added something new to her résumé: bodyguard.

Tiny rectangles of safety glass glittered across the parking lot like obese snowflakes. I shook my head, and a few pieces fell out of my hair.

Doors slammed. I looked around and watched neighbors rushing outside, undoubtedly hoping that the clinic had blown up rather than to enjoy the lovely fall afternoon. They must've been terribly disappointed judging by the glowers I was getting. Even sweet old Ember Murphy nearly frowned at me.

I felt a rush of blood to my head along with a rush of fear as the reality of what had just happened began to penetrate my brain fog. It also dawned on me that I was being an ingrate. "You saved my life, Tad. Thank you."

"Welcome."

If she hadn't chosen to walk me to the parking lot today, which wasn't her usual practice, my neighbors would have had to find someone other than me to mutter about, and I definitely appreciated her effort. A nice change, since she'd given me three kinds of headaches ever since she'd joined my staff.

My feet felt unaccountably hot, so I lifted a shoe and found the back heel half worn away. Evidently, friction was the culprit. Now that I knew what to look for, it was easy to spot the long, dual track of brown rubber leading from what remained of my car to my present position. All this confirmed my vague impression of what had just happened. My least favorite employee had dragged me backward and twenty yards away from my Volvo Hydro even as I'd pressed the clicker to unlock it. I hadn't even had time to wonder why I was suddenly zooming in reverse before the *BOOM*.

I waved apologetically at the onlookers then used my DM to call Sunny and asked her to retrieve our Alex. Naturally, she reminded me that it was my turn to perform that crucial errand, but I explained that my car was out of commission while cleverly skirting the word "fireball." She gave me her much-put-upon sigh but agreed to go. Incidentally, the first name on my wife's driver's license is "Sonja," but don't tell her I ratted her out, Pastor.

When she logged off, the reaction finally hit me full force. If I'd been using an old-fashioned smart phone rather than my DM, I would've dropped it. My hands got busy shaking, my legs gave out, and only Tad's renewed grip kept me from falling. That's when I heard the approaching sirens and realized I'd better postpone doing a proper job of falling apart.

An impressive turnout: six police cars, two ambulances, an unmarked black sedan, a fire truck, and a way too late to the party, a large van containing the city bomb squad. Five uniforms cordoned off the parking lot with green Day-Glo cones and yellow tape. Festive. Another three either engaged in crowd control or took statements from the locals; hard to tell from where I stood. After a paramedic pronounced me unworthy to ride in an ambulance, two grim officials in dark suits interviewed me and tried, unsuccessfully, to interview Tad. One, a Detective Lenz, clearly believed the incident was my fault. He was probably a neighbor. He oscillated between glaring at me and staring at the Vapabond as if about to challenge her to a bout of arm wrestling.

Luckily, the other law minion, Detective Carl Beresch, did most of the questioning and stayed reasonably polite, although from the lines on his face I guessed the man was allergic to joy. Our little chat started off awkwardly as we performed a conversational duet that's become so familiar I could do it in my sleep, and probably have.

"Doctor Al Morganson?" he asked, pro forma.

"My friends call me 'Al.' Short for Alanso."

He flicked his eyes toward Tad then back to me. "No disrespect intended. But you are the man known as 'Doctor Alien'?"

"'Fraid so." And how annoying is that since I'm not an alien *here*.

"You are the owner and operator of the—" he consulted an item practically considered incunabula since the Data Manager revolution: an actual paper notepad "—the Morganson Center for Distressed Beings?"

I hadn't chosen that name, and it always made me wince. "Only the operator; a Trader Consortium owns it."

He failed to jot down that vital, psychiatrist-exonerating fact. "We'll want a list of all your current and past clients, human and ... otherwise."

I shrugged. "I've only had one ET client this last month, and she's been here almost since we opened." Baffling case. "And I'm positive that none of my human—"

"We need to rule out every possibility," he said smoothly. "That's the routine and it works. It's in your interest to let us do our jobs."

I gave that a quick chew. "Okay, my receptionist will DM you that list, but you know I can't discuss my patients."

His eyes, already chilly, went subzero. "I'm sure you won't. But can you tell us anything that might point us in a specific direction? Any enemies? What about that one alien client?"

"Ignore that direction; she's not, um, functional. As to enemies, I'm not Doctor Popularity around here, but I can't believe anyone would actually try to murder me." My voice rang with a lack of sincerity. "Right now, Detective, I'm mostly thinking about my family's safety."

He bared his teeth, possibly to simulate a smile. "Of course. We'll make sure you and yours are protected until we find the doer."

But when the smoke cleared, as it were, the only fact anyone could determine was that an "incendiary device" had been rigged to detonate when I unlocked my car. After a damn thorough check, the clinic and its surroundings were declared bomb free. The news dot com crews appeared just as my ex car was hauled away on a huge flatbed truck with its own crane, but the interviewing cops herded me away from the cameras then drove me home. We waited in the cruiser until the bomb squad and a goofy-looking dog had gone through my entire house and its landscaping. I was certainly squeezing good use out of my tax dollars today. My wife and son showed up while we were waiting, and when Sunny heard the truth, she turned pale and kept a grip on both Alex and me that rivaled Tad's.

Three of our new pals with badges kept us company in the house for the next four hours. We served them coffee and Sunny's homemade pastries—not donuts.

The chocolate biskvi were getting scarce when four more armed personnel joined the festivities: two male FBI Special Agents, Dunn and Miller, who only accepted coffee; and two other officials, Smith and Jones if I took their word for it, from another collection of three letters, one so esoteric that even God had probably never heard of it. These last two, Smith, a white female and Jones the opposite, said little to me at first, asked less, and refused all refreshments. Soon, all four agents went into a huddle until Smith broke out to inform me that the quartet wished to interview me *immediately*. She grudgingly admitted that she was legally compelled to inform me that the upcoming session would be recorded not only by the agents' DM systems, but also—because what government agency doesn't love redundancy?—through speck-cams placed inconspicuously on their persons. All recording features of my own DM unit, she added, had already been temporarily disabled through the electronic power of federal mandate. I tested this by sub-vocalizing a recording command and got rewarded with a link-failure message flashing across my vision. Smith nodded as though she'd also seen the message and expressed her hope that crippling my DM wouldn't be too much of an inconvenience. I promised to withstand the grief of not having videos of the agents to remember them by.

Then Jones, a man who'd evidently botoxed his entire head, demanded I provide a space with privacy for their questioning, and the final four accompanied me to the dining room, where Dunn shut the French doors so that eavesdroppers would have to strain.

We all sat around my glass-top dining table. Jones handled the inquisition while the others watched me with the focused gaze of portrait painters. I didn't understand the tension in the room, and it worried me.

"Fourteen months ago, Doctor," Jones began, "NASA spent upward of two million dollars to shuttle you to the Tsf Trader mother ship in circumlunar orbit at that time. Walk us through how this happened and your experience on the mother ship."

Was this a test? "*Parent Ship*, not mother ship. When it comes to sexism, the Tsf don't have any." Maybe I'd run a test of my own. "Care to know why?"

I pretended his dismissive grunt meant yes. "They evolved as predators on a planet with food resources so scant they had to live in small, isolated groups until they developed enough social skills to raise food animals collectively." I only knew this because after I'd started working for the Traders, they'd shared some species history. "The evolutionary result is that each Tsf, unless pregnant, changes sex every few of our months, a major survival trait for small groups whose sexual distribution might be so uneven that—"

"Perhaps," Jones interrupted, "we might focus on relevant matters."

"Sure. Sorry." Which I wasn't. Test results were in: the agents weren't here on a general fishing expedition. "But why ask about my little adventure? By now, the story's grown a beard, and God knows, there's been enough info about it on the newswebs."

Jones's frown was a microscopic lip-tightening, but it was nice to see that his expression could change. "Some unreported facts pertinent to today's incident may emerge. Doctor, this will proceed more rapidly if you simply answer our questions. How did you wind up on this Parent Ship?"

I shrugged. "Tsf explorers had rescued three, um, spaceship-wrecked sentients, all from different alien species that even Traders had never heard of, all seemingly traumatized. Since we humans have apparently developed a rep among

Traders for being the galaxy's worst neurotics, Tsf leaders figured that a terrestrial shrink might—"

"That wasn't my focus, Doctor. Why *you* in particular?"

"Oh. I worked for NASA from 2025 to 2028, evaluating prospective astronauts. So when the UN passed the Tsf request to NASA, I'd already been vetted. Plus, not that many psychiatrists are fit enough to handle a space launch. Or survive the heavy gravity on a Tsf spaceship." Or manage two push-ups.

"You had no prior relationship with Traders?"

"None. I had a lot to learn. But I figured from the start that the mission was absurd."

Jones's micro-frown had evaporated. "Then why did you accept it?"

"You don't get such opportunities every lifetime."

I'd fed him an answer with all complexities strained out. Aside from the unique opportunity and enough government pressure to squeeze carrot juice from apples, I'd taken the job for the glory of being the first human to visit a Parent Ship, and because I'd been afraid that some other shrink might actually dream they were qualified to evaluate aliens.

He nodded. "Now, on to your time on that Parent Ship."

I "walked them through" at a gallop, briefly describing my three patients and confessing that I hadn't had to flex any psychiatric muscles whatsoever to effect my three cures since none of the supposed psychotics, as far as I knew, had psychological issues. Their problems were more down to earth, so to speak. I also admitted that my unearned triple victory resulted from a glut of luck plus assistance from a military-spec "brain" hooked up to my special DM implant.

"And the Traders paid you in technology," Jones said, "with the promise of more to come?"

So he knew. That shouldn't have surprised me although, during my debriefing, I'd asked NASA to withhold certain details because I'd had a hunch there *is* such a thing as too much publicity and that I'd be inundated just from having been in a Parent Ship.

I've never been more right. In fact, Pastor, if you want the remainder of my overextended minutes of fame, I'll be delighted to hand them over. What technology? Sorry, I should've omitted that part. I'd prefer not to burden you with ... irrelevant secrets.

Anyway, Jones's face could've been carved in onyx as he waited for my response, but I sensed strain beneath the mask.

"They claimed the technology was a bonus for my success. But I suspect it was mostly to, um, lubricate my way to accepting my current job."

"What did they propose, exactly?"

"To set up a clinic with various controllable environments near my home, staff it, and bring me the most interesting patients the Tsf found in their galactic travels. They said I'd be welcome to treat my human patients on site if I wished."

"Any more specifics?"

I couldn't help feeling defensive. "None. Honestly, the plan sounded wonderful at the time."

"What did they hope to gain from this arrangement?"

"My invaluable services as a trading asset."

"You said their offer *sounded* wonderful."

I explained. Flushed with triumph, giddy from one of my best days ever, and blinded by opportunity, I'd accepted without pinning the Traders down about details. I failed to ask what kind of staff they had in mind, just how close to my home the clinic would be located, how I'd pay my new employees or shelter them or feed them, and whether I'd be responsible for property taxes or rent on the new building. All of which proved that my three triumphs weren't the result of my own brainpower.

"Tsf are honest," I said with as little grump as I could manage, "but when you deal with them, it's up to you to explore and fully understand all conditions of a trade. If you don't, you're stuck because they'd just as soon dismiss verbal contracts the way Crusaders would've discarded the Holy Grail."

"How did it play out?"

Like a good concerto on a bad piano, which I didn't admit. "Could've been worse. My new employers assumed construction costs, taxes, wages, and my staff's nutritional requirements, and put me on a nice monthly retainer. But they also used the Feds to do an end run around my community's zoning and building laws, placing the clinic a mere four blocks away from Chez Morganson, and erecting it in two days with a really alien construction technique."

Jones's eyes flicked toward Smith then back. "Describe this technique. We understand the clinic appeared to build itself."

"Right. The Vapabondi, a species that trades with Traders, developed the technique. My security officer's a Vapabond."

A sore point. Given a chance to interview Tad first, I wouldn't have hired her to walk my gerbil, but she came to me as part of a trade agreement, and that was that. I shouldn't complain too loudly; my employers did better in choosing the rest of my staff, and they'd even followed my request to only inlist beings who could absorb human languages the way my fat cells absorb ice cream—didn't want my new associates dependent on artificial translators.

"Go on," Jones demanded.

"Vapabondi build things by using 'macromites,' a word coined by my receptionist combining 'mites' with 'macramé.'" Macromites are semi-organic crab-like, flea-sized machines. They communicate with each other and with their programmers with microwaves, and can reproduce faster than gossip. The weird part is that their main building material is themselves. My clinic, including floors, walls, ceilings, doors, plumbing, even the *wiring* is almost entirely interlocked macromites, self-assembled. Even what looks like glass is speciality macromites. The whole thing went up in two days, and it's not a small structure."

I could almost hear a four-part *AHA!* echo in the room. "Could enough of these machines," Jones asked in an elaborately casual voice, "detach from the building to carry an object of any substantial size?"

"Maybe. What do you mean by 'substantial'?"

He ignored the question. "Could they ... camouflage such an object while transporting it?"

I shook my head in bafflement. "Doubt it. I don't think they can change color."

I glanced over at Smith who'd sighed almost loudly enough to hear with both ears, but she'd resumed playing portraitist. The excitement level sank, replaced by an equally palpable disappointment.

Jones's non-expression didn't budge. "Since your clinic is so close, why didn't you walk to work today?"

"You're thinking I'm lazy and anti-green? You're only right about the lazy part. I had to go straight from the clinic to my son's school to pick him up on time. Really. I was once five minutes late and his second-grade teacher gave me a look to make Hitler blush with shame."

No one chuckled at my wit.

"I understand your clinic has generated some local resentment?"

"That's beneath an understatement."

He rubbed his botoxed chin, probably making sure it was still attached. "Tell us why."

I studied his face for a moment, which wasted that moment. "Partly it's because hundreds of curious souls drive s-l-o-w-l-y past the place daily, creating perpetual traffic snarls. Then there are the—pardon the unprofessional expression—crazies that show up. What I think clinches the deal, though, is that for some reason, folks dislike the idea of insane and potentially murderous aliens leaping or flying or burrowing ... or oozing into their backyards."

"Are you aware of any contact between your neighbors and extraterrestrials other than those on your staff?"

"Good heavens, no! And almost none *with* my staff. What are you getting at?"

Smith tapped lightly on the dining table. Jones didn't look at her but sat a bit straighter.

"Does any ET at your clinic have access to any form of teleportation?"

"Not as far as I know. Your questions keep getting stranger."

"Getting back to the patients you helped on the Parent Ship, tell us more about the first one."

"As I said, it looked like a cross between a tiger and—"

"Excuse me, Doctor. You mentioned that it could dematerialize enough to move through walls. Do you believe it was capable of manipulating solid objects in its dematerialized state?"

Stranger and stranger. "If by 'manipulating' you mean pick them up, I don't see how."

"Hmm. Then can you add anything concerning your third patient?" The three observing agents leaned forward a millimeter or so.

I let my puzzled expression speak for itself. "Not really. It was practically flat when I was trying to diagnose its problem, and I never saw it, um, re-inflated."

"Your report suggests that this patient may have come from another galaxy." My therapist ear detected a new eagerness beneath the smooth surface of his voice.

"That's what the Traders deduced. Since the creature's recovery they've confirmed the theory, and also confirmed their suspicion that, like themselves, that patient's species engages in trading on a colossal scale."

"Possible competition?"

I tilted a hand back and forth. "Also possible collaboration. I think the Tsf's main purpose in bringing me to the Parent Ship was all about that patient. Last I heard, they'd made progress in communicating with it and had even gotten its name and the name of its species, the Houck. At least, that's how I pronounce it. The Traders are hopping with excitement about—"

"Did you ever see any indications that this Houck, like your first patient, possessed ... unusual abilities?"

A chill brushed my spine as my subconscious caught on ahead of me. "Remember, I never even saw it after—*wait!*" Funny, how one hint following an entire parade of them could transform confusion into clarity. "You think the Houck might be playing dirty to spoil Trader operations on Earth?"

Jones said nothing but didn't deny it.

I shook my head. "Forget it. If the Houck operate on a scale only half as large as Traders, my little business would still be *far* beneath their notice. What would make you even look in that direction?"

Jones eyed Smith and got a distinct nod.

"Are you aware," he asked, "that your clinic is under twenty-four-hour government surveillance?"

I hadn't been, but it made sense; the authorities would want to stay alert for unfortunate interspecies incidents. But the presence of a video feed offered me a blazing ray of hope. "So! You've got videos of the bomber?"

Jones made the quietest snort in the history of snorts. "That's the problem. As far as our analysts can determine, no one approached your vehicle from the moment it was parked until you set off the explosive with your key-button. Therefore, we must consider extraterrestrial activity."

I studied his extra-subtle frown. "Couldn't the explosive have been planted earlier? Or maybe the key-signal wasn't the trigger and someone detonated the bomb remotely."

"Our colleagues," he gave the two FBI agents a nod, "and

the police are exploring those possibilities. However, investigators found metallic traces suggesting that your car's locking mechanism was wired, yet no evidence a timer was involved to explain your earlier successful drive to the clinic. Also, we doubt the explosion's location was random."

Now I was frowning, nothing subtle about it.

The questioning resumed, but since the cat had already exited the bag and I had nothing useful to add, the interview soon fizzled out. The session ended on a sour note: Smith finally spoke, cautioning everyone to say nothing to the police about any possible ET involvement. She didn't ask nicely.

We left to join the party in my living room and Sunny displayed her usual elegance and courtesy although I could tell she was shaken. Suddenly, phone calls started flooding in, so many we had to let our DMs handle triage and only responded to the most pressing. My insurance agent wasn't pleased.

———

A police cruiser crouched outside my house that night as my family tried to sleep. My mind refused to shut up, even for a second, and I sensed that Sunny was also keeping vigil. When we got up in the early morning, the cruiser had apparently reproduced because now there were three. One of them drove me to work and its two taciturn inhabitants, Officers Phillips and Braun, accompanied me to the front door, where Bradley S. Pearson, my dear neighbor, was lurking with some papers under one arm and a tired-looking policewomen at his side. I could feel my blood pressure soar. Never met Brad, Pastor? Count your blessings.

Thanks mostly to this one man, I've suffered through four rough meetings with the town council and some exciting times at town meetings. I've a theory about what his "S" stands for but wouldn't feel comfortable sharing it with a man of the cloth.

"Good to see you, Al," he trumpeted. "Glorious morning, isn't it? This pretty lady with me is Cathy Bennett." The police-woman gave me a wary look then winked at her fellow cops but said nothing. "Now I don't want to make any trouble for you."

Bradley always tried to radiate sincerity and likability, and never succeeded. I don't want to appearance shame, but he brought out my worst side. He was a beanpole with a pale slightly freckled complexion, an extra high forehead, thinning light-brown hair cut short, a sad moustache, and an unfortunate combination of a long but very thin nose and large, watery blue eyes. He usually smelled of solvents; perhaps his hobby involved gluing together small model lawsuits in his basement.

"What kind of trouble don't you want to make for me this time, Brad?" I asked.

He waved a bony hand at me, brushing off any tendency I might have to take offense. "Really, Al, I must remind you, *again*, that this is nothing personal. It's just that we all have to *reevaluate* the situation here; I'm sure you can see that."

The cops bracketing me radiated impatience and did a splendid job of it.

"What are you talking about, Brad?"

"That blast yesterday. A child could've been injured, or even ... *killed*! We can't have any more of that sort of thing."

"I agree. That's why the authorities are investigating the explosion, and why police cars have been parked here since it happened, and why these two gentlemen are keeping me company this glorious morning. Also why Officer Bennett is keeping such a close watch on persons of interest."

He missed my dig and waved his hand again, a bit too close to my face. "That's not enough! See here. A few of our good friends have come to me with this petition." He pulled the document from under his arm with the kind of flourish you'd expect from a magician pulling a moose out of a hat. "Now, I didn't want to bring this to you, but the entire community *insisted*, and I couldn't disappoint them. Just look this over."

He handed me the papers. I glanced at the first page and knew that Bradley had written it himself. With about triple the necessary words, it essentially stated that neither my clinic nor anyone associated with it, particularly me, were welcome anywhere near this city.

"Do you see how *many* signatures there are?" he demanded, oblivious to the significant glances the cops gave each other.

I'd already counted twenty-five names on the first page and wasn't interested in following up on pages two, three, and four. I fought to keep my twinge of guilt from transmuting to rage.

"Brad, we've been over this a hundred times. I've always understood your concerns and share them more than you may know, but I didn't choose to put the clinic here. When I learned that my employers did, I immediately asked them to locate it elsewhere and they refused on the grounds that they'd already, um, purchased the grounds."

"Then why not quit and make us all safer?"

We'd been over that ground as well. "Our government and most others around the world are pretty damn eager to keep me at this. The only reason the city council hasn't shut me down already has been pressure from Washington. Have you any idea how important the Tsf are to us? How much a good relationship with them could help us? Or what a tragedy it would be if—"

"So you've *claimed*. All I know is what's written on those papers, and you should look them over *carefully*. That's your copy; I've got the original. And I hate to say this, but it can be used in a civil case that ... I've heard may be pending, one that could have quite the impact on you."

He lifted his weak chin to look down his nose at me or perhaps to mime nobility. "That's all I have to say at this time."

Head held so far back that he risked tripping over small obstacles, Bradley S. strode past me and between my two flying buttresses and headed toward the sidewalk. Officer Bennett stayed with him until he'd crossed the street, and then she got into a parked unmarked car.

Officer Braun looked at me and held out a hand. I got the message and passed over the petition. "Nice of him to provide a list of suspects?" I said and got a hint of smile in response. I led the way through the door and into my troublesome sanctum.

I watched the cops take in everything: the absurdly large reception area, the huge and impossibly clear skylights, the 450-gallon saltwater aquarium, my multi-armed cleaning robot docked at its charging station, the full-sized olive tree, and the abstract sculptures. Then their eyes widened as they realized that the figure behind the cocobola reception desk was no sculpture. Their hands moved closer to their guns. Understandable. My receptionist, L, takes some getting used to. No doubt he's the main reason most of my human clients prefer to meet with me in the Cabin, my small separate office in back.

L isn't quite as large as Tad or nearly as weird-looking as Gara olMara the Vithy, the third member of my staff; but is hands down, not that he has permanent hands, the most intimidating of the three—to humans. Hard to pinpoint why. It's not just the way his body parts practically radiate efficiency but are, excepting for his variable eyestalks, utterly unrecognizable—to humans, I should add again. And it's not his aura of absolute confidence. Maybe it's his ... jaggedness. Where he isn't downright serrated, his body is all zigzags and sharp, hard surfaces that gleam metallically in the dimmest light. And the oddest thing about him is that the total effect of all these angles and edges suggests something ferociously streamlined: a shark, perhaps. Or the first Disney version of Captain Nemo's *Nautilus*. But you don't need prior knowledge of a Great White to know in your gut that it's not safe to pet.

After an admirably brief hesitation, Phillips forced himself to walk toward the desk. I imagine he planned to ask questions, but all he could do once he got close to L was stare. After a moment he wrinkled his nose. Under other circumstances, I would've found that comical because L uses something he calls "olfactory camouflage," constantly matching his body odor exactly to his surroundings, which meant the cop probably smelled himself—from the outside, as it were.

"How may I improve your life?" L asked him, but Phillips just turned and headed back toward me.

Braun pulled his eyes off L to glower at me. "We'll be waiting outside for the next four hours, then two other cops will take next shift. We got officers with your wife and kid. You good here?"

"Yes," I said. "And thanks for everything."

Just then, my cleaning robot decided it simply couldn't eat another joule, and it unplugged itself to scurry toward the flakes of dirt the cops and I had tracked in. The seven-foot-tall machine with its multitude of waving steel arms, designed by Tsf to resemble themselves, always made an impression on the uninitiated. So if the cops departed with a little extra haste, we must forgive them.

L extruded a limb and waved it to attract my attention. I walked over to his desk. "Such rude myrmidons." His voice emerged from the device he wore as a pendant, a personal voice amplifier. Although he could duplicate virtually any kind of noise and had proved a super genius at languages, he needed mechanical assistance to be loud enough for human ears. "Still, I ignore their slights for I have more interesting matters to discuss. But first I must ask, are you in need of therapy yourself from the recent trauma?"

"I remain sound in mind and habitually unsound in body."

"Delightful news!"

"Some detectives asked me for a client list. Can you take care of that?"

84

"With ease. And since the subject of lists has arisen, have you scrutinized your revised schedule for today? I transmitted it an hour ago."

"I'm sure my DM got it, but I haven't looked it over."

"Then I shall summarize. I cancelled all your appointments for this week save for your usual daily failure with Cora."

"You did? *Why?*"

You wouldn't think anything that appeared so alien could look smug, but L managed it. "Being reduced to fragments might be less than therapeutic for your clients."

I rubbed my tired eyes. "You're borrowing trouble. The bomb squad checked out this building from the roof down and the police have been watching the place nonstop since yesterday." I didn't mention the government surveillance or the invisible bomber on yesterday's videos.

"Are you familiar with the English phrase 'better safe than sorry'?"

"Oh. Point taken."

"Your gift of free time is adorned with lagniappe!" L shifted position to jut over the desk as if he were about to launch himself into space. "You now have the leisure to hear about my latest discovery. Doctor, are you familiar with the term 'acronym'?"

I stifled a groan. "Sure."

"Ah! Then did you know that acronyms were once referred to as 'cable codes'?" L used the temporary limb to point at an open book in front of him, one of many on his desktop including both volumes of the compact OED. L had become a serious—make that an *obsessed*—student of human cultures and languages, which in turn had become a damn nuisance.

"That I didn't know," I stated with an abundant lack of enthusiasm.

"If you wish to remember it, you only need memorize AWORTACC, which itself is an acronym standing for—"

"Acronyms Were Once, etc. L, I'm starting to understand the way you think."

"Ah! Ah! But AWOCRTACC is not *only* an acronym. In this context it is also a pneumonic! A pneumonic is—"

"Hate to interrupt," I lied, "but what came in those crates over there in the corner?" The five large boxes in question were shiny and tan-colored, certainly not cardboard or wood. They all lay side-by-side, which made me suspect they were heavy.

"A new patient. He, she, it, or something else, no judgment implied, arrived early this morning."

I glared at him. "Why can't you get it through your ... look, you're supposed to call me the minute—oh hell, never mind." I'd been down this road too many times before, and it always terminated in a dead end. Despite all my pleas, requests, and orders to inform me the instant a new alien patient arrived, L would never call me at home. He always had some rationale; perhaps the real reason involved religion.

Pastor, I'm probably giving you the wrong impression. I thought highly of L, and in most areas he was great at his job. True, his constant verbal games had gotten old enough for their beards to grow mustaches, but I loved to hear him talk about exotic beings he'd met and his own species, the Pokaroll. His take on psychological matters was always fascinating. An example? Well, he told me once that the most surprising thing that ever happens in a person's life is getting born, or in his case hatched, and that all artistic expression amounts to an attempt to handle the shock. Could be true—for Pokarolls, anyway. Back to my story!

"How," I asked through teeth trying to unclench, "did the boxes get here?"

"A Tsf Trader brought them," L said.

I went from glaring to staring. "How long ago?"

L didn't need to consult a timepiece any more than I did, but unlike me his internal chronometer was natural. "Three hours, no minutes, and twelve seconds."

"What did this Tsf say, exactly?"

The translator emitted a rapid series of clicks—Tsf speech. *Patience, Al,* I told myself. "In English, please."

"Get on the horn, pal, and tell the Doc he's got 'splainin' to do." Yep, sounded like a Tsf. Whoever had programmed their translation devices had squeezed in every cliché, slang term, tagline, and snowclone inflicted on the human race during the last century. As I'd once suspected but now knew, they'd been acting in strict accordance with the ET Operating Manual and had been monitoring our entertainment transmissions for decades.

I glanced at the boxes again wondering which one, if any, had contained my new patient; they all appeared identical.

"Did the Trader vouchsafe his or her name?" I asked, hoping that 'vouchsafe' would keep L from his daily ritual of pestering me for a new word to play with.

He generated a thin finger, used it to flip open the OED's P to Z volume, turned a few pages, extended an eyestalk to study the practically microscopic letters, and made a little squeal of joy. "Yes! The Tsf vouchsafed the name Deal-of-ten-lifetimes."

"Deal! Haven't seen him since—"

"Him is currently a her, Doctor, judging by the green cilia coloration."

"Got it. So what information did she leave me concerning the patient?"

"She vouchsafed none."

I was already regretting forking over that particular word. But that wasn't my main problem. "Hang on. I'm supposed to be treating an alien I know nothing about? *Again?*" I'd also been vouchsafed no clues about Cora, my long-term patient who'd come with Tad, but the Tsf had only been indirectly involved with that fiasco.

"Perhaps you could discuss it with the Tsf herself?"

I blinked a few times. "You mean Deal is *still here?* For God's sake, why didn't you say so right away?"

"Why rush? Life is brief and the one thing we lack time for is excess haste."

I took a slow breath. "Where is she?"

"Gara's demesne."

Well, I thought, *at least Deal won't be the weirdest thing in that room.*

––––––––

At the polished door to Gara's office, I faced my reflection and a decision. Considering Deal's presence, should I follow shop practice and knock before entering, or obey Tsf protocol and just walk in? Among Traders, only those who questioned their welcome would knock. So after glancing at the environment readout to make sure the office's present atmosphere wouldn't poison me, I touched the open-sesame plate and the door slid aside.

This room, like every room in the building, was expansive with a sky-high ceiling; after all, some clients might be gigantic. Alien equipment edged the space with oddly curved surfaces in unexpected hues, all gleaming in the morning light through the tall windows that Gara needed, but not for seeing. Her spooky computer must've been put away in whatever en suite pocket dimension Gara used for storage.

It seemed Deal was the weirdest personage in the room, although I suppose Deal might've said the same about me. He was—*she* was average size for a Tsf, a bit shorter than me while hogging more floor space, and that hadn't changed. Yet she looked so different just from the altered sexual coloration that without L's heads-up I might not have recognized him—damn it!—her. I gazed around carefully and still couldn't spot my physical therapist, which didn't prove Gara was absent. The room had shadows and she could be doing her version of fly-on-the-wall.

Deal stood in place, spinning fast enough to let most of her limbs extend straight out through centrifugal force. This gave me a splendid and unwanted peek at her gondola.

What's a gondola? Sorry, of course you wouldn't know. It's this massive, corrugated structure where Tsf keep their brains, digestive organs, and a heap of fangs. No, you don't see them on DM-TV, or on the newswebs, because Traders don't care to reveal that much of themselves, and the World Media Administration plays along. That's why the only parts of Tsf anatomy shown in broadcasts are the ten outer limbs with those seaweed-like fronds halfway down the curves. The fronds are bundles of cilia; the longest cilia act as fingers, the medium-size ones are sensory organs, and the short hairs flip like switches, making the clickety-clicks of Tsf speech. Traders also have three thick central legs to protect and support their gondolas.

If you ever met Tsf in the flesh, Pastor, I bet you'd be surprised by their curry-like aroma and how much racket all those clicking hairs generate—a sound, I imagine, that might bring a twinge of nostalgia to elderly retirees who'd once worked with manual typewriters....

Deal stopped spinning and a few dozen of her optical cilia pointed at me. Wide bands of some elastic material encircled four of her limbs: Trader pockets. One pocket held a Tsf translator. Deal started clicking and the translator spoke up.

"Doc Morganson? That you?" The English came out in a parody of a western drawl, a new variation on a consistently bizarre theme.

I smiled. "Tricky to tell humans apart, Deal-of-ten-lifetimes?"

"No way. But I reckon your mug don't look the same."

"Probably all the new worry lines." *L*, I thought, *would love this conversation.* How long has it been since "mug" was slang for face?

Deal's optics stretched out a bit further and a score of additional eyes joined in to peer at me. "Matter o' fact, you appear

89

more buoyant than I recall. Of course, back at the corral, mostly I saw you lyin' down on the job."

I nodded with sudden understanding. "Right. On your Parent Ship you mostly saw me lying on my self-propelled couch and in much heavier gravity." Tsf evolved on a world with nearly five times Earth's pull and kept some of the extra squeeze on fulltime in their space station. "I must've looked more ... saggy then. If you don't mind interrupting our reunion, where's the new patient?"

After months of experiences with various Traders, I'd come to interpret Deal's minimalist twitch either as a sign of surprise or a gesture indicating contempt for my stupidity.

"In the reception area," Deal said. "You didn't notice them there crates?"

I stared at her and not because of the fake-cowboy dialect. "You mean, my patient is *still* packed in one of those boxes?"

"In every dang one, you'd best believe."

Time out, I told myself.

Ever run your Data Manager's CPU nonstop for a year or so? The whole system gets logy and errors start popping up. In this case, my brain was the device needing a reboot. I'd forgotten my own number one rule for dealing with ETs: never make assumptions. That explosion hadn't taken me out, but apparently it had shorted my circuits.

Maybe I swayed a little. The Trader placed limbs gently on both sides of my shoulders to add support. "What's the dealio, partner? You ain't ridin' so steady in the saddle."

Distracted and irked with my own foolishness, I blurted out the question I hadn't dared ask for over a year. "Why the hell are Tsf translators programmed to make you Traders sound so *hokey*? It's annoying, not to mention frustrating. Do you know that some of the slang you throw around is so obsolete that I'd need my great-grandfather to tell me what it means?" Of course, I was instantly ashamed of myself, and I hadn't even been honest. Usually, I enjoy the varied quirkiness of Trader speech.

Deal stopped clicking. When she resumed, the voice from the translator sounded entirely different. "My dear Doctor, the programming is precisely calibrated, I assure you. We are Traders and our goal is profit, mutual profit whenever possible. We calculated that by configuring our speech patterns to make us sound colorful we would ease human reactions to our obvious physical, mental, and technological superiorities."

"I see. Smart." And how very cynical.

"We have learned that ease between species lubricates the friction of trade. With particularly frail species, we do our utmost to project harmlessness."

I tried to keep my face from expressing disappointment that Trader zaniness was all for show. Perhaps Deal couldn't read human non-verbal cues, but considering what I'd just learned about Trader shrewdness, I wasn't betting on it. "As to the patient, shouldn't we do some, um, unpacking?"

"Indeed, but first I suggest you examine this item."

She pulled a small cylindrical object from one of her elastic bands and gave it a tap. The cylinder unfolded and unrolled into a wide, stiff sheet of thin plastic. Deal passed the sheet over to me. It weighed almost nothing and for a moment was entirely blank. Then embossed patterns developed on its surface and the patterns darkened into elaborate illustrations that resembled, more than anything, those near-useless pictorial assembly instructions included in kits from, say, Ikea.

"Touch an illustration," Deal suggested.

"Okay." It was distinctly warmer than the surrounding plastic and the embossing felt taller than it looked. Also, it vibrated slightly under my finger. "Interesting. So this is a ... one-size-fits-all-senses instruction sheet?"

"Our conclusion exactly, Doctor. The beings who sent us this document were clearly unsure about the nature of our sensory organs, so they allowed for an assortment of possibilities. Even the color contains self-illuminated wavelengths well beyond human and Tsf perceptions."

"Huh. I just see an intense brown." I squinted at the drawings. "When this machine is put together, is it supposed to be a life-support unit for my patient?"

"We believe the machine *is* your patient, although it appears to be what you refer to as a 'robot.' If we obey these diagrams, you will learn why we have brought this problem to you."

I studied the illustrations more carefully; they were laid out in a spiral pattern, but the assembly order was obvious from the way the robot—assuming that's what it was—became progressively more elaborate. The reverse side of the sheet had a lengthy parts list. Even with twelve arms including my two, putting this thing together wouldn't be a quick job. I checked the time.

Not wanting any virtual buzzers, gongs, or even a quiet internal word to further abrade my nerves, I had my DM place a countdown stopwatch at one edge of my vision, where I couldn't forget it, yet it wouldn't block my view. I set this timer for an hour and twelve minutes and started it running, further validating my self-diagnosis of a mild case of OCD since I had no good reason to meet with Cora at that specific time every workday. But that was my schedule, and I was sticking to it.

"How heavy are those boxes?" I asked.

"Several outweigh us both while others are less massive. In either case, they are easy to transport due to the adaptable material coating the bottom surfaces. Apply steady pressure to any side, and those surfaces become frictionless."

"Slippery when pushed?"

"So I said. I assume from your query concerning weight that you wish to open these containers in another location?"

"I do. If this robot really needs my, um, services, I'd like to build it in one of the rooms dedicated to extraterrestrial patients."

"That is sensible since the automaton, once complete, will be far more challenging to transport. This will require several trips if we work alone."

Tad could help, theoretically, but the fastest road to chaos I'd ever found was to *have* her help; her grasp of any job tended to be more miss than hit. L knew to distract Tad if she showed up, so I wanted him at his desk. And Gara was nowhere in sight.

"Let's do it ourselves."

"Then we shall begin."

Deal was right about the boxes sliding along easily although it took a while to get them moving, and the heavier ones adored sliding straight when you wanted them to turn. Still, five minutes later they were all sitting pretty in one of my controlled-environment rooms.

We got to work, and by "we," I mean mostly Deal who was either familiar with the procedure or incredibly adept at following pictorial instructions. And of course, with all those optical cilia, manipulative cilia, and arms, her motor skills made the operation dazzling to behold.

Three boxes were crammed with smallish pieces, the other two had very few, but much larger ones. Looking at the sheet, I counted fifty-seven assembly steps ending with a completed robot standing next to the presumably empty boxes, all neatly stacked. Now and then, Deal asked me to hand over "the tetrahedron with an octagonal protruded helix" or some such, but I think she was just trying to involve me in the process as an act of pity. The gizmo kept getting more impressive and once its head—at least it looked head-like—was on, I estimated the finished project would be nearly ten feet tall and as broad as three of me. Most of its surface had a dusty, bluish gleam.

My countdown timer had reached five minutes when Deal installed the final component: a shiny, twisted strip of translucent material that went around the thing's waist like a froufrou cummerbund.

"What do you think of it?" she asked. "Can you account for its surprising variety of waveguides?"

"No, but it looks like a robot all right. Sort of man-like if I squint hard enough ... except for the three legs."

"Personally, I would assess it as an uncanny likeness of you, and see little difference between two and three legs, save for stability."

L's voice came from behind us. "The spitting image, as the locals say, of a human being." L could sidle quieter than a cat by extruding a plethora of soft little tentacles.

"Need me for something?" I asked him.

"Not presently, but I thought it prudent to remind you of your upcoming appointment. And I must confess to a whim of curiosity concerning just what those boxes contained." That must've been some whim since L had extruded a record number of eyestalks.

I opened my mouth to point out that I hadn't ever forgotten an appointment, but the robot interrupted me.

"Doctor Alanso Jose Morganson," it said very clearly, but in a voice like a squeaky hinge.

"Um. That's me."

"Doctor Alanso Jose Morganson," it repeated.

I turned toward Deal. "What's this?"

"A pity. We'd hoped for a different response than we'd gotten after prior assemblies. Now you know why we brought the robot to you; no matter what we tried, the completed machine would only stand in one place and say your name three times."

"Doctor Alanso Jose Morganson."

"Just so," Deal continued. "If it follows precedent, it will now remain silent indefinitely until it is disassembled and reassembled."

I stared at my latest patient. "Where did this thing come from, anyway?"

Deal stopped clicking but to my surprise, her translator

said, "Thinking." The translator's current mode evidently included a verbal "busy" signal.

My timer flashed discreetly and vanished just as the clicking resumed. "The issue you raise, Doctor, has convolutions. I gather you are presently under a time constraint, and suggest we return to this topic later."

"Good idea. There's a client I should see now, but I'll be back shortly. If you'd like to be more comfortable in here while you wait, my receptionist can boost the gravity while I'm gone."

"If you have no objections, I would prefer to accompany you since I have my own whim of curiosity to satisfy."

L backed out of the doorway as smoothly as warm butter gliding over an oil slick, but slowly and with his eyestalks all aimed at the robot. That gave me time to weigh the ethics of Deal's request before giving her an answer. Normally, I wouldn't consider bringing an observer to a private session, but in this case, I couldn't imagine what difference it would make.

"What are you so curious about?" I asked.

"I've been informed that this patient is a Vapabond, reputedly a most interesting species. I have seen images but have never met one before."

I looked at her in surprise as a baker's dozen eye-cilia gazed back at me. "We've got *two* Vapabondi here. Thought you knew."

"Yes, the other is your security officer."

"Supposedly. And a nurse, also supposedly. Her name is Tadehtraulagong, but I just call her 'Tad.' You haven't bumped into her yet?"

"I haven't encountered her if that was your question."

Come to think of it, I hadn't seen her today either, which was odd since she was always underfoot—if "underfoot" can apply to someone nearly twice my height.

Vapabondi are comfortable in Earth's gravity and can breathe our air as if they'd evolved here, so it hadn't been necessary to customize conditions in my patient's room. That is, it hadn't been necessary for *her*. I'd arranged for odor filtering to make the space more pleasant for me; that elephantine smell tended to build up. A Tsf translating device, programmed appropriately, sat near the vast bed in which my patient, Coratennulagond, lay supine, staring at the ceiling. If she'd been human, I would've judged her condition a twelve on the Glasgow Coma Scale—more stupor than coma.

As a female2, Cora was visibly different from Tad: shorter but wider, and her torso-shell had fancier articulation. I'd never been able to mine much information from Tad, but a helpful Tsf visitor had explained that in Vapabondi, the female1 generates an equivalent to a human ovum and retains it until impregnated by a male1. After fertilization, the egg is transferred to a womblike organ in a female2 who, if all follows nature's blueprint, is protected by a male2 until the little one is born, or more precisely, ejected.

"*This* is your patient?" Deal asked, and I wondered why the translation came out sounding surprised.

"She is. Hello, Cora," I said as always, the translator honked and growled as always, and I received the usual response. Cora's walrus-like head gradually turned toward me, and the wrinkled eyelids quivered for a moment but remained at half-mast. "I've brought a friend, the Trader Deal-of-ten-lifetimes."

Deal clicked and the translator did some honking and growing then said in English, "I am pleased to greet you."

The massive head slowly aimed itself toward the Tsf. Cora's eyes opened fully then blinked in slow motion. Surprise and excitement set my heart racing. The tip of a blue tongue appeared between her two lower tusks, licked across six inches of black, rubbery lip, and then withdrew.

As I gawked at her unprecedented responsiveness, Deal placed a few finger-cilia on my arm. "What is wrong with her?" she asked, clicking more quietly than I'd thought she could, and the translation came out as a whisper.

To my disappointment, Cora's eyelids drifted halfway down and she resumed her standard torpor. "Let's talk outside," I suggested.

Deal led the way to the hallway and after I'd closed the door asked, "What *is* wrong with her mind?"

"Wish I knew." I puffed out my cheeks and let the air out in a rush, a way of expressing frustration that always bugs my wife. "Deal, you've gotten more out of Cora in a minute than I have in the last six months. Maybe it's me, but everything about her case is ... off somehow, even the way she arrived. I assume you know about that?"

"I do not, and evidently what little information I did receive is incorrect. Soon-to-be-wealthy, a Trader in another division who is still a novice at dealing with extrinsic species, made the arrangements. I understand that your notoriety had been attracting deranged humans to this location and Soon-to-be-wealthy's solution involved a barter in which you were to be loaned a Vapabondi security specialist in exchange for your aid in treating a mentally ill Vapabond. What did you find unsettling about her arrival?"

The idea that Tad was any kind of specialist gave me an instant hit of what we shrinks call "cognitive dissonance." "You Traders brought me all the other ET patients I've had. Not Cora. She and Tad just showed up one day in a van driven by federal agents. It seems Tad had flown a shuttle down from whatever spaceship had brought them to Earth and landed it in a field fifty miles from the clinic."

Deal wriggled four limbs like pythons doing yoga, a Tsf gesture I hadn't seen enough times to make a stab at interpreting. "Vapabondi are clever but cautious beings, Doctor. They insist on autonomy in all things, so they would inevitably wish to effect the delivery. I cannot explain why the shuttle landed so far away, but I am no authority on Vapabondi behavior. Did the unexpected arrival create a problem for you?"

"I wouldn't say unexpected. Your people told me the pair was coming, just not when or how. They even gave me a micro-briefing about Vapabondi." Thank God. "But they knew nothing about Cora's condition. My *problem* was that she showed up with no documentation, patient history or previous diagnosis. The only thing I could get out of Tad concerning Cora was that Tad herself would be her nurse because only a fellow Vapabond could be qualified. In terms of evaluation let alone therapy, I've been flying blind ... without a paddle."

"Your metaphor mystifies me, but surely this Tad has oriented you by now?"

I snorted. "Anything but. One theory I have is that Tad was ordered to tell me nothing so that I could assess Cora without preconceptions." I had another theory less based on the intrinsic benevolence of all beings, namely that Tad was a jerk.

"Shall we return to your patient?"

We did, but this time Cora just lay there like a very large lump. Deal and I took turns talking at her, both of us failing to elicit any reaction. As always, I sensed that she heard but couldn't or wouldn't respond. Seeing that we were on a roll of non-accomplishment, I suggested we return to the room with the robot and continue wasting our time in a fresh venue. Deal agreed.

———

The machine, to no one's surprise, stood exactly where we'd left it.

"We have time now," I said. "Getting back to my question, where *did* this thing come from?"

The Trader aimed a few optical cilia at me but kept most of them facing the subject of my question. "No doubt you recall the unfortunate Houck you correctly diagnosed on the Parent Ship."

I managed to mate a chuckle with a snort. "Even if I habitually forgot my patients, I'd make an exception for the only one from another galaxy."

"That is why I said 'no doubt.' After you returned to Earth, this individual recovered fully and was soon able, with our aid, to converse with its fellows."

My eyebrows decided to levitate. "They must have one hell of a communication system."

Several of Deal's limbs rippled.

"Now what," I asked, "is so funny?"

She twitched, just once but all over, and more eye-cilia swung around toward me. "Your perceptiveness alarms me, Doctor, although by now I should have learned to expect it. How did you become so expert on Tsf body language?"

"I'm no expert. But I've been around you Traders enough to pick up a hint or two. The source of your amusement?"

"I will tell you, if you will remember that I mean no offense."

"Okay. Consider my skin properly thickened."

"At last, an intelligible metaphor!" It made sense to her, Pastor, because Tsf can thicken and harden the outer cells in their limbs into sword-like weapons.

Then she let me in on the joke. "I was"—the translation device paused for an instant—"tickled by something I've often observed. The manner in which a species survives long enough to become technological usually limits that technology."

"For instance?"

"Humans. Despite your many physical limitations, humans possess adequate grasping powers combined with a shape that allows fair leverage. Therefore, your earliest fore-parents depended on hurling objects both to hunt and to defend themselves against predators. Aids such as bows and guns flow from the basic idea of throwing, which has become so embedded in human perspective that in English, 'weapons' and 'limbs' are synonyms."

"I think you mean *arms*."

"I see no distinction."

"Right. What does this have to do with long-distance communication?"

"All your devices for this purpose are tools for throwing such things as microwaves, light, or radio waves. The Houck are more advanced than we Tsf in transportation, but we use identical communication tools. Distance is irrelevant when nothing has to travel."

I studied Deal for a long moment. "That's interesting. How *do* you communicate without moving anything?"

Deal raised a limb and waved it chidingly; I wasn't the only one who'd learned something about alien body languages. "This information could be the basis of a future trade. It would be irresponsible of me to supply it gratis. Perhaps we should now turn all curiosity toward disassembling and reassembling the robot. We must be certain that no mistake has been made."

My curiosity wasn't in the mood to turn, but I saw no point in arguing. "I'm game."

"You might be distressed by how your last statement was translated, but I take it you are willing so we will proceed. Observe the process with critical eyes, if you will, for the smallest blunder could result in cumulative error."

I pored over the assembly sheet while Deal followed the instructions in reverse but so slowly that I could follow the procedure and sign off on each step. From the start, though, I had a nagging feeling we'd missed something obvious. If so, we both missed it all the way to the end, where nothing but machine parts and the two of us littered the floor.

"You agree," Deal asked, "that I made no mistakes?"

"Seems that way."

"Then I shall construct it again under your few but watchful eyes."

I sighed. "One downside to having a mere pair is that they get tired but go ahead."

"Since I have memorized this process and wish to avoid automatically repeating any errors, I suggest you provide all assembly information as we proceed. I will obey your directions."

"I like it." That way I'd set the pace. I lifted the assembly sheet and tried to look at it as if for first time. "Step one. Push the three long, gray rods into the holes in the smallest cylinder. .."

With me calling the shots, the job took over two hours. I wouldn't say we completely wasted our time because when we were finished, I had the fun of hearing my name repeated three times.

After that third repetition, I noticed that my shadow was darker than it should've been considering the room lighting. I wondered how long Gara had been with us, but if she wanted to go incognito, who was I to out her?

———

That night, Sunny and I took turns reading bedtime books to our son. Finally, he drifted off, and we dared tiptoe to our bedroom. The weather had made a surprise U-turn to unseasonably muggy, but my weather widget claimed cooler air would return after midnight, so I left a window and its curtains open. We put our DM CPUs on their chargers and lay in bed with the lights off, chatting a little and watching a broad patch of moonlight on the ceiling that had snuck into our room by bouncing off the small pond in our backyard. Whenever even the mildest wind arose outside, the light above us would fill with moving ripples.

All this seemed incredibly peaceful, but I was too aware of the patrol car parked out front and too full of questions to relax. And when I closed my eyes, I kept seeing that damn assembly sheet. So I swallowed my pride and had my DM send a gentle 3 Hz pulse through my nervous system, knowing that within eight minutes my brainwaves would automatically sync to the pulse and I'd fall into a deep, delta-level sleep.

Why the pride-swallowing act? Because I usually advise against direct DM brain stimulus as a soporific. It's too easy to become dependent on it and the process, continued over months, can scramble a person's natural sleep cycle. Yes, acoustic entrainment is supposedly safe, but that night I wanted the biggest guns. I'd been awake most of the previous night and didn't want to spend another day in a fog.

So I was gently settling into a dream when a nasty thought that must've been circling my mind for hours finally landed. If the government could shut off my DM's recording function, what else could they legally make my DM do? Was I now bugged ... from the inside? I paused the delta signal and called up a virtual screen, grateful that modern technology made it possible to do online research without getting out of bed and thus waking my wife.

Having spent most of my life in the dark ages before nanobiotechnology and computer science got married, before data management systems were partially implanted, I still feel most comfortable controlling my DM with a keyboard. Oh, I can use sub-vocals just fine to input simple instructions, but strange things happen when I try the non-simple kind, and Sunny tells me that such attempts remind her of watching a bad ventriloquist. So I only used sub-V to summon what I wanted: a virtual keyboard facing me, floating in midair below an impalpable screen.

I called up my meta-search engine, raised my hands to type, and then hesitated. If my DM system *was* bugged, did I want the, um, buggers plotting the exact vector of my suspicions? I needed to take a more tangential approach. Considering how Smith et al. had prevented me from recording our session, wouldn't it be reasonable for me to research the legalities involved with that, and if the information I really wanted happened to hang out nearby...?

Figuring my best bet would be the kind of omnibus document reserved for law libraries, I forked over the twenty-five bucks for a single LexNex session and lo, the veils parted as the blindfolded lady with the scales appeared. Thanks to DM nerve haptics, I felt the projected keys under my fingers as I typed in my search parameters.

Over a million hits, but LexNex sorted them so brilliantly that my answer waited in the very first document. What I'd feared was called a "mind-tap," and it was out and out prohibited except when specifically authorized by an act of Congress.

I was semi-reassured. I dispelled my toys, closed my eyes, and of course the damn assembly sheet that I'd been staring at all day floated up again. An impressively clear image considering that my visual memory isn't normally terrific. I could practically see every detail, but it occurred to me that one detail could be missing.

Where was the power supply?

Sure, the robot had all sorts of mysterious parts, but nothing that seemed large enough to supply enough energy to move something so massive ... unless one mysterious part contained a fusion reactor. That seemed more than unlikely, but surely, the robot was *intended* to move.

Come to think of it, where was the thing's CPU?

The sheet began fading in my mind, details growing fuzzy, so I regarded the dimming image as a whole. That's when I caught on and mouthed the classic Oh My God. Could've sworn I didn't twitch or wiggle, but Sunny turned toward me and said, "What's so funny?"

Couldn't help it, I cracked up. I tried to tell her why but couldn't get the words out. After a minute, Sunny began laughing because I was laughing so hard.

"Shhh," she warned me between giggles. "You'll wake the boy."

Tears still leaking from my eyes, I finally got some control. "I told you about trying to make that robot work." The thought almost set me off again.

"Uh-huh. You and that Trader."

I was merely grinning now. "Exactly. Your big-brained husband and an even-bigger-brained Tsf. Spent pretty much the day on it. Kept putting it together and taking it apart. Followed the pictorial assembly instructions more than carefully. We were *meticulous*."

"And?"

"We forgot something." Another belly laugh got past me. "And we weren't the first ones to make the mistake. A team of Tsf scientists overlooked the same thing."

"So what did everyone miss?"

I told her and it was her turn to laugh. "That is funny," she agreed.

My cheeks were tired from grinning so hard. "It just didn't seem important at the time."

In the morning, the same two cops chauffeured me to work, but this time they neglected to come in with me. My receptionist loomed behind his desk as usual, but no one else seemed to be around unless you count the docked cleaning robot.

"Good morning, L," I said, walking up to his station.

He extruded a wad of alien tissue resembling a top hat circa 1800 on a thin stalk and waved it at me. "And a tip of the morning to you, Doctor."

"That's not—never mind. Is Deal-of-ten-lifetimes still here?"

The hat sank into nonexistence. "That is a near certainty. After you last departed, she resumed experimenting with robotics then borrowed room six for a lengthy dose of gravity therapy. It seems she spent undue time yesterday operating under Earth conditions and suffered some loss of bone density. The Tsf metabolism, if you aren't aware, is considerably faster than yours or even mine."

"Will she be okay?"

"She assured me so but mentioned it would require some ten Earth hours and two meals before she could normalize."

"Good enough." I moved closer to L and lowered my voice. "In fact, her absence may come in handy. Have you seen Tad or Gara today?"

"Both. Is there purpose in your question?"

"I think they were avoiding Deal yesterday. I want to know why. At one point, our favorite Vithy was impersonating my shadow."

"She does shadows well."

I nodded my agreement. "Have you cancelled any cancellations for today?"

"I have not commenced rescheduling."

"Then I'll try to see where Gara's hiding."

L extruded a thin limb and used it as a pointer. "Her office might be an appropriate location to begin your search."

Taking his galactic wisdom to heart, I headed to my PT's room and softly tapped on the door. Vithy lack eyes of any sort but come factory-equipped with a fantastically acute sense combining hearing and touch.

After the clinic had opened, I'd asked my employers to add a physical therapist and an analytical physiologist to my staff in case any alien patient proved to have physical problems. They brought me Gara, qualified on both counts.

"Come in, Al," she said in the contralto voice she always adopted when we were alone. No doubt she'd known who was knocking from the sound of my footsteps. Being sightless, she didn't turn when I entered but I felt a delicate breeze on my face, which implied she'd used her multi-band sonar to check on my facial expression, muscular tension, and blood flow.

Gara was ... positioned behind her acoustic DM, her tenebrous body extended into a rectangular, paper-thin diaphragm about my height and four feet wide. Her Data Manager was entirely external and a piece of technology that gave me goose bumps. It resembled a shallow circular tar pit suspended vertically in midair, a computer monitor as designed by Hewlett Packard Lovecraft. From the crisscrossing web of ripples in this oily pool, I knew that Gara was making sounds inaudible to humans and sensing her DM's response in air movements too subtle to disturb a gnat.

"I'm so sorry," she murmured, "that events recent have left you apprehensive. But I am grateful you are uninjured."

"Thanks." As usual when in Gara's presence, I felt myself relaxing. She spoke by vibrating sections of herself, which allowed her to ... heterodyne her own kind of tranquillizing entrainment into her speech. That's one reason my human patients take to her with all the enthusiasm they never show for L and Tad. Lucky, because with the paucity of alien patients that have come our way, most of Gara's work has involved traumatized humans needing physical as well as mental therapy.

Vithy don't fit into the classic categories of animal, vegetable, mineral, or fungal. But if you had to choose one of the above, you might go for vegetable because they use photosynthesis to fulfill most of their energy requirements—only they process various sulfur compounds rather than carbon dioxide. Our atmosphere neither harms nor helps them, but their unique bodies can retain enough needed gasses to keep them fit for days at a time, and without stinking up the clinic. Since any of my clinic's controllable environments can duplicate the repulsive atmosphere of your choice, and since Gara's office has plenty of south-facing windows, she can recharge at will.

What does she look like? That's a hard one. Her body is essentially a collection of shapeable, elastic, purple nanotubes dark enough to appear black except in direct sunlight. Each tube is equivalent to one of our cells and L, who's an encyclopedia about Tsf trading partners, tells me that the Vithy evolved as a gradual collaboration between individual tubes. L also mentioned, in the faintest whisper while Gara was helping a human patient in our smaller building, that some Pokaroll scientists consider Vithy to be colony creatures rather than individuals.

In a nutshell, they're dark, very few molecules short of being two-dimensional when lying flat, and can take almost any shape. When it comes to making noises, they've got *talent*, even more so than L's species. They can vibrate their bodies to produce sonic massages, ultrasound waves, or to sing hello in six-part harmony.

I decided to be straightforward. "Gara, why were you avoiding Deal-of-ten-lifetimes yesterday?"

She curled into a semicircle. "My people have had much experience with Traders. We have found some to be untrustworthy rather."

"I don't get it. We've had a dozen Traders here since you arrived, but this is the first time you've, um, kept such a low profile."

"This is the time first you have been exploded nearly."

I could feel a developing furrow between my eyebrows despite Gara's soothing influence. "What does that have to do with Deal?"

"A question excellent most. I am suspicious always of coincidences."

I shivered involuntarily. "But they do happen."

"Inarguably."

"We humans have a saying," I pointed out. "Correlation doesn't imply causation."

"Nor does lack of causation negate correlation. You may wish to know that Deal has departed now her room."

"You can hear her door open from *here*?"

"Easily."

I left Gara's office more troubled than when I'd entered—a first. And when I glanced down at the floor, my shadow was darker and more distinct than it should've been.

"With your incredible hearing," I murmured, "why do you need to, um, shadow me?"

The darkness at my feet rippled. "It is one thing to hear, another to act if necessary."

———

Gara's office and the room Deal had commandeered were in separate corridors. Tsf can hustle when they want to, but Deal must've been feeling lazy this morning; she and I reached the reception area in a dead heat, just in time for us to get a glimpse of Tad's back vanishing into the third corridor. But even without Tad, we had plenty of company.

A tall, heavyset man in a business suit that was the opposite of off-the-rack stood a respectful distance from L's desk. A large leather briefcase dangled from his left hand. I'd never seen him before, but his two outriggers were my uniformed guardians Phillips and Braun. They didn't look joyous.

Paying no attention to the aliens in the room, a trick tantamount to ignoring the proverbial elephant, the man turned toward me with a kind of slow pomp, his posture and the set of his face declaring a vast self-importance. "Doctor Morganson? My name is Skyler Penwarden Jr. I am an attorney representing an association of your neighbors." Staring at me with blue eyes obviously trying to be steely, he deigned to hold out a hand for a shake. His palm was so dry that he probably sprayed it with antiperspirant. I made a mental note to disinfect my own paw afterward. "May I DM you my business card?" he added.

"Why not?" I sub-vocally gave my DM permission to add his card to the stack but to accept no other transmissions from him. "How can I help you, Mr. Penwarden?"

He released my hand, opened his briefcase, and pulled out a ream of paper. "At the behest of my clients, I am prepared to initiate a civil suit against you. The particulars are contained in this brief, and I'd advise you to familiarize yourself with it immediately. After you do so, I would be willing to sit down with you, or with you and your attorney if you'd prefer, to discuss the possibility of settling this matter out of court."

Had I ever heard anyone else use the word "behest" in real life? The lawyer handed over the so-called brief, and I gave him my finest sardonic look. "I assume this is Bradley S. Pearson's doing?"

"He is one of the principals."

"Uh-huh. Listen to me, Mr. Penwarden. As I keep telling Bradley, this sort of harassment doesn't work. Washington, not to mention the entire UN, can't afford to let this clinic close."

The man's lips insulted the entire concept of smiling. "Our litigation is not targeted at closing your clinic. Our purpose is to simply ensure that you will not profit financially from its operation. I see no reason why the authorities should object. Please study the brief then contact my office. You have my card."

"You're wasting your time and mine. This is my *work*, and I'll keep at it even if it doesn't pay me a dime. At this point, I don't need the money." That was almost true; with a certain degree of penny pinching, I could've retired at that minute thanks to my bloated monthly salary.

Still, that bombshell failed to dent him. "Again, I advise you to study the brief. You will find that it is not merely your future earnings you may need to protect. I'll expect to hear from you very soon."

He wheeled around with the stately grace of a galleon and I'm sure would've made an impressive exit if Deal hadn't hopped forward and wrapped the end of one of her limbs around his upper arm.

"Hold up a sec, podner," Deal clicked, the translation coming out in the exaggerated cowboy twang she'd abandoned yesterday.

Penwarden made a few sincere efforts to pull away before he gave up. He stared close range at Deal, his face now suffused with an unattractive shade of red. "Release me immediately, Trader, or suffer serious legal consequences." I had to hand it to the man: he looked a mere thirty percent scared and seventy percent pissed. In his shoes, I would've hit ninety percent on the fear meter and rising. Of course, I happened to be one of the few humans who knew just how lethal Tsf could be.

Deal was immune to the lawyer's glare. "I reckon you can fergit that shet. I'm what they call a dip-la-mat in these here parts and got am-munities. But I just gotta check on if I was hear'n you right. Was you figgerin' to get yer mitts into the Doc's well-earned nest egg?"

Penwarden was one tough cookie, but the steel in his eyes was rusting fast. "That depends on how reasonable Doctor Morganson can be. I'm sure we can work something out. Let me go. Please."

Deal relinquished the man's arm and Penwarden immediately scooted to the clinic's exit. The cops became the second line of geese following their migrating leader. At the door, I thought the lawyer might turn and deliver some new legal threat, but he was gone before his small flock had caught up.

"This," I said, shaking the document in my hand, "I don't need. Are any of your people lawyers?" I asked Deal.

"We have not evolved past an occasional necessity for arbitration, Doctor." The sagebrush twang had gone. "But our arbitrators do not use our legal system as a bludgeon."

How nice for you, I thought, walking over to the reception desk. "L, would you mind tucking these papers away for now?"

L extended a pseudo-hand, took the brief, opened a desk drawer with another temporary hand, and put the vile thing out of sight. "The myrmidons," he complained, "continue to be rude, and that barrister ..." he paused to give me time to admire the latest addition to his vocabulary, "behaved no better. Not one of them spoke to me even though I invited conversation most politely!"

"That is strange," I commiserated.

Deal reclaimed my attention by gently tapping my shoulder. "After you departed yesterday," she said, "I essayed a few more experiments with the robot."

Had she figured it out? "What kind of experiments?"

"I tried constructing it from the middle of the instructions rather than what we assumed was the beginning, and in many other sequences. My results were even less successful than all previous efforts. When fully reassembled, the machine failed to intone your name even once. If the Houck sent us this item as an intelligence test, I must tilt my gondola in disgrace."

I tried to reclaim the excitement that came with last night's breakthrough, but today had killed my mood. I had so much on my mind: the pending lawsuit with attending hassles and fees, a possible bomb attack on my loved ones, and Gara still attached to my feet at the heels and matching my every step. *Shake it off, Al,* I told myself, *remember what you tell your patients. Do you want your anxieties to run your life, or you?*

"I may know how to fix the robot." Perhaps not the most tactful way to put it after Deal's IQ self-evaluation.

The Trader made a popcorn popper's worth of clicks, which the translator simplified to a single, astonished "What?"

The humor of this worked its way through my funk. "You're going to kick yourself when I tell you. Or should I say punch yourself?" I suppose Tsf limbs could swing either way.

"I am eager to proceed with this proposed auto-mutilation. Please instruct me immediately!"

I smiled and meant it. "If you wouldn't mind, could we have another joint session with Cora first? Then we'll have the whole day free."

"Certainly. This will provide a chance for me to cultivate

patience, a sadly undernourished animal in my emotional farm."

———

After our time with Cora, a note-for-note repeat of yesterday's initially promising and then disappointing performance, Deal led the way to the robot at a pace that made me trot to keep up. I wasn't in any such rush. In fact, I was feeling a distinct reluctance for my theory to be tested.

Back in Frankenstein's Cyberlab, machine parts lay cleverly organized all over the floor. Fine. We needed to start from scratch.

"Would you care to reveal your idea now?" Deal asked.

"Not yet. I'm trying to build suspense."

"Humans can be surprisingly cruel. What is our next step?"

"Reassembly for the umpteenth time. Exactly the way you first did it."

Deal aimed a platoon of eye-cilia toward me. "And you expect a different result?"

"We'll see. Put it together as fast as you like."

Practice, plus not having to wait for me to follow the action, allowed the Trader to work with such blistering speed that the robot almost seemed to implode into existence.

"And now?" Deal asked when she was finished and the robot had said my name three times.

"Now look at the instructions again. What do you see at the center?"

She regarded the sheet for a time. "No more than what stands before us."

"Really? What's that next to the robot?"

"Nothing significant. Only the empty boxes."

"The *stacked* empty boxes."

Deal neither moved nor clicked for so long that I wondered if she was hunting for a tactful way of informing me that my idea had already proved worthless. But even a psychiatrist can't read facial expressions on someone without a face. Maybe an expert on sea anemones would have better luck.

"The crates might be external DM components of some kind," I explained unnecessarily. "Maybe they need to be in contact to work. An obvious notion, I guess."

"It is obvious *now*. We Traders perceive incalculable potential in developing a relationship with the Houck and have grasped this overture by them with all limbs. So I find it maddening that so many Tsf scientists have scrutinized these instructions and overlooked the possibility you've suggested. Could I offer the excuse that the filled boxes were unwieldy in normal gravity and thus it seemed reasonable to leave each on the floor? No, even I find that unconvincing. Doctor, you are either a being difficult to overestimate or we Traders are more mentally limited than I had envisioned."

I shook my head. "Thanks for the praise, I think. But let's not pat me on the back quite yet."

"Experimental verification! Easily done." Before she'd even finished her sentence, Deal had put the boxes into a neat vertical pile.

The effect was dramatic, and by God, totally unexpected. The robot just stood there as always, but color-shifting neon streaks danced across its torso. It emitted a hive-buzzing like a gigantic step-up transformer. And those changes were trivial compared to what happened to the boxes. They spun around individually to differing orientations and then merged like hot wax into a single translucent body that glittered from within. Its final overall shape reminded me a bit of my Houck patient on the Parent Ship. Only this thing was three times larger, wasn't flat, and seemed to crackle with power.

Deal caught on fast. "It appears we'd envisioned the components reversed, Doctor. The 'robot' must be an energy generator and DM controller, while the boxes have become the actual automaton. As you surmised, the system remained inoperative until it was complete."

I swallowed hard. "Just tell me what this system is *for*."

The controller in robot disguise joined the conversation. "Doctor Alanso Jose Morganson." Its usual opening and closing gambit, but this time, it wasn't finished. "In gratitude for your assistance to one of our travelers stranded and distressed far from our native galaxy, and also to further our association with your employers, our siblings in trade, the wondrous and excellent Tsf who found and rescued our lost traveler, we have sent this energy servant poised before you. In one of our primary languages, we name such artificial entities *dhothigon*, a name you are welcome to adopt at no cost. Or you may discard it and substitute a term of your own. It is our intention for this dhothigon to be a boon in your life."

"Ah. Thanks. Very kind of you. Um, you don't happen to have an operator's manual for your dhothigon?"

The controller didn't reply. Maybe it had used up its quota of words for the year.

I turned toward Deal. "You know what I find most amazing about all this?"

"Certainly. That the Houck would understand Tsf perspective enough to know that we would regard a gift to you as a sign of respect to us?"

"That's ... not quite what I meant. What boggles my mind is that creatures living in another *galaxy* seem to have mastered English."

"I would hardly say 'mastered.' I found the controller's statements verbose and awkwardly constructed. But Doctor, Houck knowledge of your language is readily explained. They use data management techniques similar to those employed by Tsf and to a lesser degree, humans. After we opened communications with these beings, we granted them limited access to our language files. I leave it to you to make the logical inference."

I gave Deal a puzzled stare. "Why be so coy? Did you Traders, or did you not, share your knowledge of English with—"

"I should not have essayed my small evasion. The truth is that Houck protocols interfaced with ours so successfully that our DM systems automatically granted them full access to our files. As to English, the Houck helped themselves, but despite the failure of our constraints, they probed no further than our language data. We take this as a strong indication of their good will."

"Wait. Are you saying their DM technology is so damn good that it broke through *Tsf* firewalls?"

"I would phrase it in less violent terms, but essentially yes."

"That strikes me as, um, alarming."

Deal waved a few limbs around in a graceful way possibly intended to be reassuring. "Why should it?"

"Doesn't it worry you that creatures from God knows how many light centuries away have such an incredible grasp of ... communication possibilities, they can program their systems to not only interact with yours, but mesh so perfectly?" Whoops. Phrased that way, the Tsf had basically done the same thing with us. "I mean without years of monitoring your media."

"It does not although I would expect their adroitness to dazzle you considering the present limitations of human cybertechnology. Still, a logical basis exists for any effective DM design providing some measure of universality. And advanced communication skills are prerequisite for inter-species trading."

If Deal were really that sanguine about the security breach, she wouldn't have been embarrassed to admit it.

"You'd know best," I said. "But if I understand what you told me, Houck protocol networked with yours so well that your DMs interpreted its download demands as internal requests."

"Just so. Still I fail to understand why the matter upsets you."

"You really don't get it? If *your* firewalls failed, what chance do human ones have? Like mine? I have all sorts of confidential information on my system. Patient files, personal notes, debit card pin—"

"You are seeing predators where only shadows lie," she said in a series of unusually loud clicks, and I had to stop myself from glancing down at the darkness at my feet. "What possible danger," she added more quietly, "could ensue from this Houck creation accessing even your most personal data?"

"Beats me. That's the problem. Maybe this isn't true for you, but in my life, it's been the stuff I *don't* know that's bitten me the hardest."

Deal aimed a few more visual cilia at the dhothigon. "There, you make a firm point. Your experience is not entirely outside mine in this regard. I suggest we explore your measure of control over the situation."

"I'm not sure what you—oh. You mean give the controller some orders and see if it salutes?"

"I will answer yes, but tentatively since the translation of your words was unusually ambiguous."

Being unsure which one to talk to, the controller or the "energy servant," I addressed my entire mechanical audience. "I hereby name this dhothigon, um, Thoth. Thoth, will you obey me?"

Thoth had nothing to add to the conversation.

"Try an instruction," Deal advised.

"Okay." I pointed to one corner of the room. "Thoth, move over there." No response, but perhaps the Houck hadn't programmed the thing to understand pointing. Or English. "Thoth, come closer to me." Another failure to communicate. I eyed the controller. "Tell me what this servant is capable of doing."

Deal and I both jumped a little when the controller answered. "Your Thoth has one hundred and twenty possible configurations comprising variations on five basic functions, which are to serve, defend, protect, entertain, or instruct. You can select only one function at a time."

"How do I select a function or know which configuration does what? And what's the difference between defending and protecting me?" For that matter, how was it supposed to entertain? Put on a red nose and big floppy shoes?

Again, I got the silent treatment.

Deal burst into rapid clicking. "Doctor! Thus far the controller has only responded to a direct order."

My assessment of Tsf intelligence inched up, while my opinion of my own went the other way. I eyed the metal contraption and applied a voice my wife mistakenly refers to as "bossy." "Tell me how to switch Thoth to its instructive function."

"That operation is currently forbidden."

I'd often read something similar on my DMVR screen when trying to bypass the damn ads. "Why? I mean, tell me why!"

"You have configured Thoth in an aggressively protective mode that entails special security features."

As I was getting that worrisome news, flashing red letters appeared in the upper part of my vision to provide worse news: *DOWNLOAD IN PROGRESS; SIGNIFY YES IF A FILE-BY-FILE READOUT IS DESIRED.*

Not good. Without permission, Thoth was raiding my DM! I tried shutting down my system. When that failed, I yelled "yes" and watched the data zip by far too fast to read. But it wasn't quite a hyperdrive blur, which meant the interface had some sort of bottleneck. Latching onto that one buoy of hope, I whipped my DM ring off my finger and threw it on the floor. Even *that* didn't stop the theft.

"I assume there is purpose to your unusual behavior?" Deal asked.

Could be I snarled a little. "My DM just let me know that it's lying down and purring while something is stealing my private files." If there's one thing I hate, it's when my most paranoid fears come true.

"I suggest you address the controller."

"Right. Hey, controller, stop that download right now!"

"That operation is currently forbidden."

Perfect. "Then tell me what you're looking for."

"Thoth seeks information concerning threats to your well-being."

How about Thoth itself? "Tell me what it will do if it finds any threats."

"Your servant will protect you."

That didn't sound so bad at face value, but this was a face I couldn't read. "How? I mean, tell me how."

"The means depend on the threats."

Deal speared my ring with the tip of one limb and silently offered it back to me. Just as I put it back on my finger, the bizarre form of my unwanted protector drifted toward the doorway. I couldn't tell how Thoth propelled itself, but its movement was snail-smooth and rabbit-fast. Like an idiot, I leapt sideways to block the servant's exit and banged into Deal who was being an idiot in the opposite direction. Thoth pushed us aside gently, but with a strength even a Tsf couldn't resist, and headed into the hallway without bothering to use the open door. The macromite wall shattering made a noise that put Wednesday's explosion, by comparison, into the appropriate-for-church category.

Deal and I just looked at each other for a moment; macromites are incredibly tough when linked and no amount of electromagnetic muscle could've given Thoth enough traction to break the wall. But the floor was covered with tiny Vapabondi machines already scrambling to reassemble themselves. I had time for one bitter thought along the lines of *Et tu, physics?* before a second horrific *CRUNCH* ahead got me stumbling over the slippery backs of macromites to follow my supposed servant. I only fell twice.

Deal, being far more sure-limbed than any middle-aged human psychiatrist, reached the reception area ahead of me and clicked so loudly the translation was shouted, "Stop that entity!"

I leaped over a second carpet of macromites where Thoth had taken out the corner of another wall in time to see L spring through the air like an Art Nouveau rocket, the massive jumping leg he'd extruded trailing behind. He hit Thoth with a force that would've knocked a house off its foundations, but the Houck creation didn't even quiver. Impossible. L expressed tentacles and tried to latch on. Thoth flicked one ineffective-looking mini-limb and the little push hurled my receptionist across the room to smash into his own desk. Tad, likely drawn by all the noise, galloped in from one of the east-wing corridors but braked fast after spotting the glittering monster.

"L?" I bellowed. "You all right?" His silence scared me even more than Thoth.

My faithless servant scooted past Tad who'd courageously jumped out of the way. Then the shadow at my feet gathered itself up and flowed forward.

"Gara! Stop!"

I was already too late. She'd pooled herself around Thoth's ... feet or whatever it had, and her blackness turned shiny. *The old banana-peel-on-the-floor routine*, I thought. *That won't work; this bastard rolls its own traction.*

Sometimes I hate to be right. The bastard glided effortlessly over my PT and crashed through the outer wall, but at least Gara seemed unhurt in the process. Bathed in morning sunlight, Thoth slowed to a slow but relentless crawl; its body grew a few feet taller, its internal glitter flared into blinding coruscations. Nothing could've looked more dangerous.

I turned my head and my knees felt weak from relief. L had begun to stir. Then I noticed something that shoved a fresh icicle up my spine. Although the broken walls were already partly rebuilt, I could trace the line of damage. It was dead straight, aimed north by northeast and pointed directly at a certain house on the next street ahead, the residence of one Bradley S. Pearson. A sliver of Brad's gray roof shingles peeked at me from between two homes across from the clinic, as did a hint of the ocean farther beyond.

By stealing my private files, Thoth could access every conversation I'd had since my last data dump, six months ago. Something told me my alien Frankenstein's experiment would soon give Bradley, or more probably his widow, something truly worth suing about. This was shaping up to be a very bad morning for both Mr. Litigious and me.

"L," I called. "Are you hurt?"

"Not significantly."

"Good!" I turned to my supposed security officer. "Tad, that nightmare outside is a kind of robot. If you've got any Vapabondi super-weapons tucked away, get them. Now listen, everyone! Looks like our wall-breaker is just, um, moseying along now, maybe to soak up a few rays for energy. I'm praying we'll have enough time to figure out how to stop it."

"Why should we?" Tad asked.

A bad moment for Tad to suddenly get interactive, but par for her course. "Deal and I have learned that it's been programmed to ... handle anything threatening me. So it's heading toward the thing that's threatened me most often."

"Mr. Pearson," L said, using Bradley's obnoxious voice.

"Right. And I doubt the robot is planning to *negotiate*. Ideas anyone?"

"Certainly," Deal proclaimed with a single, confident snap. "The controller must be disabled. I suggest that you and I along with the Vithy do what we can to impede the robot's progress. Meanwhile the Pokaroll, who has witnessed the disassembly procedure, should attempt to dismantle the controller. Your surprising Vapabond can assist."

Surprising? No time to ask. I glanced outside. Judging from Thoth's increasing speed, I guessed it had nearly finished sunbathing. Worse, Phillips and Braun, my guardians parked on the street, were sliding out of their patrol car, weapons already drawn. I ran out the direct way, through the wall's new hole just beginning to self-heal.

"What is that thing?" Phillips yelled to me.

"Tell you later. Put those guns away, for God's sake!" Considering Thoth's Aggressive Protection mission, I figured nothing good would happen if it got the impression the cops were targeting *me*. And if the cops actually fired? While I was damn sure bullets couldn't dent a Houck energy servant, that didn't mean the robot wouldn't shoot back somehow.

The cops lowered the .38s, maybe thanks to the panic in my voice, but they didn't holster them. Bad mistake. Thoth stopped dead. A lens-like protrusion emerged from its glittering torso, pointed exactly between the two officers. I'm no sprinter, but would've surely broken some world record that day if I'd run that fast on my own. Instead, a textured shadow slid under my feet and flowed in the direction I was running like a super-speed moving walkway. I reached my destination so quickly that I stumbled trying to avoid overrunning the spot. But I got there in time.

The little lens-bubble took one peek at Dr. Human Shield before sinking back into Thoth's body, and I trusted that this danger, at least, was over.

"Thanks," I murmured to Gara, now appearing as a deep purple haze, and she gave me a don't-mention-it sort of wriggle. Unfortunately, my latest feeling of relief had a minuscule half-life. Two smaller bubbles zoomed out from Thoth, whipped around me, and settled on the cops' foreheads. Officers Phillips and Braun didn't just stop moving, they seemed to *congeal*. For a second, I was terrified that they'd been frozen stiff and would shatter when they fell over. And they did fall when I couldn't reach them fast enough, but they didn't crack. The robot started off again, still aimed at Pearson headquarters. "Gara, we can't do anything here, but I've got to get to Bradley's house before that monster does. Can you carry me that far?"

I could barely hear her response. "Sorry, Al. I'd need to recharge first."

"I can manage that small task," Deal said. I hadn't realized she'd gotten close enough to overhear. "If you wouldn't find it beneath your dignity, Doctor?"

"Hardly. Let's go! What should I do?"

"Enjoy the ride." With those cheery words, Deal wrapped limbs around my waist and legs then hoisted me surprisingly high into the air and took off bounding across the street as if Earth's gravity was on coffee break. I didn't much enjoy the experience but had to admit that Deal got the job done.

She put me down outside Bradley's back door, and I barged in.

Bradley S. sat at his kitchen table gluing snips of colored veneers to a rectangular board. He looked up at me with the ire of a man interrupted mid-marquetry and uncharacteristically let me have it, both barrels. "Knock much?"

Normally, I find his 1990s TV cliches annoying, but today my attention was elsewhere. "Brad, you're in danger! Run out your front door and keep running. Hurry!" Deal squeezed into the kitchen as I was talking.

Bradley stared at the Trader for a second too long, and then it was too late. Four glittering claws smashed through the sheetrock behind me, and then pulled most of the wall out accompanied by an ear-splitting concerto of snaps, crunches, squeals, and bangs. Thoth glided through the newborn dust cloud and over the pile of fresh rubble. It brushed past Deal and tenderly pushed me aside. One of its many claws elongated into long serrated pinchers that opened wide and began closing around Bradley's thin neck. I'd never seen anyone look so terrified and even though it wasn't my neck in the alien guillotine, my blood turned to gel.

And time seemed to freeze. Each tick of the oversized clock mounted on one undamaged kitchen wall came slow and far apart. Dust motes lazed in the morning light streaming through Thoth's demolition project. The big hole tugged at my attention. My supposed protector hadn't smashed into the house in its usual modus operandi; it had pulled the wall *out*. Why? Because I stood on the other side and would've gotten hurt. That insight told me what to do, or at least what to try....

"THOTH! If you kill this man, I will also die." I had to believe the robot would understand me even if it wouldn't obey me in its current mode. And I was counting on its protective programming.

Thoth didn't release Bradley, but its pincher didn't close. My neighbor gazed at me with eyes that were too scared to plead, and I did my best to convey a reassurance I didn't feel. The impasse stretched on and there seemed no safe way to break it.

Then, for the first time, Thoth proved that it could speak. "You will not die when Bradley S. Pearson dies." Its voice had a gelatinous tremolo but an ice-cold edge—murder in aspic.

The pinchers closed just enough to squeeze Bradley's neck without breaking the skin. Brad made a nearly noiseless whimper, and I felt sweat run down my back. "You're wrong! Killing him will destroy my reputation and career. The guilt will make me kill myself."

"I will prevent your self-destruction."

Despite that excellent rebuttal, the pinchers didn't tighten further. So maybe the Houck had a fairly broad definition of protection. "You can't save my reputation."

Thoth responded to my counterargument by doing nothing, a big improvement from what I was afraid it would do. But before I could let myself breathe again, Deal offered a few clicks of advice.

"I suspect, Doctor, that your servant is temporarily engaged in weighing the potential harm to your status resulting from this person's demise against the harm this person intends to inflict on you."

Deal's message came through perfectly: any moment now, Bradley would lose his head.

Once again, something seemed to clog the gears of time as fear whipped my thoughts into clarity. "Don't hurt him, Thoth!" I ordered for whatever good it might do as I took off running through the big hole, over the rubble, and toward the clinic. Dismantling the controller was Bradley's only hope, and obviously L and Tad weren't having much luck.

Halfway across the street, I gasped. Not because I was out of breath. In my mind, a dozen scraps of information snapped together, forming a picture I hadn't even suspected existed. My Volvo exploding, Tad saving me, the video feed showing no one planting a car bomb, Tad apparently avoiding Deal, Deal calling Tad "surprising," three shattered macromite walls, and even Cora's months of unresponsiveness added up to one stunning revelation. A truly disturbing revelation, but one that might provide a tool to save Bradley.

The frozen cops were stirring, although in slow-mo. They didn't seem hurt. In the distance, I heard sirens and guessed they were headed this way.

The front wall had nearly healed, so I had to use the door to enter the clinic but barely broke stride, sprinting toward the room with the controller. I've seen some truly weird things in my life, but the scene within that room beat them all. L had sprouted a forest of tentacles tipped with built-in wrenches, screwdrivers, hammers, and whatnot, and was twisting, prodding, and banging on the controller like an army of insane mechanics. Meanwhile, Tad occupied herself with barehanded tugging and prying. All this hyperactivity was accomplishing zilch.

"Stop!" I shouted over the racket. "L and Tad, join me in the hallway, *now!*"

I doubted Tad would obey, but L grabbed one of her arms with an extruded vice and tugged her out of the room. I slapped the wall-plate and the door swished closed.

"Have you stopped the robot?" L asked.

I kept my voice below a murmur. "Not exactly. We'll have to do that from this end."

"A glorious idea. How?"

I turned to glare at my insecurity officer. "Tad, do you have any of that explosive left? The stuff you used on my car?"

Dead silence for a moment. "You know it was me?"

"I'm positive." She'd broken her routine to accompany me to the parking lot and reacted too quickly and perfectly to what she'd claimed was the "scent" of a bomb. Also, a team of macromites, too small to be noticeable on a video feed, could've easily carried an alien version of C4 to the car in tiny batches. And who would be better at controlling Vapabondi macromites than a Vapabond? "I even know why you did it."

To make me trust her, to allay any suspicions I might be developing about her.

"If you've got any explosive left, get it now," I ordered in a nearly silent shout. "Hurry!"

You wouldn't think that something resembling a cross between an ape, a walrus, and an armadillo could look sheepish, but Tad managed the trick. Then she demonstrated that it was also possible to slink away while running. She moved even faster than I'd expected.

"You believe a detonation will disable the controller?" L whispered.

"God, I sure—wow! She's back already. Guess we'll find out."

Tad carried a large, clear jar half-full of what looked like crushed ruby dust and held it out for me to inspect.

"How do you detonate it?"

She answered by pulling out a small gadget with a miniature antenna on one end. She held this device to her mouth and mumbled something. Then she put the thing away and placed one of her sausage-fingers on the nearest wall. A tiny moving strip of ivory appeared on the finger, marched across Tad's shell, and worked its way down the arm holding the jar. I moved closer, but still could barely distinguish the individual shells of the parading macromites. A few seconds later, the ivory strip abandoned Tad to bury itself in the ruby dust.

"Will ignite at command," Tad offered.

Useful little buggers. "How fast will that happen?"

"Much quick. Three seconds. Or six. Or—"

"Okay, you stay put and give your little pals the go-ahead when I say, um, 'Go Tad." L, you're our speed-king and we're running out of time."

"You wish me to place the explosive near the controller?"

"On it. That jar should balance on a shoulder. Can you do it with extreme speed?"

"Of course."

"Good. Everyone ready?" I hated to count on Tad but had no choice.

And she came through for me, pulling out her little toy again, ready for her order, as L reconfigured himself into a low-slung torpedo with six legs and two long arms ending in enough spaghetti-like fingers for a gallon of carbonara sauce. L snatched the jar, holding it gently with a dozen spaghetti strands, and took off.

He zipped into the room so quickly that for an instant, I could've sworn he remained in the hallway.

Then he was back, triggering the door to close behind him. Even as it zipped shut, I heard the controller say, "The operation you are attempting is forbidden."

"Go Tad!"

An incredible crash came from behind us, from the reception room, *not* the place I wanted to hear a bang.

"*GO*, Tad! *NOW!*"

Like a speeded-up, stop-action demon, Thoth came charging at us just as some giant fist seemed to punch the world. The force knocked me off my feet, which probably saved my life as five empty but hard boxes flashed through the space that my head had occupied an instant earlier. L caught me in midair and set me on my feet. I think someone was talking, but at that moment my ears were on vacation.

I looked around. Both L and Tad appeared unhurt and even the walls seemed undamaged. I walked over to lift one of the boxes that had been part of Thoth a few moments before. I put it down and hoisted another, then a third. Damn. Color me stupid.

Deal bounded into the hall with Gara right behind in her spherical rolling form.

"Bradley?" I asked and only heard my own voice through a bit of bone conduction.

I could see Deal's cilia snapping but could only point at my ears while shaking my head. Then the obvious occurred to me and I switched on one of my DM's "accessibility" functions.

"Say that again, please," I asked.

This time when Deal spoke, the translated words scrolled across my field of vision: "Your neighbor is healthy save for whatever mental trauma remains. The robot released him and departed at a speed that makes me suspect it of possessing some form of interstellar propulsion. I perceive that you have succeeded in reverting Thoth to its original state."

"Thanks to L and … the Vapabond here. Deal-of-ten-life-times, may I introduce you to my patient, Coratennulagond? She's been pretending to be the security officer your people hired for me, Tadehtraulagong."

Deal hopped nearer to the party in question and stared at

her with scores of eye-cilia. "So! I'd been informed a female2 had been assigned to you, Doctor, bringing a troubled female1 along. When I saw that your patient was the wrong sub-gender, I assumed my information was faulty. Now the discrepancy is explained."

Along with plenty of other things, such as "Cora" being so unresponsive for so long. While Tad and Cora had been on their way to Earth, something had gone very wrong and the psychotic Vapabond had gained the upper grasping member.

"How do you intend to rectify the situation?" Deal asked.

I studied the Vapabond. "We'll get the real Tad off whatever meds this one's been feeding her to keep her torpid. But as for you, Cora, I believe this crisis has done you some good. I'd even say you've just had a breakthrough. This is the first time since we met that you've acted in a completely responsible way. If we work together, I'll bet we can get your mind clear and strong. Are you willing?"

"You are not angry with me?"

"A doctor doesn't get mad at the patient." That was a lie, but admitting my real feelings would help no one.

"Then I am willing."

"Great. But let's not include bombs as part of your therapy. And speaking of bombs ..."

I slapped the nearby wall-plate, exposing the room that had contained the recent blast. The floor was littered in machine parts, but none of them appeared broken or bent or even singed. Impressive metallurgy. The controller had fit together like a Chinese puzzle, so I'd guessed that a powerful explosion would break whatever electromagnetic or chemical bonds had come into play after the system was finally activated. Good thing it had worked because I had no backup plan.

"We will not," Deal said, "be assembling this device again. Or piling boxes." My ears were beginning to recover; I could hear her clicks, faintly.

"Probably not, but I think I know where we went wrong."

"Tell me."

"The empty boxes look identical, but they don't weigh the same. I bet if we stacked them from heaviest to lightest, Thoth would come to life in a far more ... amenable form. Remember the controller telling us that the servant has one hundred twenty possible configurations? That's how many different ways there are to stack five boxes if you ignore the issue of which side goes where: five factorial. Simple statistics. A clever person would've examined the empty boxes and noticed the weight discrepancy, and a logical person would've first made a pile with the greatest stability. The Houck overestimated me."

Deal remained silent for a moment. "As for me, I again find you difficult to overestimate. We Traders owe you much for the trouble our incomprehension has caused. How may we best repay you?"

I turned toward Cora. "This whole structure is made of your tiny machines. Could they tear themselves down and rebuild the place somewhere else?"

"Yes."

"Excellent." I faced Deal again. "I'm about to get drowned in lawsuits, and the trouble is that Bradley and my other neighbors are right. This institution *is* dangerous. Got an idea that might save my gluteus maximus without the Feds stepping in again and getting me even more resented. I'd like to keep treating my human patients in the Cabin, that's what we call the small building behind this one; but I want to relocate the main part of the clinic."

"To somewhere distant?"

"Not so far away that it takes me hours to commute from home, but a place that's isolated from people."

"Your desires appear to conflict. Do you have a location in mind?"

I grinned. "Not yet, but you don't expect me to solve *every* problem, do you?"

Something about the way Deal tilted a few of her limbs

gave me the impression she grinned back. "Then I may have a solution although it might mean that this structure could not simply perambulate to the new position."

"Perambulate!" L crowed, no doubt eager to rush to the nearest dictionary.

"Tell me," I asked Deal.

"We are presently not far from one of your large oceans. With Tsf environment control, I see no reason why your clinic shouldn't be repositioned some distance out to sea."

I just stood there for a moment, blinking. "You mean *floating?*"

"I mean deep underwater. Surely your neighbors would be satisfied, and we would supply you an adaptable vehicle for the short commute. Or would you prefer a sky clinic?"

———

That's basically the story, Pastor. Oh, I could blab about the subsequent meeting with Smith, Jones, and assorted tons of other officials, but even I'm getting sick of hearing my voice. Besides, you've got the answer you were looking for. So don't let those wheels fool you. Now you know exactly why I drive to work in a submarine.

DOCTOR ALIEN AND THE SPINDLES OF INFINITY

A shark glided past my office window. More minnow than Jaws, but it startled me anyway. When my clinic had first been relocated here, safely below any passing keels or propellers but far enough up the continental slope to paint my view turquoise on sunny days, the only fish I'd seen had been dead ones drifting by. Now, thanks to OH 2, the Trader-equipped Ocean Habitat Oxygen Healing project, it seemed enough gilled denizens had moved into the neighborhood to attract high ranking predators.

My grin deserved no points for humility. Traders, more specifically Tsf scientists, had modified bull kelp into hardy oxygen hoses and pollution scrubbers, and this pelagic dead zone was gradually experiencing what my assistant, L, refers to as "sub-suburban renewal." The Traders had done this for me, a bonus for my latest efforts, which puffed up my ego blowfish-style.

Just between us, I'd become the underwater version of a birdwatcher of late, and every new species I sighted reinforced the bad habit. Yes, I even carried the damn notebook, or rather a virtual equivalent. If I didn't feel so responsible for my ET patients, I could've spent all my time here fish gazing.

131

Still, I never enjoyed the process of getting here. Even after fifty-one weeks of almost daily proof of safety, diving in a Tsf submersible made me sweat. Water is heavy stuff, friends, and 220 feet down it squeezes more over each square inch than a macadamia nutcracker. Yet my sub's cabin maintains 14.7 psi, air pressure at sea level, and so does the clinic. This precludes nitrogen narcosis, but I hate to think about the pressure differential. At least the clinic is built from some of the toughest material off Earth, and while I don't know what the sub is made of, it seems too flimsy for the job.

No fins in sight, and it was time to face Haxel, my first morning patient. The prospect wiped all smirk from my face. *Another trip on the merry-go-round*, I thought, heading out the door before L could nag me.

———

I paused at the entrance to Haxel's room, giving her time to adjust to my presence. Then I stepped inside. As usual, I felt oddly ... buoyant even though atmosphere and gravity here were measurably no different than in the hallway; another unsolved mystery among many.

I could never tell which way my patient was facing—if she had a face. The Houck are aliens to the alien-eth power, and all my training and previous experience with ETs gave me no read on this one. Still, she exuded not only a presence that somehow felt charged yet peaceful, but also a pleasant orangey perfume.

"How are you feeling?" I asked.

"In general, excellent." Like my clinic's physical therapist, Gara, she spoke by vibrating parts of her surface, always using the same sweet and reedy voice. "Thank you for inquiring, kind entity. While waiting for wisdom, I have been gazing out this portal and have come to some tentative conclusions. Would you care to hear them?"

"I'd love to."

"I believe this room is surrounded by liquid, and my suspicion points at water, alcohol, or ammonia since the creatures I've seen outside do not appear adapted to cold helium or methane or—"

"It's water."

"You are certain?"

I nodded without knowing how my patient would interpret the gesture. "It's a widely held opinion. This room is part of a large structure submerged in a saltwater ocean."

"Then my doubts are resolved. Alas, I am less clear on other matters."

Here we go. "Such as?"

"I regret to say that I know not who you are, where we are, why we are here, or even what language we are employing."

"Sorry to hear it." That I was. "Do you happen to recall who *you* are?"

"My dear stranger, I fail to even comprehend what I am. And I do not wish to appear rude, but your nature is equally obscure to me although I suspect you must be amphibious."

I stifled a groan. "Any recollection we've met before?"

"Have we?"

"Many times. My name is Alanso Morganson; I'm a doctor specializing in mental difficulties. You are in my clinic, located on a planet we call Earth in this language, English. In English, my species refers to itself as 'human.' We aren't naturally amphibious, and I presently have no aquatic patients." Volunteering this information saved me at least three minutes. "After some difficulties with neighbors, my clinic was moved here to isolate it." In fact, it submerged itself, separating into its small components, which then marched over a mile to the ocean and dived in, the way lemmings don't. The weirdest parade ever.

"But I am not human?"

"You are a member of another species, the Houck, from an

extremely distant world." The entire spiel had slithered off my tongue thanks to practice.

She turned and her diaphanous folds and convolutions waved like silk handkerchiefs in a breeze before settling. Even after two months of working with her, I couldn't picture her completely unfolded.

"Thank you for this valuable information," she said per routine. "Am I suffering from mental difficulties?"

"I believe so. You think clearly and have no trouble communicating." *In four languages so far.* "You learn rapidly. But every morning, you apparently forget whatever you learned the previous day including everything you feel unclear about now."

She stayed silent for a long moment. "Then we've had this conversation before? How many times?"

"Today marks our sixty-first. Notice that you understand our numbering system."

"Most odd. Base ten, but I do comprehend it. Do I always say that?"

"Sometimes you say 'most peculiar.'"

"How tiresome this must be for you! Still, I'd appreciate it if you would educate me, again, as to my name and nature and why a doctor of an alien species has come to be tending me."

For weeks, I'd been seriously tempted to record my next lecture and play it back when the daily occasion arose. But a doctor-patient relationship should be a personal one, and any electronic shortcut felt wrong to me. But I'd sure learned to condense.

"I've been informed that your name is Haxel, as close as I can pronounce it, and that you are female. Unfortunately, I know almost nothing about the Houck, and can't explain why your own people aren't treating you. But I can supply a little background to explain how your species found out about me."

Behind her back or front or side, a school of small fish flashed past the window. I wanted to join them.

Haxel rippled all over. "I would consider that explanation a great boon."

You always do. "First off, I call this my clinic because it was set up for me, but the actual owners are different from either of us. Their species calls itself the Tsf in one of their languages, which means 'Honest Traders,' and they've been doing business with my people for over a decade. I may be the only human they employ." I paused so that she could ask the usual question.

"There is but one individual working here?"

I opened the next bag of complexities. "No, I have a staff both here and on land where I treat my human patients, but the three individuals working for me aren't Traders or humans or Houck, and all come from different worlds."

"How did such an impressive arrangement manifest?"

"Six years ago—" A new thought occurred to me. "From our previous, um, get-togethers, I know you can define the word 'year,' but do you actually have a feel for the time involved?"

One of her folds billowed upward and slowly settled. Some of the little claws on which she balanced scraped against the floor. "Perhaps not."

"Okay. We've been talking for about five minutes now. Multiply that by twelve and that's an hour. Twenty-four hours makes a day, and our year is about 365 days."

"How helpful! Please continue."

"Six years back, Traders rescued three space travelers from three damaged spaceships in three different parts of the galaxy. Each of these travelers appeared to have suffered some form of mental breakdown. Since the Tsf hadn't encountered any of these three species, they had no idea how to assess the travelers' problems and turned to my people for help."

"Why to your people?"

"Humans, it seems, enjoy an exceptionally wide variety of mental illnesses."

"Illumination arises! By necessity, your species has developed a special expertise."

Couldn't have said it better myself, but I sure could've quoted it from memory. "So the Tsf believed. Thanks to my specialty and a prior relationship with our space program, Earth's authorities chose me for the mission. Traders brought all three rescued parties to one of their outposts, a space station not far from Earth, and there I went."

Glowing red letters appeared in one corner of my vision: Text from Sunny. Accept, postpone, or reject? I subvocalized *accept*; my wife wouldn't have interrupted me at work if it weren't important.

Cobalt blue letters scrolled: 2e MOB drz crys, kn u b hm by 4?

Translation: Caroline Touey, my wife's oldest sister, still hadn't found a satisfactory mother-of-the-bride dress, which she needed by next weekend, and she'd reached out to Sunny for shopping help in this crisis. I called up a virtual touchpad, pressed the "yes" icon and the macro icon for "Love, Al," then dismissed the pad. My nine-year-old son Alex was due to come home from his after-school program shortly after four.

"Interesting patterns just emerged from you and that annulus you bear," Haxel commented. "I noticed similar incoming patterns a moment earlier. Do I perceive some method of communication?"

I stared at her. This wasn't part of the script. "You can *see* radio waves?"

"Can't you?"

"Humans can't, but you're right. My wife sent me a message picked up by this ring on my finger, and the ring relayed it to an implant in my head that we call a 'Data Manager.' I responded in reverse."

"Remarkable. Such technology is strictly for transmitting messages?"

I chuckled internally at the idea. "No, it has plenty of uses."

It often amazes me that DM systems do everything once handled by computers, TVs, telephones, cinemas, VR helmets, and radios—all images in perfect 3D when desired and with perfect clarity even for those with poor eyesight and bad ears. Yet I fear we've become too dependent on them. And their future capabilities worried me.

But why, I wondered, *would a species evolve the ability to see radio waves?* I felt a twinge of uneasiness.

"I apologize for diverting the direction of your illumination," Haxel said. "What happened on the Tsf outpost?"

"The relevant part is that one of those the Tsf rescued was a Houck—a female as it turned out. Traders had found her in a dehydrated condition, but from the absence of water and water vapor on her damaged spacecraft, they jumped to the wrong conclusion." *Wait for it.*

"They believed water was toxic to my kind?"

"Exactly. But dried out, and ignoring the vast difference in size, this Houck slightly resembled a tiny animalcule that lives on my world, and I jumped to my own conclusion."

"That she required water."

"Right." In retrospect, that was a huge and risky leap; the resemblance might've been coincidental. But it worked.

"And this Houck was cured?"

"Supposedly, but I never saw the result. I wouldn't have expected her to ... inflate into someone structured like you."

Haxel's folds tightened a bit. "Do you find my appearance displeasing?"

"Hardly. To human eyes, your form is lovely." With her multiple veils in translucent jade, coral, and amber, she was prettier than any butterfly. Even the little flexible hooks she used as fingers were rather cute.

"I am gratified to hear that. After you healed that patient, did you have further dealings with my species before we met?"

I managed not to wince. "Indirectly. They sent me a—a thank you gift: a robot of sorts. I think they intended it to become my bodyguard, but when a Trader and I finally got it working, we hadn't assembled it quite right." I'd just earned a merit badge for understatement. "It activated in this hyper-protective mode that made it so aggressive, it attacked one of my neighbors." Second merit badge of the day, this time in the "oversimplification" category.

"I begin to see why you work submerged. Did you repair the robot?"

"No, but we managed to, um, disassemble it before it hurt anyone. I thought it best to leave it in pieces." Those pieces were now distributed between four different laboratories.

"I now feel better informed, and I thank you. What do we usually do at this juncture?"

"We go on a tour. You'll meet my assistant, you always enjoy that, and then—" A faint squeak from the doorway made me turn around. *Squeak of the devil.*

Haxel was comfortable anywhere in the clinic, and we'd learned that she wouldn't leave her room unaccompanied, so we kept her door open. We didn't want her to feel imprisoned, and it bypassed issues involving announcement protocols such as knocking. L had made that noise to reveal his presence without startling anyone.

"Sorry, boss," he said. No one on my staff needed a translating machine to handle English, Spanish, Hindi, French, Cantonese, Mandarin, or Tagalog.

I shrugged. "So much for routine. Haxel, this is L, the person I just mentioned, my office manager, assistant, and receptionist."

L's current shape suggested a shark as designed by Antoni Gaudi. He'd extruded an extra pair of eyes for the occasion, probably to avoid the appearance of ignoring anyone.

"I am delighted to meet you," Haxel said.

"Always a pleasure," L responded with an extruded mouth. "Although I hate to interrupt."

"What's going on?" I asked him.

"We have a visitor arriving via untraditional channels." L picked words with the care of a doctor performing ocular surgery and I knew his use of the word "channels" had been no accident.

"Who?"

"Gaze out yon glazing, boss, and observe for yourself."

I thought the creature rocketing through the water outside might be some horribly mutated octopus until it slowed enough for me to get a clearer look. I counted ten legs flattened to ease propulsion plus glimpses of three thicker ones hidden within the outer ring. That meant our visitor was an un-mutated Tsf. And after being around Traders for so long, I'd come to recognize certain individuals and was reasonably sure my Tsf friend Deal-of-ten-lifetimes would soon be dripping in the airlock. Hard to guess which sex phase Deal presently inhabited; the aquamarine light outside hid the gender color clues. But he or she had always come here by submersible; why swim now?

I apologized to my patient for rushing off, promised to return quickly, and then sprinted to the clinic's only entrance. On the way, I nearly tripped over an appendage my cleaning robot had extended into the hallway, probably sucking up some stray dust mote it couldn't resist, while the bulky thing rested in its alcove, recharging itself from our power generator. I gave it an undeserved snarl and moved on.

———

As the inner airlock door slid aside to reveal Deal, I tried to convince my nerves to take a wait-and-see attitude. They weren't having it. Traders work hard at keeping their behavior consistent and predictable to help other species feel comfort-able with them. Good business practice. Deal had not only defied my expectations but displayed an ability the Tsf hadn't deigned to reveal to humans, namely that they could swim like a batfish out of hell. The revelation troubled me. Traders don't just play their cards close to the vest. They keep them sewn to the vest—on the inside.

Deal's "fingers," the longest of the three kinds of cilia bundled halfway down the curved outer legs, displayed a soft lavender, which meant Deal was currently male, or nearly so. He appeared bone dry, and I wondered if Tsf can absorb water through their skins. He turned slightly, perhaps to aim more of his sensory hairs at me, and a few hundred of his shortest cilia began moving back and forth, generating a clicking rather like dozens of novelty-store teeth chattering at once. A Tsf device on a limb-band handled translation.

"Doctor," Deal clicked, "it is grand to behold you. I hope you were not unduly alarmed at my mode of arrival?"

When I'd first met Deal, his translator had been set to sound ... I guess "zany" would be the word: a minor deceit to make the human feel at ease. With me these days, he didn't bother and left his machine on a neutral setting, making him sound, stylistically, much like Haxel.

"Great to see you again too, Deal. But alarm-wise, I can't answer your question until I know where 'duly' ends and 'unduly' begins."

More sensory cilia rose to bear on me. "You appear to have surpassed the scope of my interpreting machine, but I grasp your meaning. As you have clearly surmised, I come bearing disturbing news."

Wonderful. "Disturbing" news to a Trader could mean the Earth was about to explode. "Let's hear it."

Deal raised three limbs and let them fall. "What is your schedule for this day?"

I raised my eyebrows but didn't complain; Deal only provided information when he or she was ready. "Normally, I'd be spending the next two hours finishing a session with my Houck patient, and then having a shorter one with Peeps, the eDellaPe your people sent to me." Peep's memory didn't leak, but I wasn't looking forward to that meeting either.

"Peeps?"

"A nickname L coined for my convenience. Peeps has learned English since arriving here but speaks it in a frequency range so high that all I hear are squeaks and whistles. There's no way I can say its real name. One of your interpreter devices acts as a pitch-shifter so we can communicate. Peeps claims to be 'only an embryo' and hasn't chosen a sex yet."

"How sensible. This isn't my present concern, but I understand this being is over four Earth centuries old, yet has suffered a rare lapse of religious conviction, a condition requiring emergency treatment according to eDellaPe mores."

Some cures, I thought, *are worse than the disease.* "One thing about living creatures, Deal: no shortage of variety. Apparently, eDellaPe have to hang around for two millennia before they get the senior discount. I suppose that's why they're willing to use star-flight technology so inferior to yours and go on solo journeys that last so long."

"I am unfamiliar with that form of discount, but sometimes your concepts are opaque to me. Still, now that you've reminded me why this individual came here in its crisis of faith rather than attempt the far longer journey home, I recall my favorite grandparent, Best-bargain-of-all, declaring legendary profits from certain ramifications of eDellaPe longevity."

"The good *really* old days?"

"Yes, but we have more crucial matters to consider! For now, don't let my presence influence your schedule. Is there anything you haven't mentioned on today's docket?"

Docket? Was the unusual word choice a hint? "I have one unofficial patient. Remember Tad, my security officer? She's still traumatized by being helpless for so long. Tad's ashore right now, doing some bookkeeping for me in the human clinic. I usually take a few minutes every afternoon to comfort her."

Tad, a female2 member of the Vapabond species, had been transporting Cora, a female1 Vapabond patient, to my clinic when Cora paralyzed Tad with drugs and then switched identities with her, working as my security officer for months before I uncovered the deception. The fake Tad kept the real one drugged, so all my efforts to help the supposed patient failed. And in one of those gusts of irony that regularly blow my way, being put in a responsible position began the healing process for the actual patient, and a crisis brought on by a deadly Houck robot accelerated the process. After a few months of helping the real Cora regain mental stability, I felt delighted with her progress. But the real Tad remains terrified of falling asleep and losing conscious control of herself.

"Have you any human clients later?"

"It's my light day in what we call the 'dry' clinic, and my only two patients both rescheduled."

"Excellent. That provides me some temporal leeway," Deal said. "If you will forgive the delay, I am suffering doubts about confiding in you and would appreciate spending some time in solitary meditation before I risk unpleasant consequences."

Aha. So he'd swum here because if he'd taken a submersible, his superiors would know about it. Suddenly, it seemed my alarm hadn't been unduly enough; whatever Deal was worried about, it had to be huge. "All right. I'll order a gravity boost in that first room down the hall. Use the room as long as you like."

"Excellent. My bones will appreciate some challenge. I thank you."

I sent out a DM command. After a moment, a section of wall nearby seemed to shed its skin, which fell to the floor and separated into hundreds of "macromites," tiny self-powered machines developed by the Vapabondi. These quickly linked themselves into a kind of matchstick humanoid. The figure bowed in my direction and then scampered down the hallway to prepare Deal's room. The trouble I'd had concerning the imposter Tad had earned me full control over my clinic, which was entirely composed of and self-assembled by countless macromites. These little guys kept water outside where it belonged, extended filaments to the surface as antennas to enable DM communications, and were the station's gills, keeping the air inside fresh and breathable.

The oriental bow, however, was brand new. One thing for sure: today wasn't cooking up boring.

———

When I'd first begun working for Traders, I'd assumed that their super-advanced technology needed so little further improvement it wouldn't progress rapidly. I hadn't accounted for the synergy made possible by combining Tsf science with the scientific prowess of other savvy species. Just during the past month, my employers had installed new environment regulators in the clinic, technology merging both Tsf and Vapabondi advancements. Then they'd junked that system and replaced it with something even better.

Peeps breathed a nightmare mixture of carbon monoxide, nitrous oxide, and a slew of sulfur compounds pressurized to 80 psi. Getting the eDellaPe into that room had involved extra help and extra stress. After Peeps was comfortably housed, I would've needed a spacesuit to survive her atmosphere, so I managed our initial sessions through walls made conductive to light and sound. Well, not exactly *conductive*. The latest version of macromites can become windows and speakers by duplicating whatever energy patterns hit their surfaces—more a matter of projection than transmission.

Today, I simply pushed through a transparent membrane to join Peeps, and the upgraded technology maintained a bubble of Earth atmosphere at sea-level pressure around me. The system worked beautifully although the parade of floating bubbles coming and going to replenish my air were distracting.

Tsf engineers keep promising that soon they'll be adding individualized gravity. They've been promising that for almost ten years. For now, I had to put up with instantly gaining 98 pounds, which is more nuisance than ordeal on a short-term basis.

Okay. I'll try to describe Peeps, and good luck to everyone concerned. Imagine a large collection of five-foot-tall staples, thick but flexible, each standing upright and connected to the next with short garden hoses. Now imagine a multitude of smaller and even more flexible staples attached to their larger brethren here and there at random angles. Some of these small guys can make noise by rubbing against each other, producing vibrations only bats might appreciate, plus all-too-audible squeaks that make a fingernailed-blackboard sound like Mozart in comparison.

"Greetings, friend," Peeps's translator said, translating the alien's English into English I could hear. "Are you finally willing to achieve open mind and embrace truth-fact-reality?" Peeps had sure as hell recovered from whatever crisis of faith had brought it to me. But something wasn't right here.

I cleared my throat, hoping the temptation to speak my mind would pass. "Could we agree to differ on our belief systems and discuss something else today?"

"And waste one of last chances to rescue your soul? I, too, tire of debates-arguments, yet care about you too much to abandon righteousness. Have I pointed out that eleven billion of my world-mates have utter faith in written word of our prophetess, most beloved Rohmmemt? Surely, you do not dream-imagine eleven billion eDellaPe could be in error?"

As a long-lapsed Lutheran, my qualifications to judge even Earthly religions were suspect, but from what Peeps had told me, the Rohm religion wasn't my cup of chai.

"I'm not qualified to say."

"Is true! But after petitioning The Pure on your behalf, epiphany was bestowed upon me."

"Oh?"

"Your problem is merely frame of reference alien to you. I have done deep research-study and have found Earthly religion that matches sweet essence of Rohmmemt's wisdom."

I nodded, curious. "Which one did the job?"

"You are familiar with Judaism?"

That hoisted my eyebrows. I put my DM into record and report mode. "I know a little about it. You think Rohm and Judaism have something in common? How did you even learn about our religions?"

"I uncovered truth-reality because you have kindly allowed me entrance to Earthly search engines."

I did no such thing, but advanced ETs often manage to access our data systems on their own.

"Using differential engine titled 'Stone Philosopher,'" the alien continued, "I requested word for 'universe' in all collected human languages and then ran these through excellent interpreting device Traders provide."

"How did that lead you to Judaism?"

"Hebrew word for universe is *olam*, derived from root *alam*. *Alam* means 'to conceal.'"

My DM projected sky-blue Hebrew letters onto my field of vision, properly from right to left because I'd put the thing into "report" mode. But now I was hearing both the Hebrew words pitch-shifted into audibility and their English translations—an annoying facet of Trader communication technology.

After a moment, my confused brain sorted everything out. "I suppose a lot of stuff could hide behind the whole universe."

Peeps failed to break into squeaky chuckles. "Only one non-thing hides-self-effaces. In *olam*, your Jews express core of our beliefs. Universe, which comprises everything that is a thing, is merely mask. And do you know what wears this mask?"

"Let me guess: God."

"Take care! Naming that which cannot be described, categorized, or envisioned can lead even wise into error. If you doubt me, just ask angel."

By "angel," Peeps meant Haxel. Ever since I introduced these two patients to each other as an experiment, Peeps had referred to Haxel that way. At first, I'd suspected a flaw in Peeps's English. Then I'd learned that the eDellaPe species had known of the Houck long before the Tsf encountered them and held them in—let's politely call it *extraordinarily* rather than insanely—high regard. But at least Peeps had aimed all prose-lytizing efforts at L and me, apparently feeling that Haxel was already sufficiently saved. Visiting the eDellaPe with Haxel had become a daily routine.

It dawned on me that I'd never asked the obvious question. "What do you mean by 'angel'?"

"There, we believers again agree with Jewish tradition. Angels are ... I believe your term is 'applications': special enti-ties-creations that The Pure uses to accomplish tasks on cruder physical, mental, and spiritual planes. Jewish lore holds that angels have only one leg, symbolically suggesting that they cannot move, change, or improve as living beings can."

I made a mental note to research Hebrew mythology, but the main thing right now was what Peeps believed. "If I'm understanding you, you call Haxel an angel because in your view she has only one leg?"

My patient remained silent for long enough to concern me that I'd said something offensive.

"I have unintentionally misled-fooled you," Peeps finally responded. "Leg is only symbolic hint. What Houck *do* reveals their essence."

A surge of adrenaline shook my professional calmness. I felt on the precipice of some astonishing discovery.

"What is it, exactly," I asked, "that the Houck do?"

"Not my position to say-explicate. You must ask them."

Too bad the only Houck available knew nothing about her own species.

———

At 3:30 in the afternoon, Deal came out of seclusion just long enough to inform me that he still hadn't decided to take any big risks, and he wanted to "stand" on it overnight. Yes, Tsf sleep upright.

So I was free to leave. En route the sea was dark and unusually murky, perfectly matching my mental state. Even sans appointments, I usually stop at the dry clinic on my way home to chat with Gara and work for a while with Tad. Not today. My mood was all wrong. But when I walked through my home's front door, the scent of something baking that clearly featured apples, cinnamon, and the usual culprits cheered me, mostly because it meant Sunny had returned earlier than she'd expected. Tragically, I can't allow myself more than a small amount of sugar each day because of my serious blood disorder.

We both greeted Alex as he was exiting the school bus, which was rare enough to delight him. In a few more years, I suspect we'll be getting a different reaction.

We had a nice family dinner and what should've been a pleasant evening since, for once, no calls barged through my emergency-only DM filtering. But instead of basking in the Apple Kringler-scented here and now, I couldn't stop worrying about the mysterious something that had prompted Deal to sneak under the Tsf sonar, so to speak, and into my clinic. In all my years of dealing with Traders, I'd never seen one exhibit the slightest defiance of Tsf policy. I'd figured that only something important could account for Deal's visit, but my idea of *how* important kept expanding.

Alex had no school tomorrow—one of those teacher conference days that bore teachers to death but bring joy to their students—so the three of us stayed up and watched shows for an hour past Alex's usual bedtime. My boy had gotten his first DM implant on his ninth birthday, and we could've all watched different programs—standard practice for families these days. Instead, we linked our DMs and called up child-appropriate entertainment. This always reminded me of the traditional post-prandial, sitting-around-the-family-TV my generation grew up with, except that each of us saw a virtual TV directly in front of us, and the programs had the kind of three-dimensional realism that made Sunny and me apply parental filters with heavy hands.

Please forgive a brief rant. When I was a kid we had lovely devices called digital video recorders. With those, we could record shows, play them back at our convenience, and fast-forward past commercials. Today, our DMs can access all kinds of entertainment, play shows or movies or "live" events at our convenience, and fast-forward over everything *except* commercials. You are required to pay for each program by watching five minutes of ads. Sure, it makes sense. Why would any sponsor fund a show otherwise? But it feels to me like a step backward in technology just as big as the step forward. Rant ended.

As Sunny and I lay in bed, I had to admit that the DM age did offer benefits. I've always loved reading in bed, and now I could do it without holding a book or an e-reader, or going through all the labor of turning pages. My DM tracked eye movements and knew when I was ready for the next hit. Hell, I could read standing on my head with the light off and my eyes closed, if I could stand on my head. Still, during the day I prefer physical books; somehow reading a printed page feels more satisfying. But the time may be nearing when such things will go extinct except for literature intended for children too young for the implant. And that will be a damn—sorry, that's enough. Rant ended *now*.

———

Deal greeted me the moment I stepped from the airlock, and to my shock Gara hovered near him. Truly awkward. Gara considers Traders "spiritually stunted materialists," and finds the Tsf notion of mutual self-interest morally bankrupt, an excuse for rampant greed. She regards species such as the Vapabondi, humans, and even her own, the Vithy, pitifully naïve to have placed such confidence in the Tsf. For all I know, she's right.

She'd been coolly polite to Deal during their few encounters that I'd witnessed although she's a warm sort of person, but she'd never sought him or her out. I doubted that her surprise visit now during Deal's surprise visit was coincidental. She hadn't been here in months.

Due to the usual inverse relationship between preparedness and opportunity to use that preparation, Gara hasn't had much chance to apply her physical therapy magic to my ET patients despite her being hired expressly to aid arriving exotics with somatic issues. Yet she's been extremely useful. Her alien techniques and abilities have helped many of my human clientele, a boon we'd discovered almost accidentally. As a team, to brag a little, our cocktail of therapies has shown such a positive synergistic effect on human patients that other mental health practitioners have begun working in tandem with PTs, but the human sort. Admittedly, I've overheard fellow shrinks, most often when in a semi-sober state, express doubts about the value of their own part in such joint therapy.

Gara, like all Vithy, is blind; but her fibrous, rather shadow-like body, can act as a peerless echo-locator, an ultrasound delivery and detection system, a DM-quality immersion-audio projector, or the ultimate massage couch. She has, as Alex once put it, Superman ears. Gara lives on sunlight and arsenic—both to aid her version of photosynthesis—plus water and gasses guaranteed to kill an elephant in seconds. Luckily, she only needs to respire for ten minutes each day. In case you're wondering if she, too, keeps a sub in her garage, she'd beat the cetacean of your choice to any finish line.

Aside from her attitude toward Traders, the two of us

perceive things pretty much eye to ear, and we've grown close over the years. Her, I trust. Still....

"Good morning," I said to both my visitors. "Nice surprise to see you here, Gara, but I hope nothing's wrong ashore?"

If there had been, we both knew, she would've informed me through my DM rather than make a personal appearance. Her anatomy precluded a DM implant, but Traders had installed an external communications link in her office.

Always tactful, Gara didn't point out the bogusness of my question, not verbally, but she changed form—from a black, pillar-shaped cloud to a tall rectangle with a female human face protruding from the upper surface. The sculpted eyes seemed to follow me. Creepy, but I got the message: you are wearing a false face.

"Ashore, all is fine," she said, "but when you didn't make your visit daily yesterday, I concerned became."

Another strangeness. Gara makes it a practice to add subtle, comforting vibrations to her voice, designed to help humans relax. Today, something in her tone grated on my nerves, probably a warning.

"Sorry," I said. "Should've called and let you know I couldn't stop in. Nothing serious, just had to be home before my boy got dropped off."

"I am relieved," Gara claimed.

I wasn't. How the hell did she learn a Trader had shown up? Then I felt like an idiot. Deal, playing secret agent for whatever reason, couldn't inform me he was coming because even coded transmissions can be cracked, so he would've stopped at the dry clinic to see if I was there before taking the deep plunge. He would've asked Mrs. Culver, my human receptionist, about my whereabouts, and Gara would've overheard the conversation even if she'd been in her office with the door closed. Her hearing is so acute she can read my facial expressions when she's in her office and I'm in a soundproofed room.

Considering her opinion of Traders, her concern for my

well-being, and the fact I hadn't communicated with her yesterday, of course she'd come here to learn what Deal was up to. This explanation cured one worry but triggered another one, a fine example of my Conservation of Misery Principle. Best example of the Principle: The morning I'd first met Sunny, I was diagnosed with leucopenia, a bone marrow disease, that very afternoon. Another example: artificial white blood cells preserve my life, but ever since my diagnosis, I've had to eat carefully, exercise carefully, and monitor my health like a maniac. End grumble.

My problem now? I could see no reasonable way of getting Gara to leave until I could reassure her about Deal's presence. Meanwhile, Deal's reluctance to spill the beans implied that he wouldn't do so until Gara, with her hyper-hearing, was gone. The situation had gone from dicey to impossible.

I can probably guess what you're thinking: why not take Gara aside on some pretext and clue her in? Because I had no way to estimate the keenness of *Deal's* hearing. True, his sensory threads were small, but he had them in abundance. Plus, I knew that Traders equip themselves with DM-type implants. Even human DMs have sensory augmentation options for people with hearing or vision loss and the cutting edge of our technology is blunt compared to Trader tech.

While I'd been running in mental circles, no one said a word, waiting for me to take the initiative. Deal stood motionless with dozens of his sensory threads aimed my way while Gara also remained rooted, her body gently oscillating to keep upright. I had no idea what to do. A cool breeze on my forehead told me that the clinic's personal environment regulator had reacted to my distress.

Then Deal twitched a few limbs in a Tsf shrug. "I have just been ordered to meet with my superiors. Therefore my free time has ended, and I must speak now or not at all. I choose to speak and will share a secret with both of you."

The latest Tsf translators put emotional content into their

interpretations, and I could've sworn I heard a hint of giggle in Deal's artificial voice. Perhaps my favorite Trader understood my quandary.

"I only request," Deal continued, "that you decline to identify me as the source of this information if possible. Is that agreeable?"

"Yes," I said, risking speaking for us both.

"So be it. Several Earth days ago, our monitors detected a spatial anomaly somewhat beyond the orbit of your moon. Upon investigation, our scientists found no visible object in that location, but noted a partial occlusion of stars, which suggested the subtle presence of considerable matter. Naturally, they did not approach this unknown material directly, but when they sent a wide spectrum of energies toward it, one very short frequency bounced back. As a result, they assembled a visualization of the entire object."

"So what was it?"

"What *is* it, should be your question, Doctor. The overall design closely matched the only Houck starship we Traders have seen, that damaged vehicle in which we found your original Houck patient. This new vessel, however, is vastly larger."

"Wait! You're saying a giant, invisible spaceship has shown up ... um, not exactly shown—"

"It awaits."

"Any idea why?"

L's voice, on the clinic's encrypted DM channel, seemed to whisper directly into my brain. "Boss, Peeps is ready to depart but wants to speak with you first."

Perfect timing, I didn't think. I was already worried about leaving Haxel in her daily muddle for too long, and I *had* to hear Deal out.

I subvocalized, not caring that Gara would hear me. "L, I'm tied up. Tell Peeps I'll be along ASAP."

Deal began rocking on his three central limbs, perhaps a

self-comforting behavior. "We cannot guess why the Houck have come, but our concern includes both the secretive aspect of their presence, and the extraordinary size of their spacecraft."

"How big is it?"

"You'll recall the measure of a Trader Parent Ship. This Houck vessel would comfortably hold fifty such objects."

I didn't let my jaw drop quite far enough to dislocate. The Parent Ship had been immense.

"We Tsf can conceive of only two possible reasons to construct such a titan," the Trader continued. "Either as a colony transport or for conquest."

My God. "You think the Houck plan to *attack* us?"

"We simply don't know. Do you comprehend my personal crisis?"

The Tsf valued nothing more than business opportunities, and since the Houck came from another galaxy where they'd apparently set up their own trading empire, Traders gave their relationship with the Houck top priority. Tsf leaders would've ordered their subordinates to keep quiet about the Houck intrusion for fear of jeopardizing that relationship, but as my friend and supervisor, Deal felt obligated to clue me in. He'd risked his career, perhaps his freedom and life to do this. Realizing this, my throat clenched and my voice came out thin and husky.

"I sure do. Thank you."

"You will wish to relay this information to your authorities immediately, but I urge you to wait."

"Why?"

"There is little humans can do if such a ... prominent species means you ill, and any negative reaction from your people may prevent third party mediation. Skilled Tsf diplomats, using utmost delicacy, have already dispatched messages to Houck representatives concerning this matter."

"I see." *Damn!* "I'll have to ... think about this."

"Do so. Meanwhile, I shall prepare for departure while contemplating the likely consequences of my own folly."

Having "eyes" on all his outer limbs, Deal didn't need to turn to see where he was going. He put himself in reverse, leaving Gara and me alone near the airlock.

"The Bach retrieval program," Gara announced, "is progressing nicely."

Amazing how an inappropriate non sequitur could trigger what I like to call my "flight or flight" response.

———

Decades ago, human archaeologists theorized that sound vibrations conducted through a potter's hands might subtly inscribe clay being shaped on a potter's wheel. If so, and if playback could be achieved using anything from a glorified phonograph needle to laser-reflection digital analysis, a Vesuvius-buried vase from Pompeii, for example, might open a clear sonic window into the past, revealing long-forgotten cultural and linguistic truths. Last I'd heard, researchers in this field had isolated only squeaks and rumbles, perhaps the sound of the wheel itself—or not.

Gara olMara, however, has uncanny resources in the arena of acoustic science. I suppose that's because species expertise in any domain begins with the nature and acuity of perceptions, and I've yet to find the limitations of Gara's primary sense.

A Vithy's body is largely constructed of minuscule carbon nanotubes encasing bimetallic filaments that act as both nerves and muscles. Their "skin" is practically invulnerable yet so responsive to vibration that Gara can read printed material so long as a high frequency sound-source is nearby because printing reflects sound differently than the bare page. Her sense of touch is acute enough to feel starlight on her body. Which may explain why curious Vithy developed radio astronomy, although their technological repertoire never extended to telescopes.

About a year ago, when I mentioned the pottery-recording idea to her, Gara informed me that siliceous materials often contain retrievable acoustic information, particularly musical information, which tends to have a limited dynamic range and be highly organized. "Might there be," she'd asked, "any particular musical offering from humanity's past that I'd care to hear?" That's how the Bach retrieval program began, involving a network of musicologists, historians, artisans, US and German officials, and interesting shipping bills....

Exciting stuff, but its irrelevance at this moment chilled me. I understood Gara's real message: she, too, suspected Deal of superhuman hearing. Unlike me, she distrusted the Trader.

"The Tobias Trost samples at the audio-strata relevant is categorized nearly, although we can't be sure of the dates exact when Bach played. Naturally, we can only produce a guess educated concerning which tunes, if any, were actually by J.S. Bach performed."

As she spoke, she deliberately brushed against a wall; I got that message too and a stronger chill. It had never occurred to me that the macromites surrounding us could record or transmit voices, but the Tsf had commissioned this structure and had never given me the owner's manual. She hadn't been talking about retrieving noises for the hell of it....

"We'll just assume Bach was the best," I said. "I'm already late for seeing my first patient, but we can talk later. I'll be at the dry clinic this afternoon."

"Please do so. A pleasure great to hear you as always, Al. I'll be off swimming now. Take care extreme."

"You too."

My session with Haxel went on for a while as a duplicate of the previous sixty-one, but it didn't feel routine. Why would her people bring what might be a warship on a covert mission to this corner of the galaxy? After the usual usuals, she surprised me with a new comment.

"I am too ignorant to judge, but is it possible you are emotionally upset?"

I studied her shifting veils of a body, but the flowing motions told me nothing. "You're right. I do have something troubling me, but it doesn't involve you." More likely it did. "How did you know?"

"I am unsure," she said. "Simply a feeling. But would you confide the source of your trouble? Perhaps I can help."

On impulse, I decided to share a little. "Yesterday, a visitor showed up, the Trader Deal-of-ten-lifetimes, one of my employers that I just told you about." *And on a heap of other mornings.*

"What brought him here?"

Answering that was so damn tricky I almost missed the significant word. Then her words replayed themselves in my head, and a suspicion that had, apparently, been secretly gestating within me burst into certainty.

"There's absolutely," I said, feeling more stunned than angry, "nothing wrong with your memory."

"Why do you make this claim?"

"You said 'him.' Which tells me you remember seeing the Trader swim by your window yesterday, and that you knew he was presently male by his coloration. You've been playing games with me."

"Isn't it a convention in this language to apply the masculine pronoun when—"

"Don't bother. I might've figured it was coincidental except for everything else."

She drifted closer to me. For the first time, I felt a bit scared of her. All those little claws. I used my DM to send L one of our pre-loaded messages, asking him to lurk nearby, but out of sight. He DMed me back: Will do. Don't forget Peeps.

Haxel's voice came out very soft, "Kindly elucidate, I am deeply intrigued."

"Okay." I watched her very, very carefully. "Let's rehash some history. The first Houck I met had been rescued from a damaged starship."

"You said so earlier."

"And sixty-one times before, as I'm sure you recall. Bear with me." I put it together as I spoke. "The Trader rescuers gained enough access into that starship's data system to deduce that the rescued party had come from another galaxy. Traders wound up hiring me as a therapist for the castaway and two others from different species, all three species unfamiliar to the Tsf, and *all* recently salvaged from or near inoperable spacecraft."

"A remarkable happenstance."

"Oh? I once asked a Tsf friend how often non-Tsf had been rescued in deep space. Care to guess?"

"Rarely?"

"Four times. The three I mentioned and once about a thousand years ago." The Tsf, Deal claims, had started building their trade empire some six Earth millennia ago, about when Sumerians were first experimenting with scratching little marks on clay and waiting for someone to criticize the spelling. "I don't think 'rarely' covers it."

"And your conclusion?"

"You Houck arranged that last trio of rescues. Obviously, since you can travel between galaxies, you have technology the Tsf can't touch. So adding in that assemble-at-your-own-risk robot your people sent me, supposedly as a gesture of appreciation, and your own presence here, I'd guess that you good folks are"—*up to something sneaky involving a giant spaceship*—"running some kind of test," I ended lamely.

Haxel unfolded her body a bit, which startled me because it

happened so fast and because the colors in her veils brightened. "Your intuition is one hundred and nothing percent correct, Doctor. But I sense your fear. It is inappropriate. We mean no beings harm, and it is only the greatest necessity that has engendered our manipulations."

"Good to hear. So what do you want?"

"Your help, because you have proved your worth."

"My help as a therapist?"

"No. As a judge."

"*What*? A judge of *what*?" What the blue hell? Was I supposed to preside over some pan-galactic court, maybe holding a self-pounding gavel? *Never shout at patients*, I warned myself. *Especially fake ones.*

"I cannot provide you a complete answer right now."

"Terrific. How about a hint?"

"You will be asked to appraise the oldest species we know of and assess a line of reasoning of primary importance to all Houck. Perhaps 'juror' would be a more fitting term. For our jury, we are gathering a great variety of viewpoints: perceptive beings with perspectives alien to our own, particularly brilliant or creative or insightful minds, and some whose qualities encourage graceful flows of happenstance."

Years of getting pelted with L's word games helped me interpret. "Let's see if I follow. You want me to be one of your judges because you think I'm either smart, creative, intuitive, or lucky?"

"The final two qualifications assure you a place on the panel."

Right. An effective psychiatrist doesn't need high-octave brainpower so much as observational skills and good hunches; I was living proof. "How did you conclude that I was such a paragon?"

"We followed our procedure. Over time, we've learned how to identify each galaxy's species that barters most widely with other species. By setting that species a certain kind of problem, that species almost always passes the problem to the species they believe most likely to provide a solution, who in turn usually select an individual or team of individuals to deal with the problem. Such individuals have proved likely to possess the qualities we seek."

Good lord! How am I supposed to wrap my brain around this? "O...kay. I guess the Tsf must be the neighborhood traders here. But how could outsiders figure that out?"

Haxel seemed to rush through her explanation. "Easily. Although innumerable means exist for medium-range interaction, practical interstellar communication demands manipulating entangled energies. Entering your galaxy, we analyzed all such communications, divided them into language types and tallied both totals and distances involved. The Tsf scored highest in all regards."

Entangled energies?

She continued. "We then evaluated Tsf competence in choosing a candidate species. Full illumination required ninety of your years and involved approaching an associate species of theirs to ascertain their attitude toward Traders."

"Ah. Let me guess: the eDellaPe."

"The very ones. We offered them an imaging technology they lacked in exchange for information and for keeping knowledge of our presence to themselves."

"I see." Interesting that Peeps's people hadn't kept the secret just because they thought the Houck were angelic....

"Once convinced the Tsf fit our criteria, we arranged for the rescues you've mentioned so often by moving our own staged wreck and the two genuinely damaged spacecraft within detection range of various Trader outposts. Our analysis indicated Traders would indeed desire external, better-qualified help to resolve the three-part puzzle we'd set up. Thus they called on your world who called on you."

Some "procedure"! I would've laughed at "better qualified" except for Haxel's third requirement. I'd been lucky as hell.

"You didn't cause the actual disasters?"

"We do not willingly cause harm."

"Good to know."

"Your success in that challenge," she continued, "encouraged us to test you further. Thus, we sent you the automaton, but did not anticipate the way you misassembled it. Still, you dealt with it successfully and thus I came here to provide a final test."

Much thanks for the killer robot. "What were you testing me *for*?"

"The qualities I already mentioned, and also patience."

Well, you sure tried mine. "And I passed? Can you really believe I'm a good choice for this job? If so, you really do need a psychiatrist."

"What makes you trust your self-image? We find you suitable, and you are not qualified to judge that assessment. A vessel waits near your moon; we have rendered it unobtrusive to avoid disturbing your people. I beg you to join me in boarding this vessel to undertake a journey. There is something you must ... perceive before you can act as a juror."

"Where would we be going?"

"Beyond this galaxy. We would return you afterward."

The room seemed to spin around me, no doubt because my brain was flailing, trying to get a grip.

"How long would I be gone?" My voice had gone hoarse.

"No more than one of your weeks. We will arrange all needed transportation and a leave of absence from your work duties. Traders are anxious to render us grateful."

I licked my newly dried lips. "I can spare a week, absolutely, but how much time would've passed on Earth by the time I got back?" I envisioned returning to find Sunny, Alex, and possibly my great-grandchildren turned to dust. Obviously, Traders and other Milky Way commuters had found a way around Einstein's insights, but these performed comparatively short hops. Tsf astrophysicists, using Houck star charts, had established that the Houck hadn't come from any galaxy within ten million damn light-years of our own. Albert E. could well have the last chuckle at my expense.

"I included minor temporal effects in my estimate."

"Would it be possible," I asked, "to bring my wife and child along?" It wasn't that I disbelieved Haxel, but I'd had enough miscommunications with non-humans to make me cautious. The smallest misunderstanding could result in devastating consequences for my family. "Um, do you know what I mean by 'wife' and 'child'?"

"I am conversant with these concepts; Houck, too, generate offspring. I encourage you to bring your nuclear family, Doctor. Truly, you will regret it if they do not share in your experience; no description could do it justice."

That comment really set the hook in my mouth. "Look, I don't question my competence for your panel, I flatly deny it. But if you've got the gigantic jury you've implied, how much harm could I do?" That last remark should be enshrined in the Stupidity Hall of Fame, but my rationalization engine was firing on all cylinders. The chance to visit another galaxy didn't pop up most days.

"Then you accept our proposal?"

"One last issue: when your jury votes, could I abstain?"

"We require no voting."

"Then I'm yours for a week." I hoped only a week. "When do we go? My only other patient here is also leaving, just waiting to say goodbye, but I'll need to make arrangements with my family and with my land clinic."

"Some haste is essential so we shall depart at your earliest convenience, and we have two more jurors to collect on our way. Both have already agreed to their roles. I am delighted you have done likewise. We will inform the Tsf and your governments of our success. We Houck will not, therefore, render your world a burning husk. No, no, Doctor, I see by the reduction of your dermal coloration that you took my jest seriously. Our two species share at least one attribute: humor."

Don't quit your day or *night job.* "Very amusing. If it's up to me, Saturday morning would be the best time to take off." That way, Alex wouldn't miss too much school and Sunny could finish out her workweek. "Should we bring our own food?" *And air and gravity....*

"We are well prepared for human comfort and will supply details later. Please convey my farewell to the eDellaPe."

———

Peeps seemed agitated as I entered the room, its bracket-like body segments wriggling so much they kept tapping each other. These collisions were muffled, but so frequent that the noise reminded me of someone clumsy shuffling cards. I wanted to apologize, thinking my tardiness had generated this hyperactivity, but the eDellaPe didn't give me a chance.

"Doctor, I've researched Jewish lore further and have discovered something wonderful! Are you familiar with Kabbalah?"

I wondered if my newsweb horoscope, had I read it, would have warned me about today being a bad day for predictable conversations. "I'm afraid not."

"You surprise. I have learned that a major progenitor of your vocation was greatly influenced by this lore."

"Carl Jung?"

"Unexpected pronunciation, but yes."

"My training was geared more to the practical than the mystical."

"But Kabbalah is entirely practical! All about balance." With no encouragement from me, Peeps was off and running —running off at the mouth-surrogate. This time I didn't mind. I'd rather be educated than converted, even if the pedagogue involved engaged in the former to accomplish the latter.

"Moreover Doctor, and this is exciting part, system is utterly congruent with truths manifest in Rohm. Like eDellaPe, insightful Hebrews realized that each individual soul is in essence natal nutrition canal channeling—"

"What is...oh. An umbilical cord?"

"In Earth's mammals and elsewhere. Creatures on my world utilize superior mechanism. As I *attempted* to state, individual souls are not entities or parts of entities but channels for energy flows initiating from The Pure, which wise Jews refer to as *Ein Sof*: Without End. These flows, *Sephirot* in the Hebrew, radiate through four major existence planes acting as step-down transformers, from most spiritual to most concrete, and finally manifest in universe of time and space as behavior, thoughts, speech, and personality. When a being's *Sephirot* are properly balanced, that person is attuned to The Pure."

"The Pure is God?"

"The Pure is beyond conception therefore unnamable, yet without its spaciousness there would be no life, awareness, or being. This is what both Kabbalah and blessed Rohmmemt reveal. You are often interviewed by public interest media, yes?"

I blinked at the high-speed conversational turn. "True."

"When next this occurs, I would appreciate if you would convey these words to Earth's *mekubalim*, those who receive Kabbalah wisdom: The eDellaPe consider you siblings in family of truth."

"I'll try to remember."

"Thank you, and I also give thanks for curing me so quickly."

"You're very welcome, but all I did was follow the instructions your people sent me." For once, I'd been armed with sufficient knowledge concerning a patient including the appropriate therapeutic procedure. All I did was recite Rohm aphorisms translated into English.

"Those instructions, by intent, did little to effect my recovery."

This time, I blinked twice. "Oh? Then what did you just thank me for?"

"As the Masters planned, your skepticism boiled my own doubts, raising clean steam of faith. I am ready now to continue attunement quest."

"Glad to have done my part." I'd tried not to sound sour but wasn't thrilled that yet another alien race had been manipulating me.

"You will likewise be glad that angel has arranged transport from this room to quest vehicle. My departure will be far easier than arrival."

"Great."

Nice to know the hassle factor would be minimal, but the information had greater significance. Evidently, Peeps and Haxel had been conversing privately without my knowledge or approval, and it seemed that "angel" technology was up to something teleportation-ish. *Beam me up, Gabriel.* I didn't mind sounding sour in my own head.

"When," I asked, "will you be leaving?"

"Momentarily. Bless you, keep you, and may clear light of Purity shine upon you."

"Bless you, too. I hope you find whatever you're looking for."

"I have already claimed crucial element. Not speed or destination, but journey that signifies. Remember to always balance Sephirotic flows!"

Outside the room's window, part of the femur-shaped eDellaPe spaceship appeared. Peeps did some flowing itself, wobbling like an industrial-gauge Slinky, fading to a misty version of itself, and finally moving right through the wall and presumably into the starship. Years ago, I'd seen a rather scary alien do something similar and without technology. But now I'd witnessed exotic technology applied at a distance by an ET who appeared to have brought along no equipment whatsoever. Just how far ahead of human science, I wondered, had the Houck reached?

———

Alex was all sparkling eyes and grin about accompanying me on my first jaunt beyond the Milky Way, Sunny willing but cautious. As I lay in bed that night, my own enthusiasm curdled. Putting the two people I loved best in jeopardy wasn't my favorite plan. Gara's cautionary words, delivered when I'd met with her at the dry clinic before coming home, returned to bite me in the conscience.

"You are risking everything," she'd warned after I'd outlined the situation, "based on claims you cannot evaluate made by entities you now know to be devious."

I didn't dismiss her words but didn't absorb them without reminding myself how overly cautious she could be. Of course, the degree of her paranoia was a matter of opinion; no doubt she considered me reckless as hell. At 12:00 AM I was sidling over to her viewpoint.

"Can't sleep?" Sunny murmured, turning toward me.

"How could you tell?"

"You were doing your stressed breathing. A bit fast and you make this little noise on the exhale, not quite a sigh."

"My soul must be glass." A glass umbilicus, according to Peeps.

"How very poetic. But you might as well face the cruel truth: you can't keep secrets from me. To demonstrate, you're laying there, stewing over the wisdom of bringing the boy and me along."

"Untrue! I'm lying, not laying."

She chuckled. "A midnight visit from the Grammar Police, how charming. Seriously, hun, you can't take it back. If you're going, we're going no matter what. Are you ready to tell this Haxel you've decided to stay home?"

"I don't—no. It wouldn't feel right considering how much effort the Houck made to enlist me."

"So you might as well accept, relax, and get some sleep."

"Got it." Sunny was entirely reasonable and flexible ... until she made up her mind. I summoned up an imaginary triple-pan trip balance and used it to weigh the potential danger, the likely adventure, and the definite emotional consequences of leaving my family at home over Sunny's objections. That third part tipped the scales and sealed the deal. We were all going. I remained scared, but oddly enough, I felt better.

———

Saturday morning we learned that a trip to another galaxy could begin with waiting around on the front lawn. I'd put on my confident face for Alex's benefit. Before long a gray van with government plates pulled into our driveway, a nondescript vehicle except for a bumper sticker reading "I brake for shadows." Two bulky men hopped out, introduced themselves only as Carl and Steven, grabbed our four suitcases, informed us they'd be handling them until our departure, and placed them into a luggage compartment as if they were soufflés in danger of collapse. Only then did Carl suggest we climb in ourselves. The van's interior surprised me: fifteen individual bucket leather seats with racing-car seatbelts, each seat with a mounted touch screen displaying our GPS status, which seemed ridiculous since DMs these days have GPS built in. Then the side-door closed automatically, and my DM shut off without my blessing although its CPU, with two weeks' worth of charge, lay nested in my suitcase. I didn't appreciate losing my artificial resources—felt a little naked to be honest—and saw no need for draconian security measures, but my live media fast would begin soon in any case.

After Steven helped each of us with the six-point seat-belts, Carl drove with all the high-speed abandon of my grandmother whose automotive pace allowed my brother and I, in our youth, to admire individual pebbles in passing. After that excitement, we traveled no more than five miles before Carl risked going off-road and into the large and weather-damaged parking lot of an abandoned factory where a fleet of cars awaited us, suggesting that Traders hadn't lost their hunger for publicity. Among the many people standing around and radiating self-importance, I spotted two federal agents I knew and some NASA cronies I hadn't seen in years. To my surprise, Deal-of-ten-lifetimes was there, holding one limb upward to see over the mob. He waved the vertical limb at us as we disembarked. No one else seemed to notice our arrival and even Deal had more sensory threads aimed the other way, toward something glowing that I could barely glimpse between thousand-dollar bespoke suits.

As they'd promised, Carl and Steven grabbed the suitcases with Carl having the misfortune to choose two of Sunny's, who doesn't pack light.

People stood at various angles although almost all gazed toward the mystery brightness, but I recognized two over-dressed-for-the-weather US senators, a congresswoman, and one silver-haired and NBA-tall politician posing in quarter-profile for the benefit of the media newshawks jostling each other to get closer to whatever the crowd found so interesting. Some of the news crews had brought along lighting to better illuminate their DM broadcasts, and I wondered if that caused the glow.

The silver-haired head turned and the famous green eyes seemed to briefly catch my own. What had Traders told Washington that had dragged the Vice President of these United States here? The man towered, surrounded by gravitas plus a dozen burly men in dark jackets, which might as well have been embroidered with "Secret Service." More such guardians protected Deal.

"I left my POTUS in my other White House," Sunny whispered, more my kind of joke than hers so clearly an effort to soothe my nerves. And it helped, simply because it proved how well she understood me.

"Dad?" Alex said. "I can't see."

He meant that his view was mostly VIP backsides. Alex was tall, but for a nine-year-old. "I could put you on my shoulders." *You used to like that.*

He frowned. "I don't know. Kind of babyish."

Another voice chimed in. "Shuck bones, dag and nab. I reckon it wouldn't be in-fan-tile if *I* was the gentleman what did the liftin'."

I turned around. Deal had extricated himself from his guardians and inserted himself behind us. Tsf can really scoot when it suits them; it took more than a few seconds before the first security agent, puffing if not actually huffing, got back into protective position, jostling our two luggage porters. If you're wondering about Deal's stylistic jump to Southern Parody, Traders make great efforts to appear harmless when around humans, and the masquerade includes speech patterns that vary but are always distractingly colorful.

"Thought you'd gotten called in," I told Deal. "And where did you steal that demented dialog?"

"*This* is what I was recalled to do." The translation was just loud enough for me to hear. As my supervisor, Deal felt no obligation to put on a show for me. "The Houck informed my superiors of the role you'd accepted. They also requested a Tsf presence, specifically mine, at this site. As to my conversational mode, it was derived from the work of one Walt Kelly, now deceased, who created non-animated graphic works under the rubric 'Pogo.'"

"Okay. So what's everyone staring at?"

Before answering, he extended a limb downward toward

Alex, curling the end to make a seat. Deal had often visited with my family over the last two years, and I fear my boy regarded him as a combination play-toy and climbing structure. Alex jumped and spun to land on the temporary bight his play-toy had produced. He did not inherit that smooth coordination from his father. Deal hoisted him overhead, keeping the loop horizontal, with all the effort it would take me to lift a pea.

"Jus' keep up with me, Doc," Deal said at normal volume, "and see for your own self." Keeping Alex supported with forklift steadiness, Deal cleared a path for Sunny and me by relentlessly moving forward and gently brushing people aside. When those people saw what was nudging them, they became eager to be brushed; few had been around Traders in the flesh. By rights, Deal should've been the focus of interest here, and I couldn't imagine what could put him in second place.

"Excuse me, sir and madam," a Secret Service agent behind me called out. "Let us through."

Naturally, the professional guardians wanted to stay close to the Deal, the person they'd been assigned to guard, but he reached back with a limb, stretching it past my left ear, to tap the chest of the agent who'd spoken. The man got the hint and didn't bother us again.

We emerged through the human sea not far from the VP, and I got my first good look at the object of everyone's scrutiny.

The luminous thing resembled an old-fashioned movie screen, or rather the ghost of one. It looked as delicate as a soap bubble and waved around like a curtain in a mild breeze. L, I'm sure, would've described it as "filmy." Animated images of humans and various aliens, all depicted in unexpected colors, appeared on its wavering surface. The deformations and weird tints made it hard to be sure, but I seemed to recognize Deal, Gara, L, Haxel, and yours truly.

"I'll bite," I said. "What is it? A defective video screen?"

Deal waved three limbs in a shivering motion. "I *pre*-sume it's a landin' beacon, old son. But it sure beats all why *them* critters would need one."

An argument broke out behind me. I turned to look. The agents carrying our luggage and those assigned to protect Deal were in a territorial dispute. Past them, my NASA buddies gave me three big grins and one thumb-up. I grinned in return but seeing them took me back, for a strange moment, to the years we'd worked together. Suddenly, I regarded the present scene with eyes twenty-five years younger, and the cumulative changes between then and now seemed more appropriate for a gulf centuries wide.

For one thing, almost everyone regardless of gender wore makeup. Thanks to DM technology, everyone's eyes had become potential video cameras with a potentially instant worldwide audience, so most people wanted to stay ready for their close-up. And with nanofluid makeup and nanostructure hair gel and dental washes, complexions, hair, and smiles could appear perfect. Light-skinned people sported golden nano-tans; those with darker skins beamed ersatz health. No one had a single nose or ear hair visible; nary a pimple raised its head. Not everyone used eyeliner, but the whites of everyone's eyes gleamed bright white. Were we turning, I wondered, into a plastic species?

Another item stood out. I could see at least six people moving their arms and fingers as though manipulating a touch screen in front of them. Not long ago, I would've assumed these folks needed my professional services. Then there were the clothes....

Deal's clicking returned me fully to the present. "On another paw, might not be a landin' beacon. You done know what they say. When you *pres*-ume you make a pres of you and me."

Laying it on a bit thick, are we? But I heard several people giggle.

"Did you notice," he clicked very quietly, "handprints on the part closest to us?"

I hadn't, and even after he told me where to look, they weren't easy to spot on the waving surface. Once I did, it amazed me that I'd missed them since they alone were continually depicted on the screen.

I kept my own voice down. "I see them. But what species has only four human-style fingers?"

"You ask this in seriousness?"

"Oh. Thumbs don't count, huh. You don't suppose ..."

On a hunch, I stepped around Deal and walked right up to the shimmering object. This close, it made my skin tingle, and a metallic taste invaded my mouth, or maybe fright explained that last part. The section with the handprints froze in place with my approach so it proved easy to place my own fingers on the handprint graphic.

I semi-expected some flashy vehicle to blaze down from the sky. Instead, the ghost silver screen stopped fluttering, and expanded into a much larger version—vertical, and playing-card flat. This encased a garage-door-sized rectangle at ground level that was either transparent or a hole in the larger structure. Through it, I only saw the parking lot beyond. Images still played on the rest of the screen.

"Does that," I asked over my shoulder, "look to anyone else like an invitation?"

Deal responded, "Human bean type door shape, old son."

I stared at the opening for a time before I turned and rejoined the crowd.

"I'll take those suitcases," I told the agent gripping Sunny's overstuffed luggage. "My wife can handle the other pair."

"We're supposed to walk through that opening?" Sunny asked, reaching for the lighter bags.

"Let's give it a try. Deal, kindly put my boy down. Time for my family to take a stroll."

"*Un*-neck-sis-sary. I done been invited to the very same shindigs."

Mr. Walt Kelly might be rotating unhappily in his grave, but it made me feel a lot better that Deal was coming along.

"But what make you figger," he asked, "that that there hole be something to shimmy through?"

I tilted my hand toward the animations. "Those videos keep showing me approaching a room in my ocean clinic. I know it's the room we'd given to Haxel because that's the only clinic door we kept open."

"Might be a hint at that."

"Or a test."

"For smarts? Seems a mite easy puzzle for checkin' a fellow's IQs."

"Maybe a test of faith."

Walking toward the opening, I must've been more scared than I realized because my body felt so stiff and awkward. I stepped through the rectangle anyway, Sunny at my side. Deal, still bearing Alex, joined us an instant later.

Big change. We now stood behind the screen.

"That," I reported, "was one spectacular anticlimax."

"Or not," Sunny argued, pointing at a new rectangle becoming visible on this side of the screen. No empty gap, this one. Something pinkish and misty filled it, providing no glimpse of what lay beyond.

I gave it a puzzled frown. "Why the two-step process?"

"The first portal," Deal said, reverting to his normal speech now that we'd moved beyond public earshot, "likely contained analytical sensors to determine our identities and confirm our various needs. The Houck would not desire uninvited beings aboard their craft."

His explanation would've been more convincing if it hadn't dawned on me that Deal, almost as much as me, was far beyond his depth and simply trying to be reassuring. I avoided meeting Sunny's eyes. Didn't want her sensing my latest doubts, but it seemed she'd grown her own....

"Maybe," she said, "they were checking us for weapons and explosives."

"At least," I said, "we didn't have to take off our shoes. Look, these bags are killing my shoulders. Let's try door number two; we're bound to give it shot sooner or later."

Deal reached out with a few limbs. "Allow me. I will not find such weight burdensome."

I handed over the luggage without argument and sure enough, Deal didn't seem to notice that Sunny had packed an anvil into each one.

The animations on this side of the screen became consistent and specific. They showed me walking through the new doorway, then Sunny with Alex and finally Deal. After that, the screen went blank for a moment and then the pattern repeated. "Whatever happened to women and children first?" I sighed. "If you hear screaming, I'd suggest, um—"

"That we refrain from following?"

"Delicately put, Deal."

"You think it's safe?" Sunny asked so calmly that if you'd heard her, you'd probably think she didn't much care.

"You bet, considering all those hoops Haxel made me jump through. Otherwise, I'd invite the VP to test it out for us. Didn't vote for that guy."

I wasn't all that sanguine. Aliens had surprised me more than once, and the Houck were *extra-galactic* aliens, which somehow made them seem extra unpredictable. But proceeding with the confident posture of someone whose spine hadn't turned to gelatin, I stepped into pink fog and kept walking.

———

The second step was what my grandfather spoke of as a "doozy." Everything turned black and I couldn't hear, see, or feel anything outside myself including a sense of weight. The moment was nearly as brief as it was frightening, and then I was back in the pink, as it were, feeling the way you do after a close call on the highway. Without waiting for my heart to resume running in the right gear, I kept moving.

The fog-blurred surface underfoot was smooth and soft, not asphalt but a great improvement over nothing. With each pace, my body felt different: sometimes hotter or colder, and my weight and even my height seemed to vary. None of this hurt, but it didn't fortify my courage. Then I nearly turned and ran when I felt these tiny ... tugs from deep inside, as though iron pins had been inserted within my bones and magnets were orbiting my spine.

I'd taken no more than twenty increasingly uneasy steps before the internal changes ended and I emerged ... into splendor. The Houck apparently appreciated a nice view. If the floor here hadn't glowed a faint neon green, it might've seemed that I'd stepped into deep space. No visible wall or ceiling, just astronomy. Enough stars and whatnot to keep a pointillist busy for eons. And despite that gentle glow, stars blazed twinkle-free beneath my shoes. The room was immense judging by the floor and entirely empty aside from me.

To my left, the Earth hung small but bright; to my right the moon loomed, huge and close enough to appear three-dimensional. Sunny and the rest of our party joined me. We all stood in place, gawking.

Deal broke the silence. "Is everyone comfortable? I find the atmosphere and gravity ideal."

I checked my favorite faces. "We're great. Seems our hosts have got that individualized environment problem licked although the gravity seems a bit strong. And speaking of our hosts, where are they?"

A reedy voice exactly like the one Haxel's translator used

came from nowhere. "Greetings, good people. And a most radiant greeting to you, Doctor. We waited for you to become oriented before approaching your group, thus following your own protocol. May we approach now?"

This *was* Haxel, because I knew which protocol she meant. At the clinic, I'd always paused at her doorway prior to our first session of the day to let her get used to my supposedly unexpected presence. That, as it turned out, had been a waste of time, and I saw no reason to waste any now. "Come right ahead," I suggested.

Not far from us, a doorway in what appeared to be starry space gaped wide, implying the existence of a wall, and an astonishing being drifted through. I heard someone gasp and it might've been me.

"It brings me joy to perceive you again, Doctor. All of you are shiningly welcome."

"Haxel?"

"I am she."

Despite the familiar voice, I'd had to ask. This creature resembled my supposed patient less than a raisin resembles a fresh grape. Her diaphanous membranes had spread wide and straightened into multiple gossamer wings blazing with stained-glass colors. These living rainbows framed a tall, bright tubular form with the wavering quality of a candle flame.

"Al," Sunny murmured, "you've been holding out on me."

"Never seen her like this," I murmured back. "Haxel, this is my wife Sunny, my son Alex, and as you probably know, my friend and business associate, Deal-of-ten-lifetimes."

"I am delighted to receive you all. I've already met the fifth member of your party."

I looked around. "Fifth member?"

Haxel didn't appear to do anything, but the stars above our heads winked out and a high, arched ceiling came into view. I looked upward. Our bodies, blocking the illuminated floor, cast faint shadows overhead. Only mine wasn't so faint. My mind boggled.

"*Gara?*" I demanded. "Are you sitting on my shoulders?"

"Sitting, I am not. Likewise, my weight is distributed considerately on your body rather than upon your shoulders entirely."

I could visualize how she'd hitchhiked here: She'd been waiting on the parking lot, flattened and pretending to be another asphalt bump. As I'd passed, she'd flowed along with me, clinging to my ankles to imitate my shadow until I'd reached this glowing floor, which would've revealed her presence. So she'd climbed my back to perch on me, blending in with the sky scene above, hoping I wouldn't look straight up and notice something blocking the stars....

"Kindly get off," I growled, "and tell us why you're here."

Instantly, I felt lighter and Gara, condensed into her usual form, hovered near me. "I was invited."

I knew why she'd kept it secret. I might tell Deal and protecting me from him had likely been a major reason for coming along, an easier job if he didn't suspect her presence. She must be irked with Haxel for outing her.

I turned toward the Houck, but she spoke first. "Doctor, we desired you to be as clear-minded and comfortable as possible here, thus we have provided you your full emotional foundation, excepting your office manager who was needed to maintain clinic affairs in your absence."

"Foundation? You mean my support group." Strange to think of Alex in this context, but Haxel had a point. Just looking at him strengthened me. "I, um, appreciate your consideration. When does the bus leave for the next galaxy?"

"In two of your days. First, we must collect the remaining judges within this galaxy. They, and their respective supports, will be assigned to other sections of this vessel and will not be joining your group nor forming collective opinions with any other group. Meanwhile, I will be your guide. May I show you to your quarters now? Trader, feel free to set down those cases you bear. Do so and they will arrive at your destination before we do."

Deal complied and all of us non-Houck stared as the suitcases zipped along the floor as if riding a conveyor belt.

———

Haxel may have meant "quarters" literally since we were assigned three separate and species-appropriate habitats plus a common room to share, complete with three distinct styles of seating. Deal went off to explore his domain with Haxel, but Gara stuck with my family as we entered the human suite.

"How's your energy holding up?" I asked her, concerned about the lack of sunlight.

"You don't feel the radiation? Astounding! I bathe in power that touches you not." Despite her words, she didn't sound happy. "And our hosts provide me a sonic detailed of this vessel's environment stellar. I am appreciative most."

"Yeah. I think even Deal's impressed by this ship."

Human central comprised two large bedrooms, a larger living room, and a bathroom. Each bedroom had a four-poster bed with a multicolored canopy and the usual fixings, also a tall walnut-looking chest of drawers. One bedroom held all four of our suitcases—two and a half of them crammed with Sunny's "necessities." The décor suggested Arabian Nights meets Mid-Century Modern except for the bathroom, a long and galley-like affair illuminated from above by countless tiny lights in dense clusters. At first glance, I thought straw covered the floor, but it proved to be a soft mat, and the space held the usual human-style amenities all in two different sizes. The Houck, clearly, had included Alex in their planning. I don't know if the fixtures were solid gold, but they sure looked golden.

"We Three Kings of Orient Express," I commented.

Sunny laughed. "I see what you mean. We'll be roughing it in luxury. Space glamping!"

"Why," Gara asked as we paraded from the bathroom to the living room, "do you suppose Haxel accompanied the Trader?" She draped herself over a recliner not intended for Vithy. Her voice sounded uncharacteristically dry, and she articulated every word so precisely they seemed to be chiseled.

"I wish you wouldn't worry so much," I said.

"I wish you would more worry. We know not what pact our supervisor may be suggesting, but should a Trader an opportunity for profit detect, they will disregard the cost to other species and upon it pounce."

I chewed on that for a moment. "Are all Vithy so distrustful of the Tsf?"

"Only the few sensible."

If she'd been this suspicious of everyone, I could've discounted her fears. But she had a point. Deal could justifiably present himself as an ombudsman for our entire galaxy and negotiate God knows what kind of arrangement. I had no way to assess the stakes here or how high they were stacked. And I wondered if Gara's crystalline diction constituted a private message for me.

"Tell me, oh wondrous PT, what do you suggest I do?" I'd meant to sound humorous, but it came off a bit desperate.

"I suggest you maintain alertness full."

Sunny shot me a concerned look, and I batted back a try at a reassuring smile. Then I tried to reassure myself with some old-fashioned self-flattery. Wasn't I a good judge of character? Surely a better judge of character, even ET character, than a paranoid Vithy? I had no objective reason to trust Deal, but then again, why buy into Gara's fears? Yet I trusted them both, admittedly with Gara getting the lion's share of—

Aliens and trust! I'd been even denser than usual. Gara hadn't laid out her latest concerns for my ears, or not entirely. No, she guessed or perhaps knew from some squeak inaudible to me, that our hosts were listening to us, and she hoped to make the Houck cautious about bargaining with Deal. She'd tried to clue me in by using that voice.

And speaking of speaking, Alex hadn't said a word since the parking lot. Talk about uncharacteristic. His expression appeared unusually intent, and for once, he wasn't fidgeting, bouncing, or drumming on his legs.

Sunny must've noticed the same thing. "You're so quiet, child. How are you feeling?"

"I'm good, mom." His voice turned conspiratorial, which for him meant a shouted whisper. "Just busy recording everything with my DM. Gonna play it at school so I don't want to *be* the news."

"The reporter's motto," I said. "That's my boy."

Gara shifted off the recliner. "I'd suggest we repair to the room common where we can all comfortable be."

This time it was easy to read between her lines: despite her super senses she couldn't hear Deal and Haxel and hoped the common area would facilitate eavesdropping. But the moment we settled there, both Trader and Houck joined us.

"I must attend to other duties shortly," Haxel stated. "Should you want for anything, call aloud for me and I shall be here within moments. Appropriate food or Vithy-nurturing wavelengths will be served whenever you request, and menus are already traveling to your quarters."

I spoke quickly. "Do you have time to answer a question or two before you leave?"

"That depends on the questions. What would you care to ask?"

"Can you tell me more about my role here?"

"Not yet. We wish to provide no chance for preconceptions. Any other questions?"

"Yes. How do you manage to hop between galaxies?"

"I, too," Deal said, "would be interested in the answer. The energy expenditure seems impractical."

Haxel hesitated before responding. "Our technique is surely identical to your method for interstellar travel, good Trader. Doctor, I will be delighted to answer you soon, but an intelligible response will involve correcting a misconception in your present science, and my duties are pressing."

"Whenever you can."

"Before I leave, Doctor, would you mind if I make my own inquiry?"

"Not at all." Sometimes you can learn more from what people ask than what they answer.

"Speaking as objectively as possible, how would you describe the human race in terms of ethics, compassion, sensitivity, and overall goals?"

In ten words or less? Haxel's luminous wings, up until now gently sculling the air, became still, giving me the uneasy sense that this question was extremely important.

My thoughts first turned to the negatives, the violence, selfishness, greed, cruelty, and insensitivity humanity exhibited every day and night. People were starving, children abused in appalling ways, animals too, racism used as a political tool, our environment poisoned, while so many rulers and politicians with power to change our lives for the better focused on increasing or preserving that power at all costs. Hate, war, murder, degradation, shortsightedness, slavery of many kinds, the unending quest for profit ... an ugly picture.

We were self-infested with predators, scammers, and manipulators squatting in every conceivable socio-ecological-economic niche, ready to exploit every loophole in the human soul....

Then again, we had our own angelic side: immense creativity, a deep appreciation of beauty and ability to produce it, honor, self-sacrifice, dedication to healing the world's ills, dedication to serving humanity, heroism, humility, and a boundless reservoir of love. The human bell curve stretched beyond sight in both directions.

"Speaking as objectively as I can," I said slowly, "I think our species is very young and … unevenly evolved at present. Consider us a work in progress. If things go as I hope, a great work in progress."

Haxel's wings swept backward, and the shining form between them seemed to bow. "Thank you for your response and candor. I will return to you soon whether you call me or not."

———

When she left, I covertly studied Alex. Clearly his Intrepid Boy Reporter role was fraying. *Soon*, I thought, *he'll be bouncing off the walls.* Didn't know how right I was.

I turned to Sunny. "Time to unpack?"

"I'd suggest you delay that activity," said an unfamiliar Houck just then entering the common room. "Haxel is busy, so I have come to show you what humans inexplicably refer to as 'the ropes.' Armed with such priceless information, the 'unpack' can proceed more intelligently. I'll answer to the feminine name Laike if anyone dares address me."

Obviously, Laike's personality was nothing like Haxel's, and her speech patterns equally different, staccato but wordy bursts that left me unsure, at first, that my ears weren't playing tricks. No, my expectations were playing tricks. Hard to believe after dealing with Haxel that any Houck could be such a smartass, to use a word from back in the day when people said "back in the day."

Despite her style, she offered useful info. Virtually everything in our suite of suites had been made voice controllable, from color and texture to furniture and décor. All surfaces could display whatever we wished. Safety, however, was rigidly enforced and our hosts would not allow us to be harmed. To demonstrate, Laike took to the air by leaping and flapping her multiple wings. She approached a wall at an alarming speed, but the collision I braced myself to witness didn't happen. Still flapping away, she simply came to a stop.

This must've given Alex ideas, because he immediately scampered off to his new bedroom and transformed the walls and floor into trampolines. We knew this because the moment he left, Sunny ordered the nearest wall to show a view of Alex's room, just in case. So we had the pleasure of watching him bounce high from his floor and make a real stab at landing on his head. My wife and I jumped up to stop this kind of experiment, but by the time we skidded into his room, he was lying on his bed, threatening his health by laughing so hard I'd feared he'd break a rib.

"Maybe," I said loudly enough to be heard over his guffaws, "you shouldn't actually try to break your neck."

"It's okay, dad." Giggle, giggle. "Watch me!"

He leaped at a wall before we could stop him and again flipped upside down. Sunny and I both started running at once, awkwardly thanks to the modified flooring. We didn't collide only because some soft force came between us. Alex, meanwhile, only fell *most* of the way to the floor. Instead, he stopped in midair and his body rotated to the horizontal before wafting down. More belly laughs.

It was true. Alex couldn't hurt himself here to save his life. The wife and I returned to the common room feeling a tad foolish and a lot relieved.

"I admire your parental protectiveness," Laike announced. "You should rush from here like that at any possible provocation. Please continue to disregard my assurances of your safety. But I am not merely an information purveyor of questionable veracity, as you have assumed. I am *also* your menus and indeed your server; you will find my wings utile as trays. As to you, honored Vithy, your nutritional needs do not vary. So we will only focus on human and Tsf desires."

Gara extended a tendril near one of my ears to whisper, "This one wields rather than speaks English. I knew not that anyone could be at once stochastic, sarcastic, and long-winded."

"She's a charmer," I allowed, subvocalizing.

After Laike departed, Sunny and I set up our bedroom to our liking by recreating our home bedroom except that the ceiling showed stars and one wall spied on Alex. We deposited clothes and sundries in a dresser then lay down on the bed in hopes, at least in my case, that our brains would stop wobbling.

If you're wondering how the Houck obtained human food, our first onboard meal included some packaged items labeled in the hairy curlicues of standard Trader script. One minor puzzle solved.

———

The next two days flew by uneventfully but were anything but boring. Good thing in a way because as tourist fodder, our two stops within the galaxy were duds, the actual journeys amounting to nonevents. One instant we'd see a set of stars, the next—voilà!—another set of stars. We wouldn't have gotten a glimpse of those worlds where the extra judges were catching their rides if I hadn't asked Laike, on one of her visits, for a quick peek. Unfortunately, she took me literally. An intriguing image of a sulfur-yellow world dappled with brown appeared on the wall I'd dubbed the "star-screen" and we had all of three seconds to enjoy it before it vanished. Laike might've replayed it upon request, but when I asked to see pictures of my fellow judges, all her wings turned dark gray, and I didn't risk asking her for another favor. She explained, coldly, that seeing the physical appearance of other judges might lead me to develop opinions about them, and therefore compromise my decision-making process.

As a group, we were busy. Sunny worked on a law textbook she was editing; Gara repeatedly sneaked, as only she could, into Deal's room when he was elsewhere and tried her sound-retrieval techniques on various materials but came up empty; Deal divided his time between conferring privately with Haxel, and staring at Sunny whenever she took a work break and relaxed herself by knitting, a craft he found alien and fascinating; Alex turned his room into progressively more complex large-scale hamster habitats. I spent most of my hours trying to digest a heavy three-course meal of information.

The first course came from Haxel, who followed up on her promise to explain the Houck method of intergalactic travel. Deal listened in, and I could almost hear him grinding his abdominal teeth as Haxel gave away secrets that could've earned Traders a hefty profit.

"Every known species," she began, "develops errors in their understanding of physical reality that reflect the nature of their bodies, their sensory limitations, and whatever esthetic they've developed through evolutionary and social processes."

I had to ask, "What errors have humans developed?"

"Those based on your strong urge for synthesis."

"You've already lost me."

"Perhaps an example will provide clarity. For many of your decades, your scientists have sought a single formula integrating all forms of energy humans perceive directly or via instruments. We know this because Tsf have illuminated your history for us."

Not out of the goodness of their circulatory pumps, I'd bet. "Right. The Universal Theory of Whatever."

"It is possible, with sufficient cleverness and persistence, that such a theory could be constructed to withstand every test known to your species, but it would be false. Your scientific forebears learned that all frequencies from radio waves to gamma radiation inhabit specific wavelengths on the electro-magnetic spectrum. This established, they developed theories incorporating atomic and electromagnetic forces into a grander unity. Then they sought an equation that would combine this unity with gravity and time."

Didn't remember time being included in the search for the TOE, but what did I know. Deal, I noticed, had nearly all his sensory cilia aimed at Haxel.

"You're saying there's no such equation?"

"The human desire to simplify, to harmonize, to make comprehensible to the human mind is natural considering your evolution and limitations. Only recently have your scientists deduced that forces and matter invisible to your senses and instruments not only exist but comprise most of the physical universe. The electromagnetic spectrum is one of three spectra we Houck recognize, although 'spectra' may be a misleading term. Gravity, inertia, time, energy, radiation, matter, and consciousness are real effects, but any effort to squeeze these into a unitary model of existence can only lead to delusion."

"That's ... interesting." I tried to visualize what kind of "spectrum" gravity could be part of and didn't get anywhere. "How does this relate to your space travel?"

"One property of reality belonging to a spectrum unfamiliar to you is location."

That made me blink. "Location?"

"We need merely separate from time and space momentarily and it becomes simple to change location parameters. You Tsf use the identical principle, do you not good Trader?"

"Yes," Deal clicked, "but we haven't learned to apply it without invoking an energy-to-distance ratio that precludes our reaching beyond this galaxy. From what source do you summon so much power?"

Now I understood his burning interest in the topic.

"This ratio you describe," Haxel said, "is illusory, an artifact of inadequate separation from time and space."

I jumped in. "How do you separate anything from everything?"

"You may be aware there are—allow me to apply the word 'emissaries' because any notion of particles at the subatomic level is fallacious—there are emissaries of various natures that do not interact with matter."

I reviewed my scant knowledge of subatomic particles. "Like neutrinos?"

"What you call 'neutrinos' include several categories of emissary. Some are unaffected by any force humans have named including gravity. These can, however, interact with forces you haven't yet discovered. By regulating those forces, we can wrap our vessel in enough layers of these emissaries to create the desired isolation."

I rubbed my chin, which clarified nothing. "Let's see if I've got the basic idea. You blanket your ship in dark matter and then you're free to pop up anywhere?"

"In essence."

Deal had been twitching during that last exchange and he rushed back into the conversation like a berserker. "Traders would be *most* interested in grasping your exact technique. We have never managed full separation."

"Thus far, we are the only known species with such knowledge."

If Deal had come equipped with hands, I'm sure he would've been rubbing them together. "Might the Houck desire anything we can offer in exchange for this information?"

Haxel took her time before responding. "My answer, honored Tsf, must wait until after the upcoming judgment. A great many things depend on that outcome."

I found those last words ominous, but the Houck flew off before either Deal or I could pose another question.

———

The second hard-to-digest informational meal resulted from an itch of curiosity. Irrelevant or not, I kept wondering if Peeps was right about Jewish lore. So before we left Earth, I'd added a virtual pile of virtual tomes to my DM library. After our first onboard meal and after we put Alex to bed, I buckled down to some heavy reading.

Somehow, I'd gotten the impression Kabbalah was an arcane and disreputable form of Jewish mysticism concerning cosmic forces and how to control them. In my mind, I'd clumped it in with pentacles, Tarot, Golden Dawn, Thelema, and your typical 19th Century poseur magician.

The first book I dived into, chosen due to its promising title, contained nothing of the sort. Its author, a Hassidic rabbi, convinced me that Peeps had mined a genuine vein. Strange stuff, foreign to my Christian upbringing, but I saw the practical value.

Peeps had claimed Kabbalah was about balancing "spiritual flows," which the rabbi confirmed, but the specifics surprised me. Symbolically speaking, the Sephirot were organized in descending triads, each triad like a downward-pointing triangle with a properly balanced pair at each level finding full expression in their third triad member beneath. The rabbi described three "mental" flows and seven "emotional" flows, none of which I'd ever thought of as primary mental or emotional attributes.

At the emotional level for example, Hessed, the Sephira of selflessness and generosity, could operate in a negative way if not tempered by its counterpoint, Gevurah, the Sephira of self-containment, focus, and discipline. On its own, Hessed could be a spendthrift, wasting a person's energies or acting to enable other people's self-destructive behavior. Gevurah acting alone could lead to self-involvement or stinginess. Properly balanced, according to the rabbi, the two forces activated the triangle's third Sephira, Tif'eret, leading to emotional stability.

More surprising, the book contained an idea of God that struck me as improbably sophisticated. No white-bearded patriarch on a golden throne this one, but an indivisible and eternal no-thing, a hidden sacred emptiness constantly spinning the illusion of something from the illusion of nothing. This concept, I thought, was first cousin to that of the "Self" found in non-dualistic Yogic philosophy. Funny thing, I'd never thought of Judaism as an Eastern religion, but then, the rabbi claimed that Abraham's rejected sons had carried mystical secrets, with Abe's permission, to India....

—————

Now we come to the third dish on my mental plate. Gara cooked it up after one of her covert missions to Deal's digs.

Her failure to learn anything incriminating had reminded her of a question she'd been meaning to ask me. During her Bach sonic-retrieval work, she'd restored a religious argument between two men conducted in what scholars assured us was 18th century German, confirming she'd isolated the correct acoustic layer in an 18th century vase.

Gara asked me why humans would bother arguing about faith-based matters. I gave her a mini-lecture on human nature involving two concepts, both exotic to her: door-to-door religious proselytization, and the idea of a "devil's advocate." Such door-to-door work, I expounded, is primarily aimed at strengthening faith for the religious salespeople themselves, while the devil's advocate could do much the same for, well, the angel's advocate. Arguing reinforces belief.

Basic stuff, but Gara heard a possibility based on this new information that startled me. She speculated that Traders had hired her, rather than another Vithy PT, for my clinic *because* of her negative attitude toward the Tsf.

"Considering your nature human," she said, "I can hear how my doubts intense concerning Traders might cause you to defend them."

Another rug snatched from beneath my bunions. The Tsf

had already demonstrated a solid grasp of human psychology, but I found the idea that they'd been maneuvering me to this extent alarming and plausible. One thing worse than being tugged around by a ring through one's nose: being unaware that any ring is installed.

———

It might've been easier to chew my mental cud if our living situation had been more relaxed. The tension between Deal and Gara became so palpable that even Alex noticed it, asking me what I'd do if a fight broke out. I told him that would never happen and besides, the Houck had made sure no one in our rooms could get hurt. I almost convinced myself.

One incident even seemed to teeter on the edge of violence. Deal got a bright idea and asked the star-screen to show us our destination. The wall instantly turned black, and Deal complained that the Houck were "always one leap" ahead of him. Perhaps he hadn't considered the possibility we were being monitored or he'd stopped caring.

Gara asked what he perceived and when Deal told her, she suggested that his senses were "acute insufficiently." She claimed the wall couldn't be blank because it emitted a symphony of quiet but complex hums. Deal, perhaps frustrated by his latest business failures, told her rather sharply that his senses gauged reality better than hers, and the hum she'd noticed was likely an artifact of the display technology. She countered, not gently, that the hum only began after he'd made his "request destination." And so on.

On top of everything, as the hours passed, I kept getting more nervous about my responsibility here. What business did I have judging another species? Particularly one far older and, surely far more … cosmopolitan than mine. The act of judging tends to make humans feel superior to whatever is being judged. At least that was one danger I didn't face.

It was almost a relief when Haxel showed up mid-morning by my DM clock and announced that the big moment had arrived. Our hosts had so carefully isolated me from what they considered undue influences that I assumed my "foundation" would be missing this part. Instead, Haxel practically dragged my family, Gara, and Deal along, which implied some interesting things concerning the Houck sense of identity.

It seemed Haxel led us back to the room where we'd first arrived, but either I lost my bearings or the room had blown its diet. It was huge before, now it was titanic. All its walls were visible, those on one side bulging outwards like barrel staves. We had company. Hundreds of Houck floated like vivid ghosts, some tiny compared to Haxel and others larger, no two sharing the same color scheme. They cast so much light as a group that even if the walls had remained transparent, I might've had trouble seeing any stars.

"Smells like oranges in here," Alex whispered.

"These Houck have assembled," Haxel stated with a sonorous cadence I'd never heard her use, "as witnesses. Feel free to speak in your native language, everyone will understand you."

I had to swallow hard. "I'm honored to meet you all. But you should know that you've made a poor choice picking me for a juror. I doubt any human would be a good choice. We're probably primitive in many ways compared with most space-faring races; obviously, our technology is immature. So far, we haven't even found a way to travel beyond our own solar system, so when it comes to wisdom—"

"You underestimate humans," Haxel interrupted. "Technology is no measure of wisdom, and even technologically your species has much to offer."

"Really? Such as?"

"Adhesives for one. You are the first beings we have encountered to bind objects in this manner. Aren't you aware that Traders reap vast profits by exporting terrestrial adhesives?"

I gave Deal a sharp glance. He kept his sensory threads aimed elsewhere. "I am now."

"Be reassured," Haxel said. "We did not select you for your superiority or equality to us, nor do we weigh such subjective merits. You are needed to increase the variety of perspectives we require for this crucial occasion. What we desire you to judge is our solution to ... a problem we've been forced to acknowledge. We must be certain of our logic and that we are guilty of no oversight."

Must be some problem. "I'll do my best, but you can't take my opinion too seriously."

"It shall be balanced with many others. Are you ready to begin?"

I swallowed again. "Yes."

Every Houck extinguished most of its light and wrapped its wings around its body, leaving only a dim glow. Then the curved wall seemed to vanish, but no stars appeared. The blackness appeared identical to what Deal had summoned when he'd ordered our space-screen to show our destination.

Haxel moved away from me, as did her fellow Houck, leaving my group in a pool of darkness surrounded by a dim ring of light. Her voice came from a distance. "We will now turn our vessel. Please observe the emptiness before you."

I felt no motion, but a blazing crescent gradually swung into view, an elaborate object constructed entirely of countless lights in a billion colors, beyond doubt the most spectacular thing I'd ever seen. More and more of it appeared until the entire thing was revealed, outlined in purest black. The vast blaze froze in place, so I figured the ship had stopped spinning. Sunny's hand stole into mine; Alex, slightly in front of me, backed up until he pressed against my legs. Everyone remained silent. I couldn't imagine any words to match the glory.

Finally Deal clicked. "Such a pity you cannot see this, Gara."

I felt so shocked by the poverty of his response and that he'd soil such a moment with a cheap dig at Gara that I turned to stare at him. The way his limbs quivered and all his sensory cilia pointed straight ahead told me that I'd misjudged. He'd been sincere.

"Our hosts," Gara said, "have provided me a most detailed image sonic. I wish you could hear what I hear." She, too, spoke sincerely.

If this was the Houck's galaxy, it had to be the mother of all galaxies. Its profuse stars appeared strangely shaped, most were oversized and oblong, wrapped in filmy, sparkling veils in innumerable subtle tints. The galaxy seemed tilted away from us at an angle, but I could tell this jeweled empyrean was basically oval, somewhat flattened, and much longer than wide, its ends blunted. A consistently bluish streak ran along much of the internal center, but beyond that the spectrum played wild and random games. Gossamer branches of color streamed from the sides, top, and bottom. Past the main edges, diamond-like stretched-out stars, presumably closer to us than the rest, seemed to either have countless facets or a fuzzy quality that my eyes couldn't resolve.

"Wow!" Alex shouted in a whisper, and I had to agree.

Haxel drifted back to me, her wings opening. I realized the Houck had extinguished their personal glow so that we could better appreciate what was coming—courtesy on a scale appropriate to the view.

"You must have questions," she said.

I forced myself to speak. "I assume this is your galaxy?"

"No. You behold a galaxy of galaxies, one of which is yours."

My breath caught and Sunny's hand tightened. I found myself whispering. "You mean...we're looking at the *universe*?"

Haxel sang a chord of four or five notes at once before

answering. "If by universe you mean all that is, where could we be positioned at this moment? No non-Houck language of which we are aware has a term for the phenomenon we witness. Would you care to invent one or invest a human word with this specific meaning?"

"Spindle," my wife shot back as though she'd been waiting her whole life for this question. "Not only the shape, it's got threads coming off."

"An apt choice," Haxel said, and I nodded in agreement, gazing at the cosmic Spindle with new eyes. "We will now expand the image."

At this new magnification, I couldn't begin to fathom the complexities. Those eerie suns that had puzzled me weren't stars, they were entire galaxies: incredibly intricate maelstroms of effulgence, some more bizarrely configured than seemed probable. What I'd thought might be faceted stars were star clusters. The magnitude of all this made it hard to believe that my vision could encompass such a thing. Its beauty seemed to expand the more I gazed as if it was feeding my soul, growing my capacity to appreciate beauty.

Haxel wasn't done. "Are you ready, Doctor, to see more of them?"

"More *Spindles*?"

"Do you perceive, as I do, any distant lights?"

"No."

"I hear them," Gara volunteered. "They are faint."

"I expect so, good Vithy. Observe, Doctor. We will now apply extreme enlargement and image adjustment."

Suddenly, the glory expanded a thousandfold. The supracelestial object, what I'd thought of two minutes ago as the universe, shrank to provide room for hundreds more. Their luminous complexities related to the first one we'd seen, but a few were twisted into helical structures or bent into rings. The prior scene had been too tremendous for me to fully appreciate. Now I needed a major upgrade in my conception of "big."

It was impossible to take in more than a fragment of the visual symphony displayed before me, yet even that fragment filled me with ... I don't have words. Everything blurred for a moment, maybe from tears. Here was a glimpse of divinity beyond anything I could imagine.

Many, perhaps most humans have shared an experience: gazing up at a starry sky, feeling smaller than small, a grain of sand on an infinite beach. So you'd think my current view would've shrunk my self-perception to subatomic size in that same infinitesimal grain.

Instead, my emotions ran backward. *This*, I thought with a sudden joy surprisingly close to patriotic pride, *is the magnificence I am part of.*

A white circle appeared around a Spindle above and to the right of the original one. "We Houck evolved in a galaxy within this formation." *From another galaxy, all right, in another universe.* "Doctor, you may feel overwhelmed by this revelation. So I must ask, are you ready to learn of our dilemma?"

"Go...ahead." Truly, I needed something to bring me, well, down to earth.

"Do these Spindles remind you of anything on your world? Something small."

"You mean, um, like a chandelier?"

"Far smaller and organic."

What was Haxel getting at? All the hours I'd spent gawking out my office window brought a few bioluminescent creatures to mind, but no group of diatoms or jellyfish came close to resembling these cosmic fireworks. Talk about being lost at sea.

"Any more hints?"

"I had a reason for declaring your wife's use of the word 'Spindle' apt. Consider your specific field of expertise."

I frowned, baffled. While I'd had some long and skinny patients, none of them...

"Aren't there brain cells with that name?" Sunny suggested.

I nodded. "True, and other kinds of spindle cells. But spindle neurons are infinitely simpler than what we're looking at, they're—" I raised a finger and tried to draw a shape in the air—"like super skinny trees and they don't light up like the ultimate Christmas tree."

"Ours do," Haxel stated.

I looked at her, wishing she had a face that I could at least try to read. "Houck brains have axons and dendrites, and they *light up?*"

"We possess equivalents. Such forms evolve from purpose and most intelligent species possess similar mechanisms. Do you understand the function of your spindle neurons?"

"I should." One undergraduate biology professor I'd had referred to them as "cell-phone cells," a joke that would be met by blank stares from today's DM-spoiled students. "They're needed for long-distance neuron-to-neuron communication, that's why they only appear in Earth's bigger-brained—*wait!*"

"You all right, Al?" Sunny noticed my little wobble.

I'd made a conceptual leap so big it seemed to carry me from one universe to another. "Little dizzy. It'll pass."

I focused on Haxel. "Do you Houck believe," I asked carefully, "that Spindles are cosmic brain cells communicating with each other?"

"No. We are convinced they are *meant* to communicate but currently isolated. We believe that the purpose of life, our purpose, is to assist the Spindles to reach out to each other, thus producing a unified universal consciousness."

I'd been out-leaped! "That's, um, quite an idea. How would you expect the Spindles to reach out? Not using matter, I assume. And what makes you think they aren't...already communing?"

"We anticipate a sharing of forces, but our exhaustive tests have found no significant degree of energy exchange. Nor any force traversing the void beyond standard radiations."

She waited patiently as I tried to think. "What about some energy form you don't know about? Or maybe messages ... teleport between Spindles the way your ships do."

Haxel's wings briefly flared to a startling incandescence. "You justify our choosing you! But these ideas are long familiar to us. We cannot rule out unknown forces, but doubt they exist considering how deeply we have studied the folds and flows of nature. As to your second suggestion, we have identified fundamental characteristics unique to each Spindle, imprinted on all its energy and matter. Any exchange would have carried traces of foreign characteristics. We have discovered none."

"Okay. That thing you said about looking for forces 'traversing the void.' You meant energy discharged from Spindles?"

"I did."

"What sort of discharge could carry enough information?" *Peeps would've said a spiritual one.*

"Common waveforms such as light travel far too slowly to network a practical universal mind. Our search therefore has focused on higher-order behaviors primed for extra-dimensional transitions."

Those words slowly traversed the void between my ears, and somehow evoked for me the image of a stone skipping on a pond, bouncing through another dimension and coming out ahead of where it should've been. I shook my head and could've sworn my brain rattled. "I'd love to learn more about this, and I thank you with all my heart for bringing us here, but maybe I'm forgetting the main point. You mentioned a problem you had and a solution. What, *exactly*, do you want me to judge?"

Haxel opened her wings wide and the ring of silent Houck surrounding us glided closer. "Us. Specifically a logical conclusion we have reached. We are the oldest species we know of, and the most prolific in population and technology, but we recognize that perhaps our greatest asset, our ability to reach total consensus, limits our objectivity. We have, over the last terrestrial millennia, come to a painful decision we must make but dared not proceed without outside validation."

"You wanted a second opinion."

"We wanted *every* worthwhile outside opinion possible for us to gather in a reasonable time."

My throat felt dry enough to crack. I forced myself to ask, "What's this decision?"

"A most significant...anniversary approaches." Haxel appeared to be sidestepping the question, which now struck me as a fine idea. "It has been almost exactly one grand unit, about seventeen million years in your terms, since we began our quest to link the Spindles. In that time, we have explored so many galaxies, stimulating the development of life and encouraging the growth of intelligence, that we have lost count. Our entire race has participated in this project. Do you see our problem now?"

I hoped not. "You think you've failed?"

"We would prefer failure to what we have come to believe. With failure, future success might be possible."

"Please, just tell me."

"We Houck are simply incapable of producing the great awakening. Our true calling, which we have long misunder-stood, was to seed the galaxies with sentient life and then step aside to allow others to complete the final task."

I stared at her, fear condensing into a heavy ball in my stomach. "What do you mean 'step aside'?"

"An evolutionary principle is at work. Just as emptiness provides the crucial space for all existence—"

I got it but hated it. "You think the right species can't appear until yours is gone."

"Through long observation, we have deduced that reality contains, on a pan-cosmic scale, an equivalent to ecological niches. What species can evolve to fill an ecological niche when it is already fully occupied by another?"

This sounded well north of crazy to me, but it wasn't what I believed that counted. "Are you telling me you Houck plan to commit suicide, hoping a more capable species will take over?" *Please, God, let me be wrong!*

"We do not intend instant suicide but will cease reproducing. Our life spans are longer than yours, although brief compared to some. In four of your centuries, we will be gone, and the ecological vacuum will soon be filled."

I felt too cold to sweat, but that didn't stop me. "Can't you simply give up trying to link the Spindles? Why let yourselves die out?"

"Future generations could forget our insight, see the need, and resume the futile work. And our sheer numbers preclude new candidate species evolving on the billion worlds we currently inhabit. There are trillions of us, Doctor."

Calm down, Al; trillions of lives aren't resting on your shoulders. If only I could've believed it. "So *that's* the decision you expect me to judge?"

"What we ask of all jurors is to seek a compelling reason to abandon that decision. If no such reason manifests, we will consider our reasoning validated."

"Wait. You said you'd return us to Earth in a week." If my voice hadn't gone so hoarse, I would've been yelling. "You've been trying to connect universes for millions of years and expect your jury to come up with anything useful in a *week*?"

"We have vowed to restore all jurors to their home worlds before the deadline we have set. Our transportation resources are great, but some returns will involve complexities. Therefore we must dissolve the jury sooner than one of your weeks to keep our promise. If no flaw in our logic is found, we shall sterilize ourselves at the completion of the grand unit. You have two days to ponder."

"That's not …" There were so many things it wasn't, such as sane or fair, that I didn't know where to start.

Haxel continued. "We recognize the brevity of the time allotted and have compensated by assembling many jurors. Behold our fleet."

Alien starships appeared on our window to reality, hundreds of them, some barely dots and several so large, presumably close, that I could distinguish their shapes. They resembled bettas, Siamese fighting fish, so exactly that I wouldn't have put them in the same tank.

"We're inside a ship like those?" I asked.

"Yes. Each vessel contains multiple judges, each from a different world. After the experiment is concluded I shall tell you the exact number if you wish, but we believe it crucial that you feel neither overly responsible nor free of responsibility. Likewise we dare answer no further questions you may have concerning our dilemma. We will now adjourn and allow you to begin your contemplations."

I couldn't think of a thing to say.

As we followed Haxel back to our suites, I felt numb from my skin inwards. No matter how many "jurors" shared my burden, part of the responsibility belonged to me, and I had a truly disturbing idea about what was really happening here.

I figured the Houck had through their faith in this cosmic mind concept…faithed themselves into a tight corner, felt obligated to seek a way out, but didn't believe one existed. I suspected they'd gathered this jury for symbolic reasons rather than practical ones. Good luck getting a solution from me considering my limited mind and magnificent ignorance.

"Your hand is like ice," Sunny murmured. I hadn't even realized we were holding hands.

I couldn't risk glancing at her for fear that the ice around my heart, the only thing holding me together right now, might crack. But I knew she was looking at me with pity. Probably everyone was doing the same except for my boy and Gara, who'd be listening to me with pity.

"You won't fail," Sunny said. "You never do."

Even her faith in me didn't help, not much anyway. Besides, failure has gradations; there've been plenty of times when I haven't succeeded. But I'd never been responsible for untold trillions of future lives.

———

Back in our quarters, I asked Haxel if her people had considered reducing their population, maybe pulling back to a few thousand planets. Since she'd declared that question time was over, I figured she wouldn't answer but she did.

"Knowing our nature, we rejected that possibility. Our descendants would be sure to repopulate our galaxy and resume the work. All this would happen again. Also, whatever refuge worlds we chose might include the very one that otherwise would evolve the needed species."

So it was all or nothing, and I felt sick.

My mind churned all that day and night, but the only result was mental froth. I couldn't eat and sure as hell couldn't sleep. I kept asking the group for ideas and everyone tried to help, tried hard, but the only result was zero of the wordy kind. The team effort had one positive result: Gara's hostility toward Deal seemed to ease. Both were my friends, united in concern for Dr. Mess.

The second day, Gara posed a useful question. "I hear that you are desperate to preserve the Houck and agree that their absence would leave all existence poorer. Yet how can you be certain they are mistaken?"

That forced me to reassess. "I'm not. But I'm also not buying a single share of their beliefs. Honestly, this business of hooking up universes strikes me as—as a case of wishful thinking on crack. Seems to me their spiritual convictions are battling their species survival instinct and winning, but barely."

"That is an opinion confusing. Please explain."

"Look—I mean listen—obviously they're hoping us aliens will find some reason for them not to give up, and they've spent incredible energy collecting us all. That's survival instinct doing its thing. But now that they've finally laid out the problem, they won't allow us enough time to have a *chance* of finding an answer, assuming there is one."

"Haxel claimed a multitude of intellects are at work."

"So a multitude of minds won't have enough time."

"Perhaps some operate with speed great."

"I sure hope so."

I can't remember a more miserable day. Even Alex caught my mood and replaced playing with moping. All too often, I'd catch myself feeling resentful of everyone and everything, loved ones included, and it became a struggle not to snap at the innocent. By artificial evening, I'd honed self-pity to a sharp point and got ready for a second sleepless night. Sunny offered to rub my back, not a task she enjoys because it hurts her hands, and I said no thanks. She, at least, could get some rest.

Sunny had other ideas. "Al, I've been thinking about what you told me when you got back from your first visit with the Traders."

"What about it?" My snarling tone made me wince. Dr. Gracious at your service.

She ignored my rudeness. "You said that you couldn't get anywhere in treating those alien patients until you stopped telling yourself the job was impossible."

"It seemed impossible. Hell, it would've been impossible if the Traders hadn't misdiagnosed them. I see where you're going, but this situation is different. Coming up with a solution here really *is* impossible."

"Perhaps. But, Al, I've never seen you this ... agitated. If you're wrong, if there's an answer, how could you find it in the state you're in? What do you always tell me to do when I have a hard problem? Work on it, then forget about it, rinse and repeat. Let your subconscious handle the load."

There's nothing more enjoyable than hearing one's own smug words repeated.

"Remember," She said, "some other juror might find a solution. So go back to reading your books, relax, and for God's sake get some sleep," she said. "I bet you'll wake up tomorrow knowing just what to do."

Fat chance. "You're a wise woman, and I will take your prescription like a good patient." I kissed her goodnight and called up the next book on Kabbalah in the queue. I don't remember dozing off, but the night was filled with dreams about flowing lights....

———

The artificial sunrise blazing through our cloned bedroom windows woke me. I searched my brain for signs of a break-through and came up as dry as I expected. My heart filled with a crushing and irrational disappointment as I lurched out of bed, plodding to the john as if I were home. But this wasn't home. The floor here was always warm, and the bathroom always weird. I glanced at myself in a too-perfect mirror, expecting to see a face aged a hundred years and got a shock. That face, shadowed with a threat of beard, looked ten years younger, the bags I'd been packing under my eyes for the last decade almost gone. So too the fine wrinkles on my forehead.

What the hell?

Probably the lighting. I studied the galaxy-like fixtures overhead. They added up to a fairly even glow but cast webs of brightness across the ceiling. I remembered Sunny describing those luminous, multi-thousand-light-year trails radiating from the Spindles as "threads."

You know that classic cartoon image of the light bulb shining over someone head? This felt more like a thunderbolt. And the answer I'd been killing myself to reel in was so absurdly obvious that surely most of my fellow jurors had also found it. I'd even been damn close to the right track two days ago. It seemed a kind of negative miracle that the Houck hadn't seen it themselves.

Or had they? Maybe they'd fabricated some reason to reject the idea. Half of my joy balloons popped at that thought, but I refused to let the party die. Break out fresh balloons and a helium tank! I couldn't afford to let myself doubt my solution. My problem now, and it wasn't small, was how to sell it to the Houck.

When I got back to the bedroom, Sunny was awake. Her face, too, appeared much younger. She took one look at mine and nodded in a self-satisfied way. "Good for you, Al. I told you."

I perched on the bed. "And you were right as always, dear."

"Sarcasm isn't pretty in the morning, not even with a smile. Lord, you look wonderful."

"You look better than wonderful. Must be those new vitamins we aren't taking."

She smiled. "So what have you cooked up?"

"The goods, I hope. At least I'm convinced."

"But you're not sure it'll go over with aliens? Care to let me in on it?"

"Absolutely! Funny, but all the very different things I've been thinking about lately have guided me straight to this. Not sure I would've gotten there otherwise. The Kabbalah contains this idea about spiritual—"

Haxel glided into our bedroom as if she owned the place. "The proper time has arrived, Doctor, and I must summon you to the place of decision."

"Already?"

"You have slept longer than you may realize. I can smell

that you have not yet eaten and apologize that you must delay your breakfast." It was news to me that she had a sense of smell.

I'd become too nervous to eat anyway. "Can I get dressed first? And maybe my wife could grab an apple on the way?"

"If you wish, but please operate quickly. I will awaken your progeny; your associates are already alert."

Scared man walking, I thought as we paraded after Haxel. Alex bounced along with all the joy I didn't have, Sunny looked gorgeous and particularly precious to me sans makeup. Gara and Deal quietly chatted like friends, but I wasn't listening. The most important moment of my life lay dead ahead, and I wasn't prepared. I'd plunged into the classic nightmare of finding myself back in school, being tested on an unfamiliar subject. Deal could've suggested the perfect sales pitch, but it was too late to ask him.

Too soon we arrived in the huge room we'd been in two days ago, again filled with Houck. They remained stained-glass lightshows, but their bodies tended to flicker like old-fashioned florescent bulbs about to burn out. Maybe they, too, were scared. One wall still appeared transparent; its view thick with Spindles. They took my breath away; I'd almost forgotten how beautiful they were.

I tried to spot our home universe and the one Haxel had circled in white and couldn't. Too many had similar shapes. And something was nagging at me, not the incredible image, but something related to it....

"Now we ask for your judgment," Haxel announced. "Have you found any error in our decision?"

"I have."

"Truly?" She flapped her wings and the whooshing sound I heard made me suspect that every Houck around us had done the same. "Please display your ideas!"

No human would've phrased it that way, but that word "display" made all the difference. I'd never believed in miracles before; but like magic, everything I needed had come to me. Which didn't guarantee it would be enough. "May I ask a question first?"

"Only if it is brief and briefly answered."

"How many of my fellow jurors *don't* come from species who've developed the kind of interstellar, um, relocation you Houck use?"

"Twenty and six. Are you ready to proceed?"

Damn, it really might be entirely up to me. "When you invited me to join your jury, you said that I needed to see something before you could explain what I'd be judging." I waved a hand at the cosmic view. "Makes sense. Some things you have to experience to understand."

The room was dead silent.

Don't stop now. "I think there's something all of you need to see to understand the point I want to make." *Presumption, thy name is Al.*

"This will require a journey?"

"No. That display you have"—I gave the wall of wonders another vague wave—"seems capable of doing the job if you can make it show what I ask." It had already demonstrated animation ability and stunning magnification powers.

"Describe your desired result."

I licked my lips, struggling to phrase it just right. "I want an animation using rays of light and showing, over a minute or so, every journey the Houck have ever made between Spindles, but as if each trip had been made in a ... rocket ship rather than one of your teleporting vessels."

"You seek a linear visual record. Give us a moment."

It was one of the shortest moments ever before light beams began flashing between universes, just a few at first, building into a stroboscopic cascade.

My heart was racing from both fear and inspiration. I spoke just before the animation ended. "Perhaps every species has a blind spot when it comes to themselves. But you Houck may have an extreme case because of that total group consensus you mentioned."

"We may." Haxel turned completely around once, silently. Perhaps Houck could communicate via their wing-lights. "We sense a purpose to your requested animation but cannot illuminate it."

"It is audible perfectly to us," Gara said, speaking for Sunny, Deal, and maybe even Alex.

This was it. "You Houck *are* the connection between Spindles. Those trails you just saw, your own journeys, are the universe islands talking to each other. If there is or will be a pan-cosmic mind, it's been busy for the last seventeen million years, seeding life and feeding intelligence, self-assembling."

As a kid, I'd speculated on the universe being a kind of machine designed to build God through evolutionary processes. What I'd just seen brought all that back and even gave it legs.

I had one last card to play. "I can prove you've got a blind spot. Two days back, when I asked if some form of energy could be teleporting between Spindles you said that each one has a unique signature imprinted on its matter and energy, and that you'd never found any signature out of place."

"Continue," Haxel said very quietly. "You are radiating an unexpected light, and we are slow to absorb it."

I only expressed my feelings with a grin although I felt like jumping up and down making happy noises. It seemed I was getting through! "My point is that you should've found, um, an extraneous signature *everywhere* you went outside your home Spindle. You discounted the one you brought with you. Big blind spot."

As my voice died away, the room again turned silent. Then little by little, the Houck brightened and stopped flickering until I had to close my eyes against the incandescence. I didn't mind one bit.

———

If you believe my Conservation of Misery Principle, you'd think something would've gone horribly wrong on the way home. It didn't, but we hit a few speed bumps before we left.

Alex did not, and I'm going to put it mildly, care to leave his bedroom playground. No lure of school or friends or the unhealthy foods the Houck forgot to offer shifted his resolve. I'm not saying he would've stayed there without us given the choice, but he sure wasn't prepared to go gentle into that good flight. I love that boy more than my own life, but good God almighty, parental ears do not deserve such a fate.

Then Deal, all bouncy from closing some trade arrangement with the Houck, embarrassed the hell out of me by trying, supposedly on my behalf but not with my permission, to negotiate a hefty payment for services rendered.

It turned out that our hosts had a very different concept of when and how to reward someone for their work. Remember that two-stage process of boarding the Houck Siamese Fighting Ship? Deal had been partly right about that first door, the one bringing us the vast distance to a few feet farther in the parking lot. It had indeed checked our identities and individual needs, but that was the least of it. It had also performed a thorough medical evaluation of each of us, *really* thorough, and filled our bodies with appropriate energies to attract the universe-shielding "dark" neutrinos waiting for us through the second door, allowing our jump to the Spindle-ship.

The pink fog beyond door number two was the Houck equivalent to a hospital emergency room; thousands of medical repairs created the weird sensations I'd felt walking through it.

In short, I got paid before doing the job, and payment amounted to healing everything physically amiss with everyone in my party. Haxel sent my DM a full list of repairs and someday, when I have a free year, I'll read the whole thing.

But at the top of my section, among the precancerous cells excised, bone micro-fractures sealed, and heavy metals removed, was an item that jumped out at me: my leukopenia, the bone marrow disease that would've killed me long ago without nano-medical intervention, was cured. I was now the proud maker of my own white blood cells.

I think that payment was princely. Even Alex, who luckily doesn't look a decade younger, seems to overflow with health. Gara says that my new body sounds like a smoothly running stream rather than white water rapids.

If you're curious, as I was, the Houck had hired 5,832 jurors, which seemed a random number to me until Deal pointed out that it was eighteen to the third power, which should tell me something about something, but doesn't. Many jurors came up with excellent reasons why the Houck should stick around, but Haxel claimed that only mine was convincing. That scared me more than flattered me. What if I'd missed it? Sunny calls that sort of thinking "snatching defeat from the jaws of victory."

While packing for the instant trip home, Sunny asked me how I'd arrived at the solution.

"It's strange," I admitted. "You know those three things I'd been thinking about, mostly to take my mind off the judging ahead?"

Sunny paused mid-blouse-folding. "Let's see. You were reading about Kabbalah and fussing about what Gara told you, that maybe she'd been chosen by the Traders because she didn't like them. There was a third thing?"

"Yep, the technique Houck use for Spindle hopping. Everything dovetailed." I held up a finger. "Kabbalah, according to my borrowed books, is about spiritual energy flows." Another finger. "Aliens who teleport spaceships aren't likely to think of travel as a linear, ah, projective activity as we do." Third finger. "And Gara started me considering—no fussing involved!—species blind spots. The notion that she'd been planted on me to build my loyalty to the Traders hadn't once crossed my mind." Those threads of light on the bathroom ceiling had sealed the deal....

"I see. You just slapped it all together." She gave me the kind of grin that had made me want to marry her. "So what's 'strange.'"

"It's almost too neat, the way it worked out. It's like I was ... steered to the answer."

"By the hand of God?"

"Hate to admit it, but maybe. Something along those lines."

The return trip deposited us at the decrepit parking lot where we'd caught the Houck express. Agents Carl and Steve, our former chauffeurs, were waiting for us along with two reporters who'd apparently been hanging around just in case.

Deal came down with an instant terrible case of British accent, calling everyone "guv" or "love" and declaring to the live feeds that he was "over the moon" about our expedition. Tsf humor, I'm afraid.

Then we piled, hopped, or eased into the big van and Sunny, Alex, and I were the first to get dropped off.

As we climbed out, Gara told me something so complimentary that I'm too embarrassed to repeat it. And Deal offered me the Trader version of the ultimate praise: "I'm arranging a salary increase for you."

Five minutes after we opened our front door, our western neighbor, Mary, brought over a package for me that had been left at her house. I thanked her then opened it and found inside a large black hat with a wide brim, also a printed note.

"Dear Doctor," it read. "I arranged for this be delivered. Is Lubavitch Jewish headgear termed 'rain-catcher.' If you are the being I believe you are, you will forgive my verbal cascades and find essence." It had a spidery signature: Peeps. I hadn't realized the eDellaPe knew that nickname.

I had my DM look up "Lubavitch," and it listed all sorts of references to Judaism, Hasidism, and ... Kabbalah. It occurred to me that Peeps had been living for centuries, focused on "attunement with The Pure." Just how far could intuition be developed?

"Maybe it wasn't the hand of God," I said to my wife, certain that she'd place the reference. "At least, not directly."

ABOUT THE AUTHOR

Rajnar Vajra was born in the same year that Chuck Yeager broke the sound barrier, and something mysterious happened in Roswell, New Mexico. Coincidence? Perhaps.

Aside from writing, he is a professional musician, songwriter, music teacher, a practitioner of Zen and other contemplative disciplines, and has been a jeweler, a painter, a recording engineer, and much more. He follows developments in science, health, and understanding the mind's nature with the closest attention. Not, perish the thought, primarily to mine human progress for writing ideas.

He has appeared more than thirty times in the pages of *Analog Science Fiction and Fact* and has also appeared in the online stories at Tor.com and in *Absolute Magnitude*.

IF YOU LIKED ...

IF YOU LIKED *DOCTOR ALIEN*, YOU MIGHT ALSO ENJOY:

Strong Arm Tactics
by Jody Lynn Nye

Select Stories: Sci-fi
by Kevin J. Anderson

Phule's Company
by Robert Asprin

Our list of other WordFire Press authors and titles is always growing. To find out more and to shop our selection of titles, visit us at:
wordfirepress.com

facebook.com/WordfireIncWordfirePress

twitter.com/WordFirePress

instagram.com/WordFirePress

bookbub.com/profile/4109784512

Made in the USA
Las Vegas, NV
31 January 2024